the heavens may fall

ALSO BY ALLEN ESKENS

The Life We Bury

The Guise of Another

the
heavens
may
fall

allen
eskens

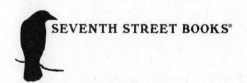

SEVENTH STREET BOOKS®

Published 2016 by Seventh Street Books®

Cover image © Seth K. Hughes / Media Bakery
Cover design by Jacqueline Nasso Cooke
Cover design © Start Science Fiction

This is a work of fiction. Characters, organizations, products, locales, and events portrayed in this novel either are products of the author's imagination or are used fictitiously. Any similarities to real persons, living or dead, is coincidental and not intended by the author.

Inquiries should be addressed to
Start Science Fiction
221 River Street, 9th Floor
Hoboken, New Jersey 07030
PHONE: 212-620-5700
WWW.SEVENTHSTREETBOOKS.COM

20 19 18 17 16   5 4 3 2 1

Library of Congress Cataloging-in-Publication Data

Names: Eskens, Allen, 1963-, author.
Title: The heavens may fall : a novel / by Allen Eskens.
Description: Amherst, NY : Seventh Street Books, an imprint of Prometheus Books, 2016.
Identifiers: LCCN 2016018139 (print) | LCCN 2016023065 (ebook) |
    ISBN 9781633882058 (paperback) | ISBN 9781633882065 (ebook)
Subjects: | BISAC: FICTION / Mystery & Detective / Police Procedural. | FICTION /
    Mystery & Detective / General.
Classification: LCC PS3605.S49 H43 2016 (print) | LCC PS3605.S49 (ebook) |
    DDC 813/.6--dc23
LC record available at https://lccn.loc.gov/2016018139

Printed in the United States of America

To Mikayla and Jon
Always remember to follow your bliss.

PART 1
The Death

Chapter 1

The courtroom had fallen quiet, the judge's words lost behind a low hum that droned in Max Rupert's ears. Max reached for his water glass, a waxy paper cup on the rail of the witness stand. It lifted empty and light. He didn't remember drinking the last of his water. He paused, the empty cup halfway to his lips, unsure what to do next. Pretend to take a drink? Put the cup back down on the rail?

And such silence; how was that possible in a courtroom full of people? So quiet that he could hear the blood pulsing through his ears, his rage thumping against his ear drums, flicking the tips of his fingers. He fought against showing any facial expression. The jury would be studying him as the echoes of the cross-examination pinged and settled into their memories. *Look at me, Sanden*, Max yelled in his mind, the words pounding like ball-peen on steel. *Look in my eyes, you sonofabitch.* He willed the attorney to raise his head, but Boady Sanden kept his gaze fixed on the legal pad at his elbow.

Max took a slow, subtle breath and tried to relax. He didn't want the jury to see the emotion that fought to break free of its tether. He saw the empty cup in his half-raised hand. He'd forgotten about it for a moment. He raised the empty cup a few more inches, tipping it to verify that it was bone dry, not a single drop to trickle onto his dry tongue. He pretended to take a sip anyway, and then he gently returned the cup to the rail.

"You can step down now, Detective Rupert," Judge Ransom said. Rupert detected a slight edge in the judge's voice—the tone of a man who'd just had to repeat his words.

Max stood, picked up his file, and exited the witness box, glancing at the fourteen jurors as he passed them. Only one, an alternate, returned his look. As he passed the counsel table, Max looked down at the defense attorney, Boady Sanden, his friend—no, not his friend, not anymore.

Sanden kept his eyes focused on the yellow tablet in front of him. He pretended to be writing something, but Max could see that the man's pen twirled in meaningless circles in the margin of the page. Max wanted Boady to look up as he passed. He wanted Boady to know that lines had been crossed and it would forever sever the connection they once shared. But Boady Sanden never looked up.

Max exited the courtroom, his thumbnail scuffing against the fold of the investigation file in his hand. He found an empty conference room, a space the size of a jail cell where attorneys fed false hopes to clients, a room where desperation clung to the walls as thick as grease in a fast-food kitchen. He spread his hands on the table, the cool metal chilling the sweat of his palms. He let his heart rate slow from a boil to a simmer as he watched a slight tremor twitch in his fingers. Anger? Sure. Embarrassment? Maybe a little of that too. But there was something more to that tremor, something that shifted his sense of balance and felt very much like doubt.

For months now Max had carried the Pruitt case around with him, its reflection looking back at him from the mirror, its scent infusing the air he breathed, its rough hem tucking up around his shoulders as he fell to sleep at night. He'd bestowed life upon this investigation, animated it in a way that gave it a presence in his world. He felt that presence at his side when he took his seat on the witness chair. But when he left the witness stand, he left alone.

Sanden had cut him up pretty good—made Max look like he'd trained his crosshairs on Ben Pruitt from the very beginning and shut out all other possible suspects. But had he?

Max opened his investigation file and began sifting through the reports, looking for the beginning, that day when they found the body. But then he closed the file. He didn't need notes to take him back to that morning, He remembered that morning all too well. It was a broken morning, torn apart by the memories that visited him every year on the anniversary of his wife's death.

Chapter 2

On that day, the last Friday in July, Max Rupert woke well before dawn. He opened his eyes and waited a moment to let wake and sleep separate in his head. A shadow in the shape of a cross floated on the wall beside him, cast there by a yellow streetlight bleeding through his window pane. Outside, the air conditioner clicked on and whirred as if this was just another day. But it wasn't just another day.

He reached a hand to her side of the bed, touching the undisturbed sheets, feeling the slight rise where the mattress remained unaffected by four years of her absence. He grazed his fingers across the soft cotton and felt the pain in his chest grow and ebb with each breath.

She used to wake up before him, a morning glory to his night owl. In so many ways, she brought balance to his life. Nobody but Jenni could cut through his wall of self-control and expose the childlike happiness he kept locked away. He'd never laughed so hard as when they were alone and she felt free to unleash her cutting wit. And she loved pretty things. Porcelain dolls, silver candlesticks, and china teacups still filled the shelves and covered the fireplace mantle. He'd learned to take care of her flowers, the chrysanthemums she'd planted in front of the house. He remembered that first year when they bloomed, how he wanted to tee off on those flowers the way Bill Murray had done in *Caddyshack*. He didn't, of course. And now, every year, Max tended to those flowers the way she had done for so long.

But there were other ways in which Jenni and Max were not counterweights but a perfect blend. She loved fishing as much as he did. They both loved black-and-white movies and heavily buttered popcorn. And they enjoyed sitting in silence together. Whether it was reading books or just swinging on the porch swing, it didn't matter as long as she was there.

Those moments of tranquility sometimes reminded him of their first date and how he fell in love with her. He no longer remembered the homecoming dance itself or the dinner before, but he remembered how stunning she looked. He remembered the way her simple dress accentuated her natural beauty in the same way that dew can make a rose sparkle. But what he remembered the most from that night was what happened after the dance.

They'd gone to a party at a friend's house. Some kids talked, others made out, and still others navigated the waters between budding relationships and breakups. He remembered sitting on a couch with Jenni, caught up in the only moment of awkward silence they had come across all evening. He had his arm stretched across her shoulders, his palm dangling in the air. He wanted to kiss her. His thoughts tangled around the logistics: how to create an opening for the kiss, how to move in—open-lipped or closed. He contemplated what he would do if she kissed him back or, God forbid, if she didn't. He had never been more nervous.

Then she moved, turning into him just enough to lay her head on his shoulder. She put her hand on his chest and sighed—not the sigh of a tired high-school girl, but the sigh of a young woman, content with the world. The struggles in Max's head vanished. He no longer thought about angles and lips and reactions. All he wanted to do was hold her. He lowered his dangling hand until it rested on her hip, his fingers gently pressing against the soft cotton of her dress. At that moment he felt more deeply for her than he'd ever felt for anyone ever before. He tenderly kissed the top of her head, and that was enough.

How many times over the years had they sat in that exact same position—slowly rocking on the porch swing or watching TV from their couch? How many times had he kissed the top of her head and told her that he loved her. And to himself, he would whisper the promise that he would always protect her. He would never let anything bad happen to her.

It had been four years to the day since he broke that promise.

On that first morning when he woke up without her, he could barely pull himself out of bed, and when he did, he crawled to her closet and wrapped himself in her sweaters and blouses, things she'd worn, things waiting to be washed on the day of her death. He pressed the fabric to his face and inhaled her essence until his last tear fell and he could again put on the façade of strength that he wore for everyone else. He returned to that closet a few times over those first months, repeating his ritual until the scent in Jenni's clothes surrendered to the dust and decay of time.

As months turned to years, he found a way to live with the sadness, but he never learned to live with the guilt. A picture on the wall, his wife smiling down at him, reminded him every day that her death had gone unsolved. Not his case. Couldn't be his case. He was the husband, and the husband can't be involved in the investigation. Rules kept him locked out, and so the hit-and-run driver got away.

Max stood, walked to his bathroom, and splashed his face with cold water. He knew from experience that he would not be able to get back to sleep. Instead he would go for a run. He would put in five miles before the sun crested the horizon, five miles of listening to the rhythm of his own breathing and the pounding of his feet on concrete, and nothing else.

July mornings in Minnesota were perfect for such a run.

After the run, Max showered, brewed some coffee, and went outside to sit on his porch swing and eat biscotti. From there he watched the day rise from behind a cluster of rooftops in his Logan Park neighborhood. He quietly absorbed the tranquility and beauty of that slow turn of the earth. She told him once that sunrise was her favorite part of the day, and now it was his.

Max finished his biscotti and was downing the last tepid sips of his coffee when the chimes of his phone went off. He could see that the call came from Dispatch, so he answered by saying, "Max here."

"Sorry to wake you, Detective, this is Carmen James in Dispatch."

"You didn't wake me, Carmen. What do you have?"

"A body in Kenwood, possible homicide."

"Kenwood?"

"Affirmative. The deceased is reported to be a white female. Officers on the scene have confirmed the death." Carmen used the formal tone and language that dispatchers were trained to use for radio calls—that calm, you-can't-rile-me resonance that gave the same weight to a murder that it did to a stolen bicycle. She read Max the address, an alley off of West 21st Street, and Max tried to remember if he'd ever heard of a murder in Kenwood. Bodies found in alleys usually took him to North Minneapolis—not Kenwood.

"Have they cordoned off the area?"

"They're doing that now, Detective."

"Call my partner, Niki Vang, and tell her I'll meet her there. Then call the ME and Crime Scene and get them on their way."

"Yes, sir."

Max ended the call, climbed into his unmarked squad car, and headed in the direction of the Kenwood neighborhood where the body of a dead woman awaited him. And as he drove, he couldn't help feeling like a monster, like his soul deserved the damnation that undoubtedly awaited him, because deep in his heart he was grateful for the call. For those few minutes, as he drove through the gray streets of Minneapolis, he was glad to have a death to think about—a death other than his wife's. He welcomed the rush of thoughts that silenced those memories.

Chapter 3

The Kenwood neighborhood—fine china amidst a collection of stoneware—started out as a mosquito-filled swamp on the southern edge of Minneapolis. At the end of the nineteenth century, some forward-thinking city planner saw its potential and convinced the City of Minneapolis to expand. They dredged out a chunk of swampland to make the Lake of the Isles and dumped the dredged-out dirt into the lowlands, raising them up to support parks and tennis courts and curbed streets. When the rich folks saw what was coming, they rushed to Kenwood to build their handsome estates.

Max wound his way through Kenwood on streets that purled past an eclectic mix of big houses and bigger ones, houses built with old money. Not all of the homes were mansions, but there wasn't a hovel in the bunch. And Kenwood had no main street, no downtown, no plazas or malls. It was completely devoid of the usual clutter of commerce like oil-change shops or Chinese restaurants. No, Kenwood was a neighborhood that prided itself on living well and peacefully, a neighborhood that liked to be left alone.

By the time Max arrived, patrol officers had blocked off West 21st and had crime-scene tape stretched across the mouth of an alley where the upscale locals hid the more unsightly aspects of their lives, like garbage cans and cluttered garages. Max parked a block away, slipped on cloth booties and a pair of latex gloves, and walked slowly toward the alley, taking in what he could.

West 21st held one of the few storefronts in all of Kenwood, a short, half block of commerce that consisted of a bookstore and an art gallery. Max had been in the bookstore once, back when Jenni was looking for a book written in Ojibwe, something to give to a client—

probably a child. Jenni considered being a social worker a calling, not just a job. He remembered the store and he remembered the smell of lilacs on that spring evening and the feel of her slender hand in his as they left the store. Those were the tides that moved through his head every year on the anniversary of her death.

The alley opened just to the east of the bookstore, giving access to a parking area in the rear. As he made his way down the alley, he could see his partner, Niki Vang, in the parking lot, talking to a crime-scene technician named Bug Thomas. When Niki saw Max approaching, she nodded her greeting and then nodded toward a bundle of cloth at her feet. She didn't throw a joke his way as she normally did, a sure sign that she understood that Max carried the extra burden of a thousand memories on his back that day.

Across the alley from the parking lot, the neighbors had cultivated a wall of trees and bushes and vines, a privacy barrier to keep the book-store patrons and others from gawking into backyards. Max glanced around and wondered if this might be the most secluded location in all of Kenwood.

Bug Thomas knelt beside a dumpster to inspect the ground for footprints or other trace evidence. The dumpster's lid was open, its belly filled with bags and empty boxes, leaving no room for hiding a body. Max put his hands on his knees to examine the bundle, a blanket edged with a pink ruffle and with horses and stars across its face, the kind of pattern you'd find on the bed of a young girl. It was obvious that the blanket held a body.

"This has to be one of the cleanest alleys I've ever seen," Max said.

"This is Kenwood," Niki said. "Even their crime scenes are nicer than everyone else's."

"Who found the body?"

"An early-morning jogger," Niki said, pointing to a man wearing a 1970s-styled headband and standing just beyond the crime-scene tape.

Max pulled a corner of the blanket back to uncover the woman's head. Her hair, a paprika shade of red, was the same color as Jenni's, and for a razor-thin moment, he saw Jenni's face peeking out from behind the mess of red hair. He dropped the corner of the blanket and stood up—the movement filling his chest with a queasy sensation as if he'd just stepped up to the edge of a high precipice.

The bedspread had fallen open and Max could see that the woman was not Jenni. He glanced at Niki to see if she had seen his reaction. If she had, she didn't show it. Max replaced the spread to wait for the medical examiner. "Hey, Bug, you didn't happen to find a purse or ID lying around by chance?"

Only in his twenties, Bug looked like he just stepped out of a *Dragnet* rerun with his flat-top haircut and thick, black-rimmed glasses. His real name was Doug, but everyone called him Bug. Max had heard that Bug got his nickname by publishing an important paper on insect entomology. Max preferred that explanation to the possibility that some asshole in the department started calling him Bug to highlight the kid's many quirks: the way he tapped his thumb and fingers together when he thought, or the way he struggled with small talk like it was an unpracticed foreign language.

Bug stopped his examination of the parking lot, pausing as if he had to process the question. Then he stood up, giving his full attention to Max before answering, and said, "I didn't find anything yet."

Max wanted to say "at ease" or "carry on" to let Bug know to go back to his inspections. Instead he just nodded and looked down at the bundle. "That looks like a little girl's bedspread, not something a grown woman would have on her bed."

"I had the same thought," Niki said.

Behind them came the shuffle of tired feet, and they both turned to see Dr. Margaret Hightower making her way down the alley—the grand dame of the Hennepin County Medical Examiner's Office. In her mid-sixties, Margaret moved with the gait of an eighty-year-old woman, carrying her hard life on her shoulders and in her face. For the past six years now, she wore a sobriety necklace, a silver dog tag with the inscription "one day at a time" etched on its face, and she no longer came to crime scenes with a hint of single-malt scotch on her breath.

"Hey, Maggie," Max said. "Isn't it a bit early for the day-shift to be on duty?"

"You know me, Max; I get up at the butt crack of dawn. Besides, we're a bit short-staffed, so I'm on call. What do we have?"

Niki peeled the blanket back to show a pale-skinned woman, attractive, athletic, with a thick tangle of red hair wrapped around her face as though she'd been walking through cobwebs. Half-opened eyes stared through the web of hair, and the eyes had dark-yellow lines forming where they had grown dry. A thick smear of blood surrounded a wound on the right side of her neck. Niki unwrapped the rest of the body to show that the woman was naked.

"Caucasian, female," Niki said. "I'd guess mid-forties. One obvious wound on the right side of her neck."

Maggie made her way to the woman's head and started to kneel down but then stood back up. "Jesus Christ, my knees suck. Max can you give me a hand?" Max held Maggie's arm as she went down to her knees, then flopped to her butt. "I used to be a dancer, you know . . . a ballerina. Did I ever tell you that, Max?"

She had, but Max said, "I don't think so."

"Yeah, back in college. I could pirouette 'til the cows came home. I was flexible as all hell. And now I can't even kneel down without a crane to hoist my fat ass back up. Don't ever get old, Max."

"I'll do my best, Maggie."

Maggie gently pulled back the woman's hair to get a better look at the wound. "Yeah, that's our frontrunner for the cause of death." Maggie carefully touched the skin around the wound. "Probably a knife. That's a perfect location if you're looking to cut the carotid or jugular. Either one would be enough to kill her. Your suspect either knew what they were doing or got lucky."

Maggie lifted one of the woman's arms; it didn't move easily. "Rigor's set in. Could you guys tip her onto her side just a bit?"

Max lifted the woman at the shoulder as Niki did the same at the woman's hip. The skin on the woman's back had turned a deep red.

"Lividity," Maggie said. "Help me up, would you?"

Max and Niki each grabbed one of Maggie's arms and lifted her to her feet.

"Preliminarily, I'd say that this isn't your crime scene," Maggie said. "Not enough blood loss. A cut to the throat like that . . . if it's the internal jugular, it might not bleed all that much, but the carotid . . . no, I'm thinking she was killed somewhere else, bled out there and then brought here. Besides, why wrap her in a blanket if you're not transporting her?"

Maggie continued, waving a finger above the body. "Rigor and lividity both set in here in this parking lot. She would have been laid out in this position within an hour or two after death. My rough guess on time of death would be late last night or early this morning, probably within an hour either side of midnight. As soon as we can get her on a table, I can take a reading of her liver temperature. I should be able to give you fairly precise TOD after the autopsy."

Max nodded, then said, "Mind if we take a minute with her here?"

"Absolutely. She's all yours." Maggie stepped back to let Max and Niki have full access to the body.

They knelt down beside the woman, one on each side, and Max nodded toward Niki to give her the go-ahead. Niki started at the woman's feet. "Pedicured toenails." Then she ran a gloved finger along the woman's leg and brought her finger to her nose to smell. "Lotion . . . vanilla." Niki lifted the woman's hands to see long fingernails painted with a professional touch. "Expensive manicure, clean, no obvious scrapings under the nails. No immediate signs of defensive wounds." She looked closer at the hand. "This indentation on her ring finger suggests that she usually wears a ring, maybe a wedding band, but it's not there now. Possible robbery, but the whole dumping-of-the-body thing makes me think robbery's not our motive."

Max took great delight in watching Niki work. Her observations and inferences came quick and certain, as though she'd been working Homicide for three decades as opposed to just three years. For her part, she couldn't have been happier escaping Vice and the misogynistic jokes that floated behind her back. Her supervisor in Vice, a thick-necked man named Whitton, once told Max that Niki's appearance made her the perfect Asian prostitute, the kind of Geisha-girl that every traveling salesman wanted to screw. That was back when Whitton was fighting to keep her in Vice and Max was fighting to get her assigned to Homicide.

Max first met Niki when Chief Murphy temporarily assigned her to Homicide to deal with a glut of murders in North Minneapolis three years earlier. They had been called to an apartment complex where a woman was found murdered in her fourth-floor bedroom. The building had a security system with cameras showing that no one had entered or left the apartment near the time of death.

Max couldn't figure out how an intruder entered or exited without being seen. That's when Niki noticed that the dust pattern on the window blinds suggested that the blinds were not in their normal position. That discovery led to the arrest of a man in the next building over, who had climbed from his window to hers using a telescoping pole he'd designed just for that purpose. He'd been hiding in the poor girl's apartment when she came home after bar closing.

That began the tug-of-war.

Whitton told the chief that he needed Niki as bait. When he saw that point failing, he argued that the cohesiveness of the unit demanded that she stay, portraying them as a family. Whitton lost the battle when Max asked Whitton to speak Niki's Hmong name. He couldn't. He'd never taken enough interest in Niki as a detective to learn that her real name was Ntxhi, a name she converted to Niki because most Westerners tripped over their tongues trying to pronounce it. Max uttered her given name and sealed her transfer to Homicide.

Niki moved to the dead woman's head, leaning down to smell a strand of her hair. "Smells like fresh shampoo, like she just showered." She peeled back more strands of the matted hair and unveiled the woman's attractive face with no makeup or lipstick. Niki thought out loud. "She showers . . . maybe puts her hair up in a towel . . . puts vanilla body moisturizer on . . . and gets stabbed in the neck before she can brush her hair."

Max nodded in agreement. Then a glint of light caught Max's eye as Niki moved the woman's hair back. "Well look at that," Max said, lifting an earlobe mounted with a large diamond stud—a stone that had to be at least two carats. "You're right about this not being a robbery." He leaned in to get a closer look at the earring, then he pulled the hair away from the woman's other ear to show the pair. "Do women wear earrings into the shower?"

"Sometimes . . . sure."

"I think your shower hypothesis has legs." Max turned to Bug, who was taking pictures of the earrings. "Hand me a gem bag and a forceps, would you?"

Bug reached into a tackle box, pulled out the items, and handed them to Max. Max then carefully pulled the earring from the woman's ear and dropped it into the paper bag.

"A gift for the missus?" Bug said with a forced chuckle.

Max closed his eyes. Bug must have had no idea that Max's wife was dead or that today was the anniversary of that death. Bug was just trying to crack a joke. Max also knew how hard it was for Bug to make any attempt at humor, so he didn't hold the faux pas against the awkward technician. But that didn't mean that the words didn't cut Max anyway.

When he opened his eyes again, he could see Niki at the far edge of his periphery mouthing something to Bug. He couldn't tell what she said, but he saw Bug shrivel and walk away. Max felt bad for the kid and tried to get everybody's attention back to the investigation.

"Our best theory right now is that we have a dead woman, stabbed in the throat after getting out of the shower. The killer brings her here, intending to drop her into the dumpster, but unloads into the parking lot instead. So, who is she, and where was she killed?"

"And are there any other victims?" Niki added. "If that indent on her finger is from a wedding ring, she may have a family."

"We have to find that crime scene."

"I'll canvass," Niki said. "Maybe someone around here saw something last night, or maybe they know her from the neighborhood." She pulled her phone out of her pocket and snapped a close-up of the woman's face. "Not the best picture, but it'll do."

Max waived an ambulance crew over to transport the body to the Hennepin County Medical Examiner's Office. "I'm going to borrow Bug." Max said. "I have an idea on getting an ID." Max slipped the specimen bag with the diamond stud into his pocket and gave it a pat.

Chapter 4

Max pulled into the parking lot of the Ballistics Lab at 8 a.m., the time that his normal shift should have been starting. That was the thing about being a homicide detective, dead bodies never waited for the start of a shift to turn up. Unpredictability came with the job and had been the one aspect of Max's chosen profession that bothered Jenni. One time, they were celebrating their anniversary at a nice restaurant, and just before the meals came to the table, Max got a call.

He tried to read her face as he kissed her good-bye. He knew that she had to be embarrassed to have to cancel such an elegant and expensive meal, disappointed at having to spend the rest of their anniversary at home, alone. Then there was the time that they were hosting a Christmas dinner for her family, twelve guests in all. Max left home about the time that Jenni was putting the twenty-pound turkey into the oven. He expected her to be angry when he came home nine hours later. But if she harbored any resentment, she never showed it.

The only time Jenni had ever voiced reluctance at Max's job was when the topic of having children came up. She wondered if a child would understand why their father had to run out in the middle of a school play or a soccer game. How would a child feel when he or she looked into the audience to bask in the glow of a father's admiration, only to find an empty seat? Yet every one of those conversations found its way to their first date, back in high school, when Max shared with Jenni his dream of being a homicide detective. She bought into that dream from the very beginning, and no wife could have been more supportive. "I understand," she would say about his disappearances. "But I don't have to be happy about it."

In the end, those conversations didn't matter. There would be no children.

Max and Bug walked into the Ballistics Lab, Bug swiping his ID badge to get into the heart of the facility. The Ballistics Lab was separate from the main crime lab and focused on matching bullets to gun barrels or tools to an injury. Max didn't have a bullet or a tool, but he had a diamond and the lab had a microscope.

Bug sat down at one of the microscopes and turned on a computer screen where the image would appear. Max handed him the gem package that contained the diamond.

"Look on the girdle of the diamond. If this is a real diamond, it might be branded."

When Max had asked Bug to accompany him to the lab, Bug didn't utter a word. Nor had Bug said anything when Max asked him to fire up the microscope. Now as Bug worked to secure the diamond in place below the lens of the microscope, his fingers twitched as though he were more nervous than usual.

"You okay, Bug?"

Bug stopped fiddling with the diamond. The muscles of his mandible flexed as though trying to utter words that would not come out. Finally, Bug said, "I forgot your wife is dead. I didn't mean . . ." He stopped talking and took a breath.

Max put a hand on Bug's shoulder and tapped lightly on muscles pulled rigid by the young man's crushing anxiety. "It's okay, Bug. That was a long time ago. Don't kick yourself over it."

Bug seemed to relax as he refocused on his task. Once he set the diamond in the mechanical stage, he focused the lens onto the side of the diamond, a flat, thin strip that separates the diamond's crown from its pavilion. Bug turned the stone under the lens and Max watched on the monitor until a laser inscription appeared. First he saw an image of a bird with long, elaborate wings. Beside the bird was the name Hercinia, and beside that a serial number.

"Bingo," Max whispered. "Ever heard of Hercinia Diamonds?"

"No," Bug said. He wheeled his chair to another table with a computer and typed in the name. "It's a diamond company out of Toronto, Canada." Bug read some more. "They specialize in diamonds mined in the tundra. No blood diamonds."

"Should we give them a call?"

Bug used a phone in the lab to dial the contact number from the website. He handed the phone to Max.

"Hercinia Diamonds Incorporated. How can we help you?"

"Detective Max Rupert calling from Minneapolis, Minnesota. I'd like to speak to your records department."

Pause.

"Or your boss, whichever is easier." The words came out sounding like a threat, but they weren't meant to be one.

"One moment please."

A click, a few seconds of Karen Carpenter singing "Close to You," and then another click. "This is Richard Holerman of Customer Relations. Can I help you?"

"Mr. Holerman, I'm Max Rupert, a homicide detective with the City of Minneapolis, Minnesota. I'm investigating a death here and I thought you might be able to help."

Silence.

"Mr. Holerman?"

"Yes . . . I'm not sure how I could—"

"The victim is a woman and she was wearing a pair of earrings with Hercinia diamonds. We have the serial number from the diamond. We need to identify her. If you could tell us who those were sold to—"

"Oh, Detective . . . I'm sorry . . . what was your name again?"

"Rupert. Detective Max Rupert."

"Yes, Detective Rupert. I don't think I can help you. We aren't a retail store. We don't sell directly to the public."

"You sell to stores, though, right? If we knew which store you sent these particular earrings to, we can take it from there."

"I'd love to help, but I'm not sure if I can give out that information. This is a rather unusual request."

"I'm not asking for trade secrets here, Mr. Holerman. I just need a place to start. This is terribly urgent."

"I'd have to ask my legal department and get back to you. I don't want to run afoul of the law."

Max could feel the grip of his hand on the phone growing tight. He closed his eyes, exhaled, and loosened the grip. "Mr. Holerman, we have a dead woman and no idea who she is. We don't know if we have other victims somewhere, maybe a husband or a child who might be clinging to life, waiting for help to arrive. We could have a murderer cleaning up his crime scene as we speak. If you need to talk to your legal department, do it, but for God's sake, do it quickly. These earrings are our best source of finding her identity. We need to move on this, and you're the key."

"I . . . I'm sorry. It's just that I've never . . . I'll call you back shortly. At this number?"

He must have been looking at a caller ID. "No, call my cell." Max recited his cell number, thanked Holerman, and hung up. Then he wrote the diamond's serial number on a piece of paper and headed for City Hall, leaving the diamond earrings with Bug to be processed.

At City Hall, Max pulled up a blank administrative subpoena on his computer screen and began filling in what he could, which wasn't much. But he would have everything ready for when—or if—Holerman called back. Max called over to the Hennepin County Attorney's Office and spoke to an attorney in the Adult Prosecution Division, a woman he'd never worked with before, and gave her a heads-up that he'd be e-mailing the paperwork for her signature as soon as he heard back from Holerman. He hung up the phone and waited, tapping his fingers on the desk of his cubicle, a two-person space that he shared with Niki Vang. He thought about calling Holerman back but called Vang instead.

"Got anything yet?" he asked.

"Nothing that helps us. I've knocked on all the doors in the immediate area and no one heard or saw a thing. No surveillance cameras. None of the neighbors recognized the picture, but the bookstore manager, who came by to open up the store, thought our victim looked familiar, like she'd been in the store browsing around at some point, but she couldn't put a name with the face. If she's been to the bookstore, it's more likely than not that she has some tie to Kenwood. Any luck on your end?"

"Nothing yet, but I'm waiting to hear back from a diamond merchant in Canada. The earrings were branded and had a serial number. We might be able to get a name if we can track that serial number. But for some reason, the guy from Canada is reluctant to—"

The phone buzzed in Max's hand. He looked at the screen and saw the number from Toronto.

"Gotta go, Niki. This should be him." Max switched callers, and a voice he didn't recognize, a woman's voice, greeted him.

"This is Victoria Lowell. I'm the vice president in charge of customer relations here at Hercinia Diamonds. I've been authorized to help you locate a store that sold a pair of our diamond earrings. If you give me the serial number, I can tell you which retail outlet sold them, but I'll have no way of knowing the buyer."

"That's okay," Max said. He read the serial number and listened to the sound of her keyboard clicking.

"Those earrings were purchased from us by Galibay Jewelry in Minneapolis."

Max had never heard of the store. He did a search on his computer and read that Galibay Jewelry was a small shop in Uptown that catered to high-end jewelry buyers. No store hours, the only way to see their merchandise was by appointment. The website had a phone number for making appointments, but no e-mail address or fax number.

"Ms. Lowell, I don't suppose you have a fax number for Galibay on file?"

There was a pause at the other end of the line. Then, "Yes, I do have a fax number." She read the number to Max, who typed it into the subpoena form, along with the other pertinent information about the store. After he ended his call from Toronto, Max sent the completed subpoena to the County Attorney's Office for a signature and called the number for Galibay Jewelers. A pleasant-sounding woman answered the phone.

"This is Detective Max Rupert of the Minneapolis Police Department. Could I speak to the owner or manager there?"

"This is Miriam Galibay. I own the store."

"Ms. Galibay, I'm trying to ascertain the identity of a woman found dead this morning."

Ms. Galibay gave a slight gasp.

"I need your help."

"Certainly, but how . . ."

"The deceased was wearing a pair of Hercinia diamond earrings. We contacted the company, and they informed us that the earrings were purchased by you for resale. We need to find out who bought those earrings."

"Oh . . . Oh my, I . . . I'm afraid I cannot help you. Our clients rely upon us to protect any information given to us. I mean, you're just a voice on the phone. I can't give out client information to anyone who calls. You understand, don't you?"

Max looked at his inbox and saw the completed administrative subpoena scanned into an e-mail. He sent it to the printer. "Ms. Galibay, I'm going to fax you an administrative subpoena. It requires you to provide me with the name of the owner of those earrings. I understand your situation, but this is important."

Max walked to the printer with his cell phone pressed to his ear, pulled the subpoena, and sent it to Galibay as they talked.

"But, Detective, how do I know that you are who you say you are? I don't know what an administrative subpoena is. I have a reputation to protect."

"Ms. Galibay, call the Minneapolis Police Department and ask for Detective Rupert. They'll connect you back to me so you know that I am who I say I am. If I have to, I could drive down there and hand-deliver the subpoena, but this is urgent. Can you just call me back? You'll see that I am who I say I am."

"Okay. I'll do that." The line went dead.

Max went back to his cubicle and waited for his phone to ring. Thirty seconds. One minute. A minute and a half. Two minutes. Finally, after two minutes and fifteen seconds, the phone rang.

"Max Rupert here."

"Detective Rupert, this is Miriam Galibay. I have that information for you. The name of the person who purchased those earrings is Benjamin Pruitt."

Max nearly dropped the phone. "Ben Pruitt, the attorney?"

"Well, I don't know if he's an attorney, but I have an address on Mount Curve Avenue, if that helps."

Max scribbled the address down, thanked Ms. Galibay, and ended the call. The urge to spit caused Max to tighten his lips together.

Max typed Ben Pruitt's name into the computer, and the Internet fed Max thousands of responses. He did a search for images and found dozens of pictures of the man he knew to be Ben Pruitt. About halfway down the page, he saw a picture of Ben standing next to a stunning redhead—the woman from the alley. Max clicked on the link and read a caption identifying the couple as Ben and Jennavieve Pruitt, attending a political fundraiser.

Max called Niki as he ran out the door, giving her the victim's name and address. He would meet her there.

Chapter 5

On the drive back to Kenwood, Max thought about the last time he saw Ben Pruitt. It had been in a small conference room in the office of the Minnesota Professional Responsibility Board two years earlier. Pruitt's disciplinary hearing lasted a little over an hour, but the road to get there took the better part of a year.

It began with the trial of a man named Harold Carlson, a roofing contractor who crushed his girlfriend's skull with a roofing hatchet, a particularly evil-looking tool with a hammer head on one end and a small axe on the other. Her sin had been to kiss another man, one of Carlson's employees, a man who also owned a roofing hammer. Carlson would take the stand and swear that he never touched her. He had no idea how her arms and legs became burned with road rash and other marks consistent with being thrown from a moving vehicle.

A motorist discovered the woman's body in a heap along the road, and before the sun rose that morning, a trail of suspicion brought Max to Harold Carlson's home.

Max found Carlson asleep on his couch, the stench of hard liquor seeping from the man's pores. Max also found the roofing hammer, with the girlfriend's hair and blood on it, lying in plain sight on the seat of Carlson's truck. Max had been alone when he found the hammer, and one of the techs had walked past the truck without having noticed it. Both sides knew that the case rested on Max's testimony about finding the hammer.

On cross-examination, Carlson's attorney, Ben Pruitt, grilled Max, suggesting that Max found the hammer along the highway where the body had been found. Pruitt accused Max of then planting the hammer in Carlson's truck. Pruitt's questions pointed out that Max had the opportunity to plant the hammer. He'd been at the scene where they found the body. There had been moments when he hadn't been observed and could have secreted the hammer into his car. He was alone when he claimed to have found the hammer in the truck, a location where a crime-scene tech, a woman trained to observe and find murder weapons, had walked past without seeing the large silver hammer. Max swatted the questions away with honesty. It happened the way it happened, and he didn't have to explain it any further.

But then Pruitt asked for and was granted permission to approach the witness. He held a single-page document in his hand, and as he walked up to the witness stand he spoke in a loud clear voice so that everyone on the jury could hear.

"I'm showing you defense Exhibit 42. Do you recognize this document?"

Max took a moment to read the document then answered. "I've never seen this document before."

"You don't remember receiving a reprimand from your superiors for falsifying evidence in a case just two years ago?"

Max looked at the Assistant County Attorney and wondered why the man hadn't jumped up to object.

Pruitt continued. "Falsifying evidence, just like planting evidence, is a serious thing for a police detective to do."

Max glared at Pruitt, wanting more than anything to shove that forged document down the man's throat. "Mr. Pruitt, I've never seen this document before because this document never existed before. I've never received—"

Finally the prosecutor stood up and shouted, "Objection, Your Honor. Lack of foundation. Lack of authenticity. This document has never been disclosed—"

"Approach! Now," the judge ordered. Both attorneys walked up to the bench. The judge pressed a button that filled the court with white noise so that the bench conference would not be heard by the jury. Despite the white noise, Max could hear occasional words or phrases as the exchange grew heated.

"It's cross-examination, I don't need to disclose."

"This document has to be a forgery. Detective Rupert said he's never seen it before."

"Detective Rupert's a damned liar."

At that last one, the judge piped in and pointed a finger at Pruitt. Max couldn't hear the words, but the redness in the judge's face spoke volumes. After sending the two attorneys back to their respective tables, the judge instructed the jury to disregard Exhibit 42 and the statements of Mr. Pruitt. He was asking them to not remember Pruitt's assertion that Max had been reprimanded for falsifying evidence. And by asking them to disregard that point, he was embedding Pruitt's words in the brain of each juror.

At the end of Max's testimony, the Court took a short recess during which Max convinced the prosecutor to get the Court to order that Pruitt provide the State with a copy of Exhibit 42. Pruitt argued against it, saying that because it was not received into evidence, he had no obligation to share his work product. The judge was not in a mood to put up with that, and the State got a copy of the document.

Exhibit 42 turned out to be a carefully forged letter of reprimand confirming that Detective Max Rupert had been found to have planted a syringe in the purse of a woman whose roommate died of a heroin overdose. The case never existed. The letter of reprimand had been the creation of someone's desperate imagination. But whose?

At Pruitt's disciplinary hearing, Pruitt testified that his investigator produced that document as part of standard background research on Detective Rupert. Pruitt went on to suggest that his client, the roofing contractor, must have paid the investigator to forge that document.

The investigator denied it and was facing a licensing board himself at the time. In the end, the Board of Professional Responsibility took Pruitt's license to practice law away for sixty days and issued a public reprimand. The Board concluded that Pruitt knew or should have known that the document was a forgery. It chided his failure to use due diligence to confirm the authenticity of the document before presenting it to a court. His act, in the end, was a fraud upon the court.

Pruitt's reprimand was a public one and made it into the business sections of both the *Minneapolis Star Tribune* and the *St. Paul Pioneer Press Dispatch*. Max smiled when he read the articles. He thought the newspaper articles would end the attorney's career, but somehow it seemed to have the opposite effect.

Now, Pruitt's wife was found naked and dead in a parking lot in Kenwood, and a theory was taking shape in Max's mind.

Chapter 6

The Pruitt's house may have been a mansion to some, probably not in the eyes of someone who lived in a true mansion, but it was big and square and solid, as though it had been cut from a single block of stone. It stood on a corner lot raised up from the street by a retaining wall that had the appearance of a pedestal upon which the trophy house gleamed. Pruitt had never impressed Max as being an attorney of such a stature that he would be able to afford that kind of house.

Niki stood at the door of the house with a uniformed officer at her side. Two more officers stood on the sidewalk at the base of a set of steps cut through the retaining wall. One more officer arrived just behind Max. Max signaled for the officers to follow him up the steps to Niki's position.

"I've rung the doorbell and knocked. No answer."

Max turned to the small group of uniformed officers. "Okay, we're doing a welfare check here. We found a body this morning; we believe foul play is involved. We've identified the victim as Jennavieve Pruitt, and this is her house. We don't have a warrant, so we're going in just to make sure that there are no other victims, like maybe a family member in need of help. No going through drawers or cupboards. Just look for bodies. If you see anything else in plain view, call Niki or me, got it?"

The officers all nodded.

"You two," Max pointed at two of the officers. "Go around back and check the garage and any out-buildings." Then he addressed the remaining two officers in turn. "You go with Detective Vang, and you with me."

Everyone drew their weapons. Max tried the handle on the door, and the door clicked open. Unlocked.

"Benjamin Pruitt!" Max yelled. "This is Detective Max Rupert of the Minneapolis Police Department! We're coming in! Mr. Pruitt, are you here?" Max entered the foyer and turned to the left, his companion officer behind him. Niki turned right.

"Mr. Pruitt, it's the police!" Niki shouted. "If you're here, call out. We're here to help!"

Max's path took him into a study, a room with mahogany walls and twelve-foot ceilings—a corner office with paintings on the wall, the blurry kind that Max knew to be the work of an impressionist, the kind of painting that his Jenni loved so much but that he never quite understood.

On another wall Max saw a row of family photos, one of Pruitt standing beside Jennavieve. Next to that, a picture clipped from the *Minneapolis Star Tribune*, with Ben Pruitt standing next to Jennavieve. The caption identified the couple as well as a third person in the picture, their daughter, Emma. Max hadn't even noticed the girl, about eight, maybe nine years old, peeking out from behind her mother's black evening dress, the girl's lower lip pulled into a bashful bite.

"They have a daughter," Max yelled to Niki. "Her name is Emma."

Max passed through the study to a mudroom and back porch, rain boots, three pair, in a neat row, unused slickers hanging on hooks, the smell of cedar and cloves rising from a wooden bowl of potpourri in the corner. Nothing amiss.

Max continued to call out his presence, as did Niki from the other side of the house. The mudroom connected to a pantry stocked full of canned and dry goods, organized by category, then content, then size. Max passed though the pantry and entered the kitchen at the same time that Niki entered the kitchen from the dining room.

"Anything?"

Niki shook her head no and opened the last unchecked door, which led down to a dank-looking basement. Niki called down. "Mr. Pruitt? Emma? It's the police. We're coming down."

Max motioned and led his officer back to the entry and the staircase leading upstairs. They took the stairs two at a time. The first bedroom they came to had been turned into a storage room, filled with boxes and Christmas ornaments and old exercise equipment. The officer went to check the closet and shook his head no to Max.

Across the hall, Max found Emma's room, painted in little-girl colors with a canopied bed, its sheets—horses and stars—matching the spread that had been wrapped around her mother at the bookstore. Whoever killed Mrs. Pruitt had used Emma's bedspread to haul her out of the house.

Max looked around the room. Emma played soccer and had won four trophies, which filled a corner of her dresser. She'd pinned pictures of her and her mother and father on the wall above her bed, pictures taken on a warm beach with a bright-blue ocean in the background. Another set of pictures captured her and her father riding on horseback in a jungle. On her dresser, next to her soccer trophies, stood an eight-by-ten of Emma, a school portrait.

At a minimum, this little girl's bed was now connected to a murder. It was possible that he might also have a missing child on his hands. He had probable cause to issue an Amber Alert. Max eased the back off the frame and slipped the picture out.

At the end of the hall they came to the master suite. There Max found his crime scene. To the left of the king-sized bed, blood spattered in a broken arc hitting the wall, spraying the keepsakes on a bedside table, and ending in the middle of the high-end Amish-built bed that had been stripped of its bedding. In the middle of the bare mattress, a large towel lay half folded, half wadded. Max pulled latex gloves from his pocket, snapped them on, and lifted a corner of the towel to expose a stain of blood the size of a turkey platter.

Max motioned for the officer to stand still and not move while he checked the bathroom and walk-in closet. He stepped carefully so as not to disturb anything, and he made no move beyond what was absolutely necessary to make sure there were no other bodies. Then he pulled his phone out and called Niki.

"Anything in the basement?"

"Nothing out of place."

"Come on up here to the master bedroom. I found our crime scene."

Max instructed the officer beside him to go down and check in with the two officers searching the out-buildings. "Tell them to finish the search for bodies, then secure the perimeter. Stay put until we get a search warrant."

When Niki entered, Max pointed at the first traces of blood in the carpet between the master bedroom and the master bath. "It starts here. I think your shower theory works. The blood seems to follow a path, as if the victim was stabbed here and was then thrown onto the bed, where she bled out. The bedspread we found on the victim came from the daughter's bed down the hall."

"So where're the husband and daughter?"

"I have a theory, but I'm not a big fan of Ben Pruitt, so I don't want to jump to any conclusion too quickly. We'll need a warrant."

Niki glanced around the room as if taking mental notes for her probable-cause application, then nodded. "I'm on it."

Max handed her the photo of Emma. "Also, do an Amber Alert. Let's assume that Pruitt has the child and is running."

"Kills the wife and takes off with the child?"

"It's as good a theory as any at this point."

"But why take the bedding? Why haul the body to the bookstore parking lot?"

"I don't know. But the best I can come up with is either Pruitt killed his wife and is on the run with Emma, or Pruitt didn't kill his wife and the odds of us finding another body go way up."

Chapter 7

Max stationed one officer at the front of the property and another in back, then called Bug to tell him that they found the crime scene. Bug and his partner, Dennis, had just finished combing through the contents of the dumpster behind the bookstore. As expected, they found nothing of interest. They would be at the Pruitt house shortly.

Max went to his squad car, an unmarked Dodge Charger, and slipped a digital recorder out of his jacket pocket. Then he used his phone to search the Internet for Ben Pruitt's office number. He found it right away. He turned on the digital recorder and dialed.

A woman answered. "Pruitt Law Office, how can I help you?"

"I need to speak to Ben Pruitt."

"I'm sorry, but Mr. Pruitt isn't available at the moment. Can I take a message?"

This didn't surprise Max. He'd have been surprised if Pruitt had been in the office. "Is he at court, or do you expect him back soon?"

"I'm sorry, but I don't discuss Mr. Pruitt's schedule. Can I take a message, or would you like his voice mail?"

"Can you give me his cell-phone number? It's vitally important that I reach him."

"I'm sorry, but I cannot give out his cell-phone number. Let me put you through to his—"

"Miss, my name is Detective Max Rupert of the Minneapolis Police Department. I'm not calling Mr. Pruitt about a case. I have a matter of life and death I'm dealing with, and it involves Mr. Pruitt. I need to reach him immediately. This isn't a matter to go to voice mail. Do you have the ability to reach him or not?"

"Well, I . . . I could have him call you."

This came at odds with what Max expected. "So you know where he's at?"

"I do, but I am not at liberty to say, seeing as I don't know who you are for sure. Give me your number, and I'll get a message to him to call you. That's all I can do."

Max gave her his number and hung up to wait for a call he didn't believe would come. After five minutes, his phone rang. Max turned on the recorder again and answered.

"Detective Rupert?"

"Mr. Pruitt?"

"Yes."

"I need to talk to you, and I'd like to do it in person."

"No problem. Just stop by my room, number 414 at the Marriott on Michigan Avenue."

"Michigan Avenue?"

"Yeah. Chicago. So you can either fly down here to chat, or you tell me what this is all about over the phone."

"Is your daughter with you?"

"What?" The tone in Pruitt's voice lost its edge of cockiness. "My daughter? What do you mean, 'is she with me'? No, my daughter isn't with me. What's going on? Is Emma missing?"

"Mr. Pruitt, calm down."

"You're scaring me, Detective. What's—"

"Mr. Pruitt, we're trying to find your daughter. Do you know—"

"Where's my wife? Let me talk to Jennavieve. She'll know. She has to know."

Max searched Pruitt's voice for any hint of pretense. He sounded genuinely upset and confused. "Mr. Pruitt, your wife isn't here. We need to know where your daughter might be. Do you have any idea?"

"No. I don't know where Emma is ... I ... I don't understand."

"Mr. Pruitt," Max paused for a second to put the words together in his mind before he spoke them. "Mr. Pruitt, a body was found this morning, deceased. We believe it's your wife."

"My . . . but . . . I . . . I can't breathe. Give me a second. I just need to . . . breathe."

"Do you have any idea where Emma might be? Any at all?"

"My God. Detective Rupert, you have to find her. You have to find Emma."

"Where could we look? We need a place to start."

"What happened? When did she go missing? I . . . I have to get home."

"Mr. Pruitt, we're doing all we can to find your daughter. Does your daughter have a cell phone?"

"No. We were going to get her one for her birthday in October. What happened to Jennavieve? How'd she . . . I mean . . . are you sure?"

"We'll need you to make a final ID, but we believe it's her. I can't discuss any more right now."

"I'm on my way. I'll catch the next flight back. If you hear anything, I mean anything, you'll call me, right?"

"Sure, but in the meantime, if we could look through your house, maybe there's a note or something else that will tell us where Emma is."

"Absolutely. You can search anywhere you like. Do what you need to do to find my daughter."

Max disconnected with Pruitt, tucked the recorder back into his pocket, and called Niki. "How's the warrant coming?"

"I'm just getting ready to run it over to the courthouse."

"Add this to the probable cause: 'The victim's husband was located by phone, but the victim's daughter is still unaccounted for. The victim's husband claimed to not know the whereabouts of their daughter.'"

"You believe him, Max?"

Max thought about the fear he heard in the man's words. Pruitt was either genuine, or very good at playing the part. "I'm holding off making a judgment right now. He seemed shaken up. He even granted consent to search his house."

"We have consent? So we don't need a warrant?"

"Get the warrant anyway. You don't know this guy. I don't want him pulling his consent and screwing with us. Also, get an order to

seize his business computer. He'll probably claim attorney-client privilege, but let's secure it so he can't delete anything. We'll let the County
Attorney figure out what we can look at later."

"You think Pruitt's a good bet for this?"

"He says he's in Chicago, and he sounds like he's freaking out about
his missing daughter, but that could all be bullshit. He could be on the
level, but the guy's a snake. Let's be extra careful on this one. I don't
want to step into any traps."

Chapter 8

The open front door of the Pruitt home was thick enough to stand up to a medieval battering ram and smelled of wood oil. Max stood just outside of the door and watched as Bug and Dennis inspected the runners of the mansion's elegant stairway for footprints. Niki arrived with the search warrant just about the time that Bug gave them a nod that it was okay to enter the house. Max and Niki slipped cloth booties over their shoes, put on gloves, and made their way upstairs to the master bedroom.

Nothing in the room gave the impression of a fight. Books on the nightstand stood next to a water glass and a charging cell phone. Knick-knacks, a jewelry box, and pictures on the dresser appeared orderly. The bed, with its missing sheets and bloody towel, held the only signs that something bad took place in the room. Max waited for Bug to snap a few pictures of the towel in the middle of the king-sized mattress before picking it up and inspecting it. He found three long strands of red hair matted into the blood in the towel. They were consistent in both color and length with the hair he'd seen wrapped around Jennavieve Pruitt's face that morning.

Max pulled out his digital recorder and began dictating notes for his report. "Three strands of red hair were matted within the area of dried blood on the towel found on the bed in the master bedroom. These strands appear to be visually consistent with the hair of the deceased, Jenni Pruitt."

"Jennavieve, you mean," Niki said. She was on her hands and knees looking under the bed.

"What?"

"You called the deceased 'Jenni.' Her name is Jennavieve."

"Did I say Jenni?"

"I'm pretty sure." Niki reached under the bed, her arm buried up to her shoulder, her eyes focused on something at the end of her reach. "Hey, Bug, come get a picture of this."

Bug got on his belly and snapped four shots of whatever it was that Niki found. Then Niki pulled out a second towel, white with splotches of blood, in long oblique patches, staining half it. Niki turned the towel sideways as if she were going to wrap it around her body, and the blood stains matched up to where the blood would have spurted out of Jennavieve Pruitt's neck.

Max pointed at the towel in Niki's hands. "She used that one to dry her body and this one for her hair," he said.

Niki sniffed her towel and nodded. "Body wash." They put their towels into paper evidence bags.

"Detectives?" Bug had stopped taking pictures and was looking at a wooden display case about the size of a cereal box centered on the fireplace mantle. Niki and Max joined him. The mahogany shadow box had a blue felt interior that appeared to have been molded to hold a missing, ceremonial dagger. Max could tell from the shape of the mold that the dagger's blade was long and angled on both sides to suggest a double-edged blade. The handle, also long with a walnut-sized pommel at the end, gave the impression that the knife was more of a decorative piece than an actual weapon. The cross guard, the piece of metal that keeps the hand from sliding from the handle to the blade, curved toward the blade almost in a perfect *C*. An inscription on a gold plate attached to the bottom of the display read: "FOR CARVING OUT MORE PROTECTED LAND."

"Get a picture of that with measurements and send it to my phone. I want to show this to Maggie. Also check for prints. If that missing knife turns out to be our murder weapon, someone had to hold the box to pull it out."

Max went back to the bed and followed the blood trail, which started at the side of the bed and led to a bathroom larger than Max's bedroom, complete with a hot tub, a double-sink vanity, and a tiled shower big enough to host a small party. The floor was dry, but a wash-cloth wadded up on the floor was still damp. Niki watched from the doorway of the bathroom as Max narrated his thoughts.

"Mrs. Pruitt takes a shower . . . the washcloth is still damp, so some-time last night fits with what Maggie said. She wraps a towel around her body and another around her hair. She . . ." he walked to the vanity, where a bottle of vanilla body lotion lay on its side, and next to it, a hair dryer and night cream. "She puts body lotion on her legs, maybe some night cream on her face. But she doesn't dry her hair."

"She's interrupted," Niki said. "She hears something."

Max nodded agreement. "She walks into the bedroom to check." Max walked to the spot where the blood trail began, just past a corner that separated the bathroom and walk-in closet from the rest of the bedroom. He stood facing the bedroom door. "She turns the corner and sees her killer. The killer stabs her in the neck. Blood hits the wall as she is moving toward the bed. We have blood on the towel around her body. The towel falls to the floor, and she falls onto the bed?"

Niki looked at the trail of blood spanning about seven feet and shook her head. "Maybe the force of the blow sent her to the bed, or maybe the killer pushed her there. She didn't have defensive wounds, so no struggle."

"She was either surprised, or she knew her attacker. Either way, the attack happened quickly. There's very little blood on the floor. She'd have been pushed onto the bed right away. She lands with her throat in the middle of the mattress and bleeds out. The towel around her body falls off or is pulled off and gets kicked under the bed. The killer lets her bleed out here and then wraps her in Emma's bedspread to haul her to the bookstore." Max crossed his arms over his chest, bringing his right hand up to grip his chin in contemplation. "But why take her to the bookstore?"

"And where's the bedding from this bed?" Niki asked. She stepped into the walk-in closet. "It's not up here anywhere, and it's not in the laundry room. It looks like Jennavieve Pruitt was getting ready for bed, so logic suggests that the bed was already made."

"And where is Emma?" Max asked. "No sign of a struggle. The killer took Emma's bedspread, but the rest of her room is untouched. If she was taken, where's the fight?"

"She left voluntarily?"

"Left with someone who's carrying her dead mother wrapped in a blanket?"

Niki, who'd been looking down at the trail of blood in the carpet, suddenly jerked her head up. "Her bed was made." Niki skirted past Max and into Emma's room. "Look. Her sheets are still tucked in. Emma didn't go to bed here last night. If Jennavieve Pruitt was killed within a couple hours of midnight, Emma would have likely been in bed. She didn't sleep here last night."

"And, if she wasn't here, Mrs. Pruitt would have known where she was." Max went to the nightstand and picked up the cell phone.

Bug, who still stood beside the knife case, piped up. "You'll mess up the metadata if you turn that on."

"We have a missing child." Max said. "I suspect that Forensics will forgive me this once." He turned on the phone and saw that it was not password-protected. He also saw an icon for text messages. He touched it and read the most recent text, which came from Ben Pruitt.

At 5:30 p.m. Ben Pruitt texted: "Going out with some folks from conference. Tell Emma I love her and give her kiss good night for me."

At 5:35 p.m. the reply from Jennavieve Pruitt: "OK."

"This makes it sound like Emma was going to be here all night," Max said. "Someone's plans changed?"

Max was about to dig into older text messages when a uniformed officer called up from the bottom of the steps. "Detective Rupert, there's a little girl out front. Says her name is Emma Pruitt and that she lives here."

Chapter 9

Max hurried down the steps, stopping briefly at the front door to remove his latex gloves and booties. At the bottom of the outside steps, standing on the street curb, was a little girl talking to a female officer. Max took a couple deep breaths, not wanting to alarm the child, and strolled down the walk to her.

Emma looked like her picture, strawberry-blonde hair, cut with bangs, skinny arms and legs, gangly and awkward in her stance. She glanced back and forth between the crime-scene tape and the female officer until she saw Max walking down the steps, then her attention turned to him and stayed there.

"Hi, are you Emma?"

The girl nodded her head, but said nothing.

"I'm Max. I'm a police officer." He slid his jacket aside to show her the gold shield in his belt. "How are you?"

Emma shrugged her shoulders and glanced again at the crime-scene tape behind Max.

"We're here to meet with your father. He was worried about you."

"He's in Chicago," she said.

"I know. I talked to him on the phone. He didn't know where you were, so he called us. Where did you just come from?"

Emma pointed up the block and said, "Catie's house."

"Does Catie live up that way?"

Emma nodded.

"Is Catie a grown-up, or one of your friends?"

"Friend." Emma's eyes danced from Max to the officer then to the house and all of its activities. "Where's my mom?"

"Do you know if Catie's mother is home? I'd like to talk to her. Could you show me where she lives?"

Emma looked at the female officer then at the ground. "I'm not supposed to talk to strangers."

The female officer went down on one knee so that she could be at Emma's level. "That's right, sweetie. It's important that you be very careful, but we're the police. We protect little girls like you."

Max had seen the female officer around, but he couldn't remember her name, so he glanced at her name tag. Sandra Percell. "Emma, would you feel better if Officer Percell walked with us?"

Emma nodded.

"Okay. Why don't you show us where Catie lives?"

Emma walked up the block, the way she'd pointed earlier. As they walked, Max sent a text to Ben Pruitt. *Emma is okay. Was at neighbor's house.*

Two blocks later, they approached the front gate of a house that looked like a grown-up version of a doll's house, two stories of blue siding and white trim capped with cedar-shake shingles. The place even had a turret. Emma led them to the front door, and Max rang the bell. The woman answering the door froze halfway through the motion, a look of fear taking over her features.

"Oh my. Is something wrong?" The woman looked back and forth between Max and Officer Percell.

"Everything's fine, ma'am. Would it be alright if Emma stayed here for a little while?"

"Of course." The woman opened the door wider to let Emma pass. "Catie's upstairs in her room. Go on up." Emma started running up the stairs but paused near the top to have one last look at Max. Her expressionless face couldn't hide her understanding. She knew something was wrong. Max could see it in her eyes. She knew he lied to her. Max held her stare for all of two seconds before he looked away and she disappeared up the stairs.

"I know I probably should have walked Emma home," the woman said. "But she's ten, and that's old enough I think. When I was ten, I was babysitting and everything, so I didn't think there'd be anything wrong—"

"Ma'am, can we talk . . . somewhere that we won't be overheard?"

"Um . . . sure. Come on in."

Max nodded to Percell, who nodded back and left to return to the Pruitt house. Catie's mother led the way through the house and out the back. She brought Max to a gazebo painted the same blue and white as the house and that overflowed with an array of flowers. On the gazebo they took seats opposite one another.

"My name is Detective Max Rupert." He held out his hand and the woman took it.

"I'm Terry Kolander," she said. "Am I in trouble?"

"Not at all, Ms. Kolander. I'm going to tell you some things that I need you to keep to yourself for a little while. Can we have that understanding?"

"Of course. I used to be a nurse. I understand confidentiality."

"That's good." Max leaned forward in his chair so that he could talk in a hushed tone. "Did Emma spend the night here last night?"

"Yes."

"What time did she come over?"

Terry thought for a moment. "A little after five. Jennavieve called and asked if I could watch Emma for the night. She said she had something she had to attend to. I said yes, of course. Catie and Emma are best friends."

"Did Mrs. Pruitt say what she was going to do last night?"

Terry raised a hand to her lips. "Has something happened to Jennavieve?"

"Was it a business meeting or something personal?"

"Oh, no. I mean, um . . . I don't think she said. She just said . . . she said 'Can you watch Emma for the night? I have . . .'" Terry furrowed her brow in thought. "'I have some things to take care of.' That's what she said. I just assumed it had something to do with her foundation."

"Her foundation?"

"Yes. Jennavieve is the director of a foundation that restores wetlands.

She's always having meetings in the evenings. She was in the paper not too long ago. Her foundation won a big court case." Terry stopped talking, as if a new thought kicked its way to the forefront of her consciousness. She locked her eyes on Max's. "What happened? Why are you here?"

"When's the last time you saw Mrs. Pruitt?"

"Detective Rupert, what happened to Jennavieve?"

Max dropped his head, knowing that his conversation would not continue until she had an answer. He raised his head back up, looked her in the eye, and said, "We found a body this morning. We believe it to be the body of Mrs. Pruitt."

Terry gasped and looked toward the house, to an upstairs window where two young girls stood, watching the gazebo.

"I need you to be calm, Ms. Kolander," Max said, drawing her attention back to him. We haven't had an ID of the body, and we're waiting for Mr. Pruitt to get here from Chicago. I'm hoping you can watch Emma until we get things squared away."

"Absolutely." Ms. Kolander's eyes began to tear up.

"And I need you to act like nothing has happened. If it turns out to be Mrs. Pruitt, we'll let her father decide how best to let Emma know."

"Sure." Terry slid a fingernail under each eye, catching the forming tears in the corners and wiping them on her pleated shorts.

"What can you tell me about Mrs. Pruitt?"

Terry took a breath to settle her emotions before answering. "She's incredible. I know she comes from a wealthy background. Her family owns a bunch of businesses. I think they made most of their money in paper milling. They own a ton of land up north and a handful of paper mills. But Jennavieve isn't the corporate type. I mean, don't get me wrong, she's a powerful woman, on the Board of Governors for the Minneapolis Club, a big donor at the Guthrie and Hennepin Theater Trust. She's very involved with just about every important local charity, but her baby was the Adler Wetland Preservation Foundation."

"Adler?"

"That's her maiden name. She devoted a lot of time to that foundation."

"And what about Mr. Pruitt? What can you tell me about him?"

"We weren't close friends with the Pruitts. Not that we disliked them. People live busy lives. We'd see them around the neighborhood, they seemed nice. They came out a couple weeks ago for the Fourth of July. We have a little get-together every year. Nothing fancy, just drinks and steaks."

"How'd they seem?"

Terry scrunched her face—the look of a woman who had a thought but wasn't sure about sharing it.

"Anything you can tell us might be helpful," Max said.

"Well, it's probably nothing, but when they were here, Ben was being very attentive to Jennavieve."

"Was that unusual?"

"I don't know if it was unusual . . . I don't know them well enough. He just seemed . . . I don't know . . . maybe 'overly charming' might be how I'd describe it. He can be a charming man to begin with, but that day he was floating around here like Gene Kelly. Kept asking Jennavieve if he could refill her drink or get her a napkin, that kind of thing."

"And how was Jennavieve?"

"She was her normal self. Between the two of them, she's the serious one. At one point, Ben found an oleander blossom that one of the kids must have broken off, and he brought it over and put it in Jennavieve's hair. I said 'Wasn't that sweet.' And Jennavieve said 'It's all for show.' I wasn't sure how to take that. I mean, Jennavieve can be so serious. I didn't know if she was joking or not."

The chime on Max's phone dinged, and he looked to see a text from Maggie Hightower. *Starting the postmortem. You want to be here?*

"Excuse me," Max said. "I need to respond." He texted Maggie back. *Go ahead and get started. I'll be there in a bit.* "Sorry about that. So, do you think the Pruitts were having marital problems?"

"Not to my knowledge, but like I said, we weren't close. If it weren't for the children being inseparable, we'd probably never see the Pruitts."

"But people hear things."

Terry shrugged. "I don't engage in gossip. There are some neighbors who are nosier than others, but I don't care to hear that kind of prattle. People know that about me, so I'm usually kept well out of the loop."

"Suppose I were to track down these nosey neighbors, what might their names be?"

Terry gave Max a look of disapproval. She had no idea how important nosey neighbors were to solving crime. Max held her gaze then raised an eyebrow.

"You might start with Malena Gwin. She lives right across the street from the Pruitts. She tends to have her nose in most things going on around here."

"I appreciate your help, Ms. Kolander." Max stood to leave.

Terry walked Max to the front door, and partway to the street, pausing there to have one last moment of privacy. "What's going to happen to Emma?"

"Her father will be here in a little while. We can put him in touch with professionals to help him break the news to Emma. It's not going to be easy for her."

"She's very quiet, and sweet. This is going to be very hard on her." Terry glanced over her shoulder at the house. The windows were all empty. "At least she has her father," Terry said.

Max didn't respond.

Chapter 10

Max Rupert remembered his first autopsy, the hint of formaldehyde and rotting meat barely noticeable behind the acidic pungency of bile. He watched a doctor pull organs from a dead man's body, examine them, weigh them, and then put them in jars. The ME worked with an efficiency that could only come from years of experience. It reminded Max of a day when he was a child and he watched his father replace the carburetor on their Dodge Dart. No wasted movements. Every part set aside on the garage floor in an orderly formation. It was nothing to get emotional about—just a task that needed doing.

In the years since that first postmortem, Max found that if he harkened back to that day in his father's garage, he could better handle watching autopsies. They were bodies, not people. They had parts that needed removing, parts that had been damaged, parts that sometimes held the secret to finding a killer. Any personality, any spark of individuality that had once inhabited those bodies, had departed long ago, expelled in that last, silent exhale.

When Jenni died, however, the delicate wall that separated him from these victims splintered into a thousand shards. He hadn't watched his wife's postmortem, of course, but every time he entered that room, he knew that she had been there. She had lain on a stainless-steel table. She had her ribs cut open—ribs that Max used to tickle as they lay in bed on lazy mornings. They had lifted her heart out of her chest—just a handful of dead muscle. How many times had he listened to that heart beat against his ear over the years? She had been dissected by a doctor just doing a task that needed doing. The hands that cut her apart had no idea how special she was. How loved she was. They had no idea of the magnitude of loss her death meant to the world—to Max.

He and Jenni were going to see Europe. They were going to have a child—adopt if necessary, or maybe become foster parents. They were going to grow old together. Everything they were working toward still lay ahead of them. On the day she died, Max learned how crushing the sheer weight of those dreams could be. Everything ended so abruptly that it felt as though he had driven into an oncoming train. And in the days immediately after her death, there were moments when he would forget to breathe and times when he was sure his heart would stop beating.

In that impact, not only did he lose the ability to see the bodies as just bodies, but they began to follow him around. He would hear their whispers in the breezes that passed by his ear. Their reflections would beckon to him from muddy puddles or dirty windows. They judged him as he fought to find sleep at night. How often had they come to him in his dreams, the black stitching, the gray eyes? No matter how handsome or beautiful they had been in life, they came to Max as he had seen them on that examination table.

Max thanked God that he had never seen the pictures from Jenni's death. He was the husband, not the detective. He was prohibited from having anything to do with the investigation of her hit-and-run, but that didn't stop him from hearing things. It didn't stop him from taking a peek at some of the reports. The detective in charge was a friend, a man okay with turning a blind eye.

But Max never looked at the photographs. He couldn't bring himself to do that. He had read enough of the reports to understand why her funeral had a closed casket. He understood why she had to be identified using dental records. Her death had been messy, not the clean bounce-off-the-car that the stuntmen do in the movies. The car that hit Jenni had dragged her before it took her life. Then the car sped away and no one ever paid for her death.

Now the body of Jennavieve Pruitt lay on a stainless-steel table in the center of the room, with a stitched-up incision in the shape of a Y starting at her shoulders and ending at her pelvis. Another incision, not yet stitched shut, opened the side of her neck where the knife wound had been. A strand of the woman's red hair had fallen across her face, and Max had to resist an urge to brush it back.

"The wound on the neck was the cause of death," Maggie said from her seat at her computer. "Cut both the carotid and the jugular."

Max turned to her as he cleared away distracting thoughts. "We have a preliminary ID on the body," he said. "Jennavieve Pruitt. She's the wife of a criminal-defense attorney named Ben Pruitt."

"Ben Pruitt? That name rings a bell. I think he's cross-examined me once before." She turned away from the computer monitor to give the name her full attention. "Yeah, if I recall the right guy, he'd be middle to late forties now, dark hair, kind of handsome—when his mouth is shut?"

"That's him."

"You got him figured for this?"

"I wouldn't put it past him. He pulled some shit on me during a case once. Let's just say I wouldn't lose any sleep if I had to send him to prison. Did you get a TOD?"

"I can give you a fairly tight range. I'd put her time of death at pretty close to midnight. Body temperature can do only so much, especially because we can't be certain when she was moved outdoors."

"What caused the neck wound?"

"A blade." Maggie turned back to her computer, clicked past a number of photos of organs being extracted and weighed, and stopped at photos of the neck. "I cleaned the wound, and if you look at this close-up, you can see that the incision is about an inch and a half wide. And look here." She pointed at the ends of the cut with the tip of a pencil. "This blade is double-edged. No flat side."

"Like a dagger?"

"Generally speaking, yes. And the killer stabbed the blade all the way in." Maggie pointed to a couple dots about the size of a pencil eraser equally spaced on either side of the incision. "This dagger has a cross guard that's curved in toward the blade in an arc. The tips of the guard left bruises on her neck."

Max pulled his phone out of his pocket and brought up the photo

Bug had sent him of the knife display case they had found in the bedroom. "Any idea on the blade length?"

"Not for sure, but it was long enough that it penetrated through to the other side of her neck." Maggie clicked to a picture from the left side of the woman's throat and a small half-inch incision.

Max showed her the display-case photo.

Maggie compared Bug's measurements to her own. "The incision is a few millimeters wider than the blade you have here, but with a double edge like that, you're going to cut on the way in and on the way out. The length of the blade fits and the points on the tips of the cross guard are a perfect match. I'd say that if this isn't your murder weapon, it's a dagger very much like it."

"Excellent," Max said. "What else you got for me?"

"Some unusual bruises." Maggie again moved through her computer photos to a series taken of Jennavieve Pruitt's back. "It's here." She circled an area of the woman's shoulder with the tip of her pencil. "It's hard to see through the lividity, but there is a definite bruise on her right shoulder and here on the back of her left arm, and some finger-shaped bruises on the back of her head and neck. You can almost see a handprint."

Max looked at the pictures and moved his hands around to try and match the bruise pattern. Then he got down on one knee and looked up at the picture again. "If the killer held her down . . . if she was face-down on the bed and the killer held her down like this, with a knee on her right shoulder, one hand on the back of her head, and the other on her left arm . . . would that explain the bruise pattern?"

Maggie went through the photos again, comparing them to Max's simulation. "I think that fits pretty well. You think she was held down?"

"We found the crime scene. She was stabbed a few feet from a bed, but then either fell or was pushed onto the bed, where she bled out."

"And the killer held her down while she bled to death. That would explain the lack of blood on the bedding you found her in."

"Any chance of prints from the skin?"

"We can try, but it's very unlikely."

"Any indication of sexual assault?"

"Nothing definite. If she had sex recently, it was with a condom and not rough enough to leave a mark."

"What about stomach contents?"

"She had a salad for dinner—I'm guessing a late dinner—and wine."

"She had wine in her stomach?"

"I didn't sip it to verify, but I sent a sample in for a toxicology test."

"Any sign of defensive wounds?"

"No bruises, other than the ones I showed you on her shoulder, arm, and neck. No skin cells under the finger nails. Her death came quickly. With both the carotid and the internal jugular cut, she would have lost consciousness in a matter of seconds."

Max walked over and looked at Jennavieve Pruitt's body, taking in the contrast between her cold white skin and the black zigzag of the stitching that held her chest and abdomen together. He looked at her face, knowing that it would come to him in those moments when sleep and wake lived in equal parts in his mind. He wanted this face to come to him. He wanted her to speak to him in those quiet moments of the night. If Ben Pruitt killed his wife, Max would make sure he paid for that crime. Although the math didn't add up perfectly, Max could sense a certain equilibrium to it. He may never be able to bring his own wife's killer to justice, but this man squandered a gift. He killed his wife, a woman who loved and trusted him. Pruitt threw away that which Max would kill to have back.

If he could bring Jennavieve Pruitt the justice denied to his own wife, she might help him find some small measure of peace. He knew this bordered on fantasy, maybe even insanity, but deep inside he hoped it to be true.

Chapter 11

Max was finishing up with Maggie when Niki called him. "Ben Pruitt's here," she said, "at his house."

"How's he acting?" Max asked.

"Maybe a bit over the top but not out of control. I have him waiting outside."

"Is his car there?"

"I let him park in the driveway so it's covered in the search warrant."

"Excellent. I'd like to get a look in his trunk and in his suitcase, so don't let him take anything out of the car."

"I already sent an officer to secure it."

"Have I told you lately that you're a damn fine detective?"

"Can never hear it enough."

"I'll tell you what. I'll buy you a parrot and teach it that one phrase. I hear parrots live to be about sixty."

"And I hear parrots taste like chicken. In the meantime, what should I do with Mr. Pruitt?"

"Have a squad car bring him downtown. I'll see if he's interested in talking. Depending on how long that takes, I should be back in time to canvass the neighbors with you."

"See you then."

Max hung up, said his good-bye to Maggie, and headed back to City Hall to prep for his interview with Ben Pruitt.

Pruitt arrived twenty minutes later and was led to the interview room by the unit staff officer. Pruitt looked unsure of himself as he sat across the table from Max. Max held out a hand and Pruitt, with some hesitation, shook it. *Rule one: make them comfortable*, Max thought to himself.

"I'm truly sorry for your loss," Max began.

"Are you sure it's Jennavieve? I mean there's been no positive ID."

Good one, Max thought, *don't tip your hand that you know for sure it's your wife.* Jennavieve's murderer would know that she was dead and exactly how she was murdered. An innocent man would be asking questions. "You'll have to go make a positive identification, but I have a photo I could show you, if you want to see her."

"Yes . . . I . . . I need to see."

Max opened his file enough to pull out a black-and-white picture from the autopsy. He turned it around and slid it across the table. *Now watch his reaction.*

"Oh my God!" Pruitt began to shake, his fingers clamped tightly on the edges of the picture of his wife's pale, dead face. "Oh my God, it's Jennavieve. I can't . . ." He put the picture down, leaving it face up, not as Max expected. A guilty person would feel compelled to turn the picture over, to hide the face of the person they killed. They wouldn't want to see their victim looking back in judgment.

"What happened? Who did this?"

"I assure you we're doing everything we can to answer those questions." An answer but not an answer.

"Anything you want from me, just ask."

"I appreciate that. It'll help a lot if we could exclude you as a suspect. Can we get your fingerprints and DNA?"

Pruitt straightened up. "Exclude me? You know you'll find my fingerprints and DNA all over that house. How will that exclude me?"

"You know how this works. It's standard procedure. If we know what's yours, we can figure out what isn't yours."

Max could see a hint of anger pass behind Pruitt's eyes.

"I'm the husband. I know I'm gonna be the first person on your list of suspects. That's standard procedure too. Or am I wrong?" Pruitt's eyes stared into Max's, waiting for a response, a response that Max refused to give. "And, by the way, don't think I didn't notice that you didn't answer my question. How did my wife die?"

"I'm afraid I can't discuss an active investigation."

"Bullshit, Detective." Pruitt continued to stare at Max and spoke in a controlled tone. "I know it's technically confidential, but I also know that you release information all the time if it helps you. Well, I want to help you. I did not kill my wife." Pruitt leaned harder into the table and calmly said it again. "I did not kill my wife. I know you don't like me. I know we've crossed paths before and it left a bad taste in your mouth. I'm a criminal-defense attorney for God's sake. It's my job. I wouldn't be doing my job if I didn't piss off a cop or two along the way. You may have it in for me, but as far as I'm concerned, that's all water under the bridge. I want to help you find who did this. And to that end, you need to know that I did not kill my wife."

"Mr. Pruitt, I never said that you killed your wife. I never said you're a suspect. I just want to get as much information so that I can find the person who did this."

"Then tell me what happened. How'd she die?"

A lab tech knocked on the door and entered with a portable fingerprint scanner. "May we?" Max asked.

"Sure," Pruitt said. "But you're wasting your time."

Max glanced at the camera above the door, and gave a nod to his commander, who was watching the interrogation on a computer monitor and had sent the tech in. Pruitt looked at the tech, then at the camera over the door and offered his hand to the tech before returning to the conversation.

"I was in Chicago," Pruitt stated. "I was attending an NACDL convention."

"NACDL?"

"National Association of Criminal Defense Lawyers. It was a conference on white-collar crime. I flew down yesterday, Delta Airlines. Check it out. They'll confirm it. Got to Chicago about eleven a.m. The first panel discussion didn't start until two in the afternoon."

"How'd you get to the airport?"

"Park-and-ride." Pruitt pulled his wallet out of his back pocket and produced a receipt.

"Can I hold on to this?" Max asked.

Pruitt narrowed his eyes, as if calculating advantages and disadvantages of Max's request. Then he answered, "Sure, if it'll help find my wife's killer."

"What hotel did you stay at?"

"The downtown Marriott."

"Is that also where the convention is being held?"

"Yes."

"Did anyone see you?"

"Absolutely, I have a few friends I see at those things."

"Can I get some names?"

"Um . . . let's see, there was—"

The tech, who had been taking Pruitt's fingerprints as he spoke, now waved a long-stemmed cotton swab in the air to signal that he wanted a DNA sample. Pruitt hesitated as though confused by the interruption, then opened his mouth. When the tech finished, Max slid a legal pad and pen across the table, and Pruitt wrote down two names. As he did, Max looked at Pruitt's hands—no marks, no cuts, nor were there any on his face. Max didn't expect to see any, though, as Mrs. Pruitt showed no signs that she struggled with her attacker.

"What about last night?" Max continued.

"I'm an old hand at these conferences. They had a social hour at one of the hospitality suites, but that's for the young guns. I don't need to do any of that politicking. A couple friends invited me to join them for a drink. At first I planned to, but then I felt tired, so I ordered room service—a club sandwich and some fries—and stayed in for the night."

"What time did you go to your room?"

"Around five or so. I called Jennavieve to touch base. She didn't answer, so I sent a text. Told her to kiss Emma good night for me. You can check the cell-phone records for the exact time. For that matter, check the cell-tower data. It'll show that I'm telling the truth."

"Is it common for her not to answer when you call?"

"No more common or uncommon than anyone else with a cell phone, I suppose."

"And you didn't leave your room after that?"

"No. Not until I got up this morning. I started for the conference, but I forgot my schedule. Went back, grabbed it, and was in the big room by the time the first speaker took the stage. Nine a.m. if I recall."

"So no one saw you between the hours of five yesterday evening and nine this morning?"

Pruitt dropped his head and sighed in apparent exasperation. He paused, then raised his head, looked Max in the eyes, and spoke in a slow, clear voice. "Listen, Detective Rupert, if a client called me and said that his wife was murdered and that a homicide detective wanted to talk to him, I'd tell him not to go. I don't care how innocent that client is. I'd tell him not to talk to the cops because the cops are good at getting perfectly innocent people to say things that make them sound guilty. And if I call up any criminal-defense attorney worth his or her salt, they'd tell me not to talk to you, especially given our history. I mean, you have a problem with me, I know that. But here I am. I want to talk to you because my wife was murdered and I didn't do it."

Pruitt's face reddened as he spoke, his pitch rising with each new statement. "I want you to find the sonofabitch that killed my wife—that took my Jennavieve away from Emma. I want to be helpful. But if this is just some bullshit attempt to hang this on me—to get back at me—then we're through. So ask me what you want, but make the questions productive, because if I think you're not interested in my help—if I sense that you're just laying some kind of trap for me because you have a problem with me—then I'm done here."

"Mr. Pruitt, I'm not trying to hang this on anyone right now. I'm just gathering information. I don't know what's important and what's not." *Keep him talking.*

"Whether or not anyone saw me after I went to my hotel room won't help you find my wife's killer. Of course I was there alone. I read a book. Fell asleep early. No friends stopped by. No one-night-stand with some lonely lady at the bar. No escort. Just me and my book and no fucking way to get from Chicago to here and back by morning."

"Mr. Pruitt, there's no need to get riled up. Like you said, it's standard procedure. We need to exclude you."

"Well, you have what you need. Now do your job and find the person who killed my wife. And, by the way, where was Emma when all this happened? Is she safe?"

"She stayed with a neighbor last night, the Kolander family. She had no idea. She's still at Terry Kolander's house."

"Where was Jennavieve killed? At the house? Is that why it's swarming with cops and lab techs? Jesus, what if Emma had been there?"

"Did your wife have any enemies? Do you know of anyone who might want to hurt her?"

"No...I mean..." Pruitt brought his hands up to his forehead and rubbed his temples. "She had some enemies, but I can't imagine anyone resorting to murder."

"Who?"

"Jennavieve ran a foundation that fought to restore wetland habitat. They would coordinate efforts among conservation groups and the federal government to stop development that might impact a wetland. Jennavieve's group brought the lawsuits. They were always pissing people off. She got threatened all the time, but we never took them seriously."

"Anything recent?"

"No. None that I can think of right now."

"Anybody from your side of business have a beef with you?"

"Like one of my clients? No. You'd be surprised how accepting my clients can be of the trouble they get themselves into. They appreciate anything I can do to lessen that trouble."

"Business must be doing well. That's one hell of a house you have."

Pruitt didn't respond.

"You two weren't having any kind of financial issues, were you?"

Again, Pruitt just stared at Max.

"No marital issues?"

Pruitt dropped his head and sighed. "These are not productive questions, Detective. I told you to ask productive questions, questions that might help you find my wife's killer. I didn't kill her. I loved my wife, so quit trying to bring me into this. I had nothing to do with Jen-navieve's death. I know you'd love nothing more than to come after me, but you'd better start asking questions that will actually help find her killer, or I'm leaving."

"I'm just trying to see a full picture, Mr. Pruitt. I mean, every couple has the occasional disagreement. That doesn't paint you as a bad husband."

"Detective, we're done." Pruitt stood up. "I'm still free to leave, am I not?"

"You are."

"Then I'm leaving. And for the record, I'm invoking my right to deal with you through an attorney." Pruitt headed out, but he stopped halfway through the door and turned to look at Max. "I would have stayed here and talked, you know. I would have done everything I could to help you. But it's clear why you brought me here. You want this to be on me, and to hell with any other possibility. Well, if that's the way you want to go, then screw you. My attorney will be in touch."

Ben Pruitt walked out of the interview room. After he'd gone, Max looked up at the camera and signaled to shut down the recorder before he slammed his fist onto the table.

PART 2
The Defense

Chapter 12

Professor Boady Sanden sat on a rocking chair on his front porch, soaking in the warmth of the late-afternoon sun and listening to the chatter of birds in the two massive oaks in his front yard. Beside him lay a stack of papers, notes, and cases he'd collected over the past year, changes in the law handed down by various courts, sharp-pointed edicts that he needed to add to the syllabus for his criminal-procedures class, a class he'd been teaching for six years.

He took a break from work to look up and down Summit Avenue to see if anyone else had a job that let them sit on a porch on such a nice afternoon. He saw no one. He propped one foot up on the porch rail and smiled. Summers off. It was one of the best perks of being a law professor. Of course, he could teach summer term—and had in the past—but not this year. The time had come for the meniscus repair in his right knee, and even though he felt he could have been back teaching in time for the summer session, he was under strict orders from his wife, Diana. And Diana was the boss. She assured him that they didn't need the money, although he noticed that she'd been hinting lately that she might want to stay home for Christmas and not take their usual winter-break trip to the Caribbean.

She always took care of him like that, and he loved her for it.

Even back in the day, back when Boady had a private law office in Minneapolis with a small army of law clerks and associates, back when he gave keynote speeches at criminal-defense conferences and brought home paychecks so big that it sometimes made him giggle, it had always been Diana who called the shots at home. It was Diana who orchestrated the numbers so that they could buy a house on Summit Avenue, a stretch of pavement they shared with the governor's mansion and the Cathedral of St. Paul. Their house was a decent-sized Victorian, bigger than what the two of them needed, but smaller than what the gawkers expected to find on the street where James J. Hill once ran his Great Northern Railway and F. Scott Fitzgerald wrote *This Side of Paradise.*

It was Diana who put Boady's mind at ease when he needed to quit practicing law. It was she who convinced him that they had set aside enough money that he could walk away from his law practice and move to a tiny faculty office on the second floor of Hamline University School of Law. She had watched him struggle under the weight of a client's death for two years before, finally convincing him to give up his law practice. In those two years, she watched him drop twenty pounds. He couldn't eat, couldn't sleep. The practice of law had become more deadly to Boady than a malignant cancer, and Diana feared every day that his drive to work might end in a car crash that only she would know had not been an accident. She'd told him this when she begged him to apply for the law-school opening.

She had saved his life, and he loved her for that, as well.

Boady liked the city of St. Paul. Being the older of the twins, St. Paul bore the deep scars and hunched shoulders of experience. The city was thoughtful and somber and had nothing to prove. It may move a bit slower than its brother to the west, but there was no city on Earth more sure-footed.

Boady had once been a man of Minneapolis. He moved through its halls with a naïve confidence completely undeserved. There had been a time when it seemed as though every decision Boady made, no matter how reckless, ended well for him and for his clients. He felt like one of those action heroes who could run through a warehouse full of flying bullets and never get hit. He was untouchable—until the day he wasn't. Now he understood. Now he was a man of St. Paul.

Boady had let his mind drift away from his syllabus and onto a couple squirrels chasing each other across his yard. They scurried up a tree when the black car pulled up and parked in front of the house. Boady looked up to see Ben Pruitt heading up the walkway.

Boady smiled and waved. "Well, shut my mouth. If it isn't the great Benjamin Lee Pruitt himself."

Ben waved back with no smile. He walked like a man at the end of a long journey even though he had just stepped out of his car. The sadness behind Ben's eyes caused Boady to stand to greet him, a serious greeting for what suddenly had the feel of a serious meeting.

Ben embraced Boady in a hug. "Jennavieve's dead," he said, his voice tripping across the words. He pulled back from the embrace, his eyes thick with tears ready to fall.

"What?"

"She's dead. They found her body this morning. She was murdered."

Boady motioned to a second rocking chair, Diana's chair, and the two sat down. "Are you sure?"

"I just came from the morgue. I identified her."

"What happened?"

"I don't know. I was in Chicago. I flew down yesterday morning for a conference. I got a call today from your buddy, Max Rupert, saying that Jennavieve was dead and Emma was missing."

"Emma's missing?"

"They found her. She spent the night at a neighbor's house. She's alright. I haven't seen her yet, but I'm going there after I talk to you. They tell me she doesn't know her mom's dead yet. I . . . I don't know what to say to her. Her mother was everything to her."

"I'm so terribly sorry . . . Jennavieve . . . I can't believe it. Have they told you anything about how it happened?"

"Not much. I managed to get the ME to tell me that Jennavieve was stabbed. When I viewed her body, she had stitches along the right side of her neck. I've seen autopsy photos before, and I knew that wasn't part of the normal procedure. I pushed until the ME gave in and said that's where the knife . . ." Ben's eyes glazed over and tears began rolling down his cheeks. He wiped them on the sleeves of his white button-down shirt.

"Where was she killed?"

"I don't know. They won't tell me anything. I think she was killed at our house. There's an army of cops there. They won't let me go home."

"If you need a place to stay—"

"No. That's not why I'm here. I'm here because I think I need a lawyer."

Boady started to say something. He wanted to tell his friend to look elsewhere if he needed an attorney, but the words knotted up in his throat.

"I'm afraid Rupert's going to try and hang this on me." Ben shifted in his seat, as though settling in for a longer conversation. "I mean, you heard about the problem between Max Rupert and me, I assume."

Now it was Boady's turn to settle in. He leaned back in his chair, crossed one leg over the other, and tried to recall what he could about the bad blood between Pruitt and Rupert. "I read something about it in the *Minnesota Lawyer*. I also read the Board of Professional Responsibility opinion." Boady tried not to look disappointed, but he must have failed because Ben dropped his eyes as Boady spoke. "You were suspended for . . . was it thirty days?"

"Sixty. But I didn't know that document was a forgery. I swear to God, Boady. My investigator gave that document to me and told me it came from Max Rupert's disciplinary file. I had no way of knowing. It looked legit. I had no reason to question it."

"I'm not saying you knew anything like—"

"Wait. Boady, listen to me. I would never knowingly commit fraud on the court. I would never do that. When you left the practice, you entrusted me with your clients. You said that you knew you were leaving them in good hands, my hands. Did you mean that?"

"Of course I did."

"In all the years we worked together, did I ever do anything to make you believe I would intentionally introduce a forged document into a trial?"

"No."

"Not one of your clients, not one judge, not a single prosecutor has ever accused me of unethical behavior—except that one damned document. That's because I didn't know it was a forgery."

"I believe you, Ben. And you're right, I turned my practice over to you because I trusted you. I never doubted your integrity for a moment.

When I read that you'd been publicly reprimanded, I wanted to call. I should have—"

"I understand why you didn't. I can't blame you. The opinion was so one-sided, I'd have believed it if it weren't about me."

"No, Ben. I should have called. You could have used my support and I . . . well, I dropped the ball."

"Boady, I need your support now. Rupert's never forgiven me. He's the lead on Jennavieve's case, and I know he'll try to find a way to charge me with her death."

"Have you met with him yet?"

"Yes, earlier today."

Boady scratched his chin. "You think that was wise?"

Ben shook his head and looked out to the street. "I know. I would have told any client to stay away from Rupert. It's stupid, but dammit, Boady, I'd just found out that my wife was dead. I wasn't thinking like a lawyer. I just wanted to help find the sonofabitch that killed Jennavieve. If I can help with that, I want to."

"And did you help with that?"

"Probably not."

"What did Rupert want to know?"

"He started by asking me where I was last night. I told him the Marriott in downtown Chicago. I told him that my last communication with her was around five o'clock yesterday. And then he started asking about our marriage and I told him not to."

"Looking for a motive, marital discord."

"If he'd asked me questions that I thought might lead to the person who killed my wife, I'd still be there. But he kept bringing it back to me, so I left."

"And you think he's gunning for you?"

"Boady, I didn't kill Jennavieve. I don't know how he could possibly hang me with this, because I was in Chicago. I had no reason to kill her. I don't know what Max Rupert might do, but I think I need someone on my side. I'm a mess and I need you to help me get through this."

"You know I don't practice law anymore. Except for moot court and my practicum classes, I haven't been in a courtroom in six years."

"You kept your license, didn't you?"

"Yes, but—"

"Boady, you're the best attorney I've ever seen—myself excluded, of course." Ben gave Boady a slight forced smile. "And more important than that, I trust you."

"But I'm not a defense attorney any longer. I don't do that . . . and you know why."

"Boady, you knew Jennavieve. You know me. You and Diana have been to our house. You ate at our table. For God's sake, you were at the hospital when Emma was born. I'm not asking you to get me out of a DWI here. I'm terrified that Max Rupert is coming after me. He's going to ignore any other evidence and dig up anything he can to point this at me. He hates me. He's the one who pulled the strings that led to my reprimand. I need you. I need someone who can help me find the truth, even if Rupert isn't looking for it."

"You know Max and I are friends, right?"

"I know, but I also know that there's no one better than you in a courtroom. There's no one better than you at digging the truth out of a mess of lies. I've seen you do it. Who knows, they might not even charge me. They might find whoever did this and Rupert can go fuck himself. But if Rupert doesn't find the real killer, you know he'll come after me. I'm convenient. I'm the obvious target. I'm the husband. You know how this works."

"I have to teach this fall. I can't do both."

"Can you take a sabbatical? I have your retainer right here." Ben reached into his shirt pocket and pulled out a check and handed it to Boady.

Boady read the number: $200,000. "Jesus, Ben, that's way too much."

"If this case goes to trial, that amount won't cover it. We both know that. If they don't charge me, you can give me back what you want. But I'll demand that you keep at least what you would have made as a law professor for the semester. If I get charged, I'm going to trial, fast and hard. I want you to have the time you'll need to prepare. There'll be no plea bargains. It's either conviction or acquittal. I didn't kill Jennavieve. I'm not pleading guilty to anything, no matter how much they reduce the charge. There'll be no face-saving plea bargain. I need you to understand that, Boady. I'd rather go to prison a wrongfully convicted man than to say a single word that even hints that I had anything to do with Jennavieve's death. Emma has to know that I didn't kill her mother."

"I can't make a decision like this without talking to Diana."

"Absolutely. I wouldn't want you to. Talk to her and get back to me."

Ben stood and held out a hand. Boady took it and pulled Ben in to embrace him. When they parted, Ben's eyes were once again full of tears. He turned to make his way down the steps and back to his car but stopped after taking only a few steps.

"I have to go pick up Emma," he said, looking over his shoulder at Boady. "How do you tell a little girl that her world has fallen in?"

Boady wanted to say something helpful, but he could find no words. He simply shrugged his shoulders, shook his head, and watched his friend walk away.

Chapter 13

The Pruitt house looked smaller the second time Max Rupert pulled up to it. Maybe it was the bright-yellow tape stretched around it, marking it with a police-department stamp of ownership. Maybe it was the familiarity of the squad cars and the crime-scene vehicles and the smooth, mechanized efficiency of the lab techs bent to their tasks like the cobbler's elves. Or maybe it was the evolving thought of Ben Pruitt, not as the high-powered master of the house, but as prey to be tracked and cornered. Whatever the reason, Max approached the house with an odd sense of comfort.

He paused at the opened door. Inside, Niki sat on the staircase, her knees pulled together, creating a table of her thighs on which she filled out the search inventory sheet. Her black hair fell across her face, hiding her eyes.

"Find anything helpful?" Max asked.

"No murder weapon and no bedding. We found a laptop and phone that both appear to be hers, and we took his computer from the study and sealed it. How'd the interview go?"

"Great . . . for him. He professed his innocence, laid out his alibi, said everything he'd want a jury to hear. Once I started asking him specific questions, he accused me of having a vendetta against him and shut it down. He's managed to put his version on tape and nothing more."

"Is his alibi sound?"

"No. He can't account for his whereabouts from about five thirty yesterday until nine this morning. It takes, what . . . six to seven hours to drive from Chicago to here?"

"Maybe he mapped it out on his computer. We'll need to seize his office computers as well. He's going to go ballistic if we do that. You think we have the probable cause we need?"

"I don't know. If he drove back here to kill his wife, he'd need a car. He says he parked in the park-and-ride. No cameras, but he has a receipt. We can check their records. We can also check his credit cards and see if he booked a flight back or rented a car in Chicago to drive back, but I'm guessing he didn't. He's not stupid."

"Maybe he hired it done—set it up so his wife would be killed when he was in Chicago."

"That's a possibility. He has access to that kind of criminal element through his law practice. If it was a hired gun, maybe someone around here saw something."

Max turned and stepped out onto the front stoop. He gazed up and down the street. Neighbors, pedestrians, and gawkers had gathered in little pockets to talk and speculate as to why the army of squad cars had set siege to the Pruitt house. Reporters were milling around, undoubtedly asking their usual questions and trying to get quotes for the evening broadcast. Directly across the street, Max spied a lone woman sitting on her porch with a coffee mug in her hand. Malena Gwin, the nosey neighbor, at least according to Terry Kolander. With a nod of his head, he signaled Niki to join him, and they walked across the street together.

Ms. Malena Gwin stood up as the two detectives mounted her porch steps. She reminded Max of an actress whose name he didn't know, one of those faces you'd see on a sitcom or commercial who is famous enough to be recognized but not known. She had dark hair and a tomboy face, the kind of face that doesn't steal attention but draws it in over time—attractive for her forty-something age.

"Malena Gwin?" Max said.

"Yes. That's me."

"I'm Detective Max Rupert, and this is my partner, Detective Vang. May we have a word with you?"

"Of course. Is it true that Jennavieve Pruitt has been murdered?"

"Would you mind if we stepped inside? Away from prying eyes and ears?"

Malena glanced over Max's shoulder at a photographer snapping pictures of them on her porch, and she showed them in. Ms. Gwin's house was not nearly as large as the Pruitts', but its modest shell hid within it a trove of architectural treasures: wood-paneled walls with elaborately carved crown molding, French doors of cherry wood and stained glass through which Max could see the bottom few steps of a staircase that reminded him of the grand staircase in the *Titanic* movie, only in a smaller scale. A blue, claw-footed sofa sat across from two matching armchairs. Malena took a seat on the sofa, and Max and Niki sat in the armchairs.

"A reporter asked me this morning how well I knew Jennavieve," Malena said. "I asked him why he used the past tense, and he said that Jennavieve Pruitt was dead. He said that his source told him that she'd been murdered. Is that true?"

Max pulled out a notepad and pen and leaned forward. "Ms. Gwin, I would like to ask you some questions, and I am hoping that we can keep this conversation between us for now. We're conducting an investigation, and it would be helpful if the world didn't know some of these details. Can I ask you to keep this confidential?"

"Of course, Detective. I have no desire to be in the news. I told that reporter to get off my property, and I'll tell him that again if he comes back."

"I appreciate that," Max said. "In answer to your question, yes, Jennavieve Pruitt is dead, but we don't have an official cause of death yet." A lie, yes, but withholding details was a necessary part of any proper investigation. "You live right across the street from the Pruitts. I was wondering how well you know them."

"I know . . . I knew Jennavieve a little better than I know Ben. I moved here in 2008. My husband's family owns the house. When his parents died, we moved in."

"Is your husband around? We'd like to talk to him too."

"My husband died four years ago. It's just me."

"My condolences," Max said.

Malena nodded her acceptance. "I've known Jennavieve and Ben for about eight years now. We're not close. I run into them at neighborhood functions and the like. Jennavieve and I are both into fitness, so we see each other in passing when we run." Malena wore a blue sundress, and she crossed her legs as if intending to show off her well-toned calves. "Jennavieve was a wonderful person. I can't imagine how devastated Ben and Emma are right now. They're okay, aren't they? They weren't hurt?"

"They're fine," Max said. "How well do you know Ben?"

"Like I said, not as well as I knew Jennavieve. They were pretty quiet neighbors. I suppose I'm pretty quiet myself. I know he's an attorney. He's always struck me as a good father. I'd see him going for walks with Emma or playing in their yard. It seemed like he spent more time with her than Jennavieve did, but like I said, I only know what I saw on the outside of the house. I didn't spend time with them inside."

"When's the last time you saw Ben Pruitt?"

"Last night . . . about . . . oh, it had to be around midnight."

Max and Niki shared a look, both being careful to withhold any facial expression.

"At midnight?" Max repeated.

"About then, yeah. I was up because . . . well, I just couldn't sleep. It was such a beautiful night out and fresh air helps me fall asleep, so I went out onto my front porch. I was sitting there, about ready to come in, when I saw him pull up in a red car."

"You actually saw Ben Pruitt?"

"Yes. I remember because it just seemed odd. The car wasn't the black Lexus that he usually drives. I thought it might be a loaner from a mechanics shop or something."

"Do you know the make of the car?" Niki asked.

"Well, I'm no car expert. It was red and a four-door I think, maybe a little older but not too old."

"Are you sure it was Ben?" Max said "It was dark out, after all."

"I'm sure. He parked on the street instead of pulling into the driveway, which seemed strange. There's a streetlight on the corner, so I could see that it was Ben. Is that important?"

Max scribbled Ms. Gwin's words onto his notepad as he envisioned Pruitt's alibi turning to rot and crumbling through Pruitt's out-stretched fingers. Max pressed back a smile. "Every little bit helps," he said. "What did Mr. Pruitt do next?"

"He kind of looked around—he didn't see me—then he walked up to his house."

"What'd you see next?"

"Nothing. I got my fill of fresh air and was feeling sleepy, so I went to bed. Stayed there until this morning."

"Did you hear anything after you came inside?" Niki asked. "Any commotion or arguing, or maybe Ben Pruitt pulling away?"

"You think Ben killed Jennavieve?" Malena brought her hand up to her mouth. "Oh my. Is that what happened?"

"Ms. Gwin, we don't know what happened," Max said. "We're just gathering information right now. We want to be as thorough as possible. Did you hear anything?"

"No. I went to bed and fell asleep. Do you really think . . . oh my God, poor Emma."

"Ms. Gwin." Max leaned forward. "We need you to think hard. Is there anything else you can tell us?"

"No. I saw the red car pull up. Ben got out, looked around, and walked up to the house. Then I came in. That's all."

Max stood up and Niki followed his lead. "I appreciate your help, Ms. Gwin. And as I said before, we'd appreciate it if this conversation remained private for now. There may come a time when you'll be asked to repeat it, maybe even in court. I'd like it if you wrote down what you remember, and if anything else comes to you . . ." Max held out his card. "Please call me or Detective Vang." They shook hands, and Max and Niki made their way back across the street toward the Pruitt house, pausing beneath a streetlight a few feet from the edge of the Pruitt property.

"He parked here," Max said, looking back and forth between Pruitt's house and Malena Gwin's porch about one hundred feet away. "He's driving a red car. Why?"

"He can't fly back from Chicago," Niki said. "We'd be able to track that down. A bus or a train would take too long. He'd never be able to get to Minneapolis and back in time to set up an alibi. He needs a car."

"So, what, he rents one? Buys one?"

"On Craigslist, or a classified add." Niki said. "If he shows up with cash, he could buy one on the spot. It's more likely that he arranged it online. If he did, he may have left a trail on his computer or phone records."

"I like where you're going, but, remember, Pruitt's clever. He's not the kind of guy to leave a trail. If he's going to call Chicago to buy a car, he's smart enough to use a throwaway phone. So let's assume he drives back from Chicago, he parks here and not in the driveway."

"The driveway passes beneath the bedroom window. Mrs. Pruitt would have heard the car pull up."

Max nodded. "And with Malena Gwin's statement, we have enough probable cause to seize his office hard drives and search them to see if we can find proof to back up the theory."

"You think the judge will let us look at the hard drives of an attorney?"

"I'm sure that Pruitt will scream about the violation of attorney-client privilege. But we can get around that. I did it once before. The judge ordered an independent third party to go through the evidence and determine what we could see and what was protected. If we find any evidence that he was planning a car purchase in Chicago or researching the best routes to get back here, that won't be protected."

Niki looked at her watch. "I can get the warrant knocked out before court closes for the day. I'll take care of collecting the computers."

"No. It's my turn. I'll—"

"Max," Niki interrupted. She didn't say any more than his name, letting the force of her tone hang in the air until he looked at her. Her eyes told Max that she remembered what day it was and the significance that that square on the calendar carried. She knew that he'd be watching the sunset from Lakewood Cemetery, surrounded by the pale stone markers that shared a slight knoll with his Jenni. Max could feel the mood shift as the chill of their unspoken conversation moved them across a threshold separating the bustle of the day's events from the wistful approach of sunset.

"You going to be okay?"

"Yeah," Max whispered. "I'll be alright."

Chapter 14

Boady Sanden stayed on his porch long after Ben Pruitt left. He watched kids pass by on bicycles. He watched joggers getting in their daily run after work. He watched the shadows of his oak trees spread across his yard. All the while, he contemplated Ben Pruitt's offer. He tallied the numbers in his head, weighing the loss of his teaching income against the fees he would get from Ben, the scales tipping overwhelmingly in favor of taking the case. But then again, it had never been about the money.

The question he grappled with as he sat on his porch was, could he go back to that world? The high points of his years as a criminal-defense attorney came back easily: the victories, the accolades, the money. But he forced himself to remember the dark days, the last couple years when his guilt caused him to tremble as he approached a jury. He had made the mistake of believing in his own invincibility, which cost him dearly—and it cost his client his life.

As he watched the evening start to crawl across St. Paul, he wondered if he could honestly go back to that life, and he wondered if Diana would permit it. She had been the one to insist that he leave his practice.

Boady had been sitting on the edge of his bed at three in the morning, unable to sleep and unable to think straight. He had put on a suit, but couldn't remember why. He'd lost so much weight that his pants crinkled into small folds under his belt. Then he felt Diana's hand on his shoulder. She pulled him gently to her and held him like a mother might hold a scared child. She told him that he had to quit practicing law or it was going to kill him. He didn't fight it. He knew she was right. And he did what she asked.

Diana had texted Boady to let him know that she had a house showing that evening, a prospective buyer who couldn't be available until after normal work hours. So goes the life of a realtor. Boady had long ago become the family cook because of Diana's frequent absences, a role he was glad to take on. He expected her home around seven, so shortly before that, he rose from his seat on the porch and went to the kitchen to start preparing a stir-fry.

As he cut green and red peppers into thin strips, he thought about Ben and Jennavieve and the many times he watched them together, two people as perfect for each other as he believed he and Diana were. He'd come at the thought of Jennavieve's death from as many angles as he could, and every path led to the same conclusion. Ben would never hurt her. Boady believed that to his core.

He remembered when he'd first met Ben and Jennavieve. Ben had just put in his twelfth year at the Dakota County Attorney's Office when a case they had against each other went to trial. It had been a burglary case where the victim and the accused had been boyfriend and girlfriend at one time. She broke up with him and he didn't take it well, breaking into her apartment to confront her about it, pushing her to the ground, and skinning up her elbows.

Boady went to trial on the demand of his client, who was certain that he'd prevail. Boady didn't see how. What neither Boady nor Ben knew was that by the trial date, the couple had reconciled. These lovebirds weren't even supposed to be talking to each other, and they orchestrated the boyfriend's acquittal. All the attorneys could do was watch.

At trial, the girlfriend took the stand and confessed that she'd made the story up because she was angry at her boyfriend. She swore that he'd never been there that night and she busted the door lock with a hammer to frame him. Because he'd been long gone before the police arrived, his guilt rested on her testimony alone.

Ben didn't see the flip coming and he did what all young prosecutors do: he tried to introduce the girlfriend's original statement. Boady, ten years Ben's senior, objected and explained to the judge and to Ben Pruitt the *Dexter* problem. *Dexter* was a case that prohibited a prosecutor from putting a witness on the stand only to impeach her with a prior statement. "The prior statement can come in," Boady pointed out, "but it can only be used to impeach. In other words, he can use it to show that the witness is lying, but he can't use it to show that the burglary ever occurred. If there's no substantive evidence that the burglary actually occurred, then all you're left with is proof that the witness lied—nothing more. There is no evidence upon which a jury can legally find my client guilty."

The girlfriend was the State's last witness. After her testimony, Ben rested his case and Boady moved for a judgment of acquittal. The judge took the matter under advisement, and while Ben and Boady waited for the judge to return and issue the acquittal, which they both knew was inevitable, the two men struck up a conversation.

They talked about some recent cases handed down by the Supreme Court, and Ben, like Boady, disagreed with restrictions the Court had been placing on Fourth Amendment rights. Ben talked more like a defense attorney than a prosecutor. It was in that conversation that Boady floated the idea that Ben should come to work for him.

Ben asked for a week to think about it, but called Boady the next day to ask if they could have dinner together to talk about the offer, a dinner that would include their wives. They met at the University Club in St. Paul, a beautiful, private club that overlooked the southern edge of St. Paul. Boady had been a member since moving to Summit Avenue, just a few blocks west of the club.

It had been his plan to impress Ben and his wife with the fine meal and extravagant surroundings. He had no idea that Jennavieve Pruitt, formerly Jennavieve Adler, was a member of the Minneapolis Club, an equally swank private club in Minneapolis. Not only that, but Jennavieve's mother and father had both served on the Board of Governors for the Minneapolis Club. She practically grew up in the place.

But Jennavieve didn't come across as someone who gave a lick about clubs. Boady got the impression that they could have just as well been meeting at a fast-food joint for all she cared. Jennavieve was beautiful and gracious and completely levelheaded, and Boady took to her immediately. When Boady asked what she thought of the club, a question born of a momentary and uncharacteristic conceit on his part, Jennavieve never mentioned her illustrious upbringing. It wasn't until months later, after Ben had made the leap from prosecution to defense that Boady learned of her family position.

Boady saw Diana's car pull up the driveway just as he finished slicing the chicken. He poured a touch of oil into the pan and turned on the heat.

Diana entered through the back porch as she normally did. Boady met her at the door to the kitchen and gave her a kiss. But as she went to pull away from the kiss, he held her gentle brown hands in his pale white hands. He pulled her back in and embraced her, squeezing her tightly against his chest.

"Have you caught any news today?" he asked.

A look of concern eased into the edges of Diana's smile. "What happened?"

"Jennavieve Pruitt is dead. She was murdered last night."

"Oh my goodness. Murdered? Are you sure?"

"Her body was found this morning. She was stabbed in the throat."

"That's horrible. Are Ben and Emma . . . ?"

"They're okay. Ben came by after he identified her body."

"Ben . . . came here? Why would he come here?"

Boady went to the stove, where his oil was hot and ready for the chicken. He laid the chicken strips in and stepped back as the oil crackled and spit. He spoke now without turning to face Diana. "Ben wants my help."

Diana crossed to the kitchen counter next to the stove. "Why does he want your help?"

Boady still didn't look at Diana. "He thinks they may try to point the finger at him. It's standard procedure to suspect the husband. He just wants to have the benefit of my advice."

Diana put her hand on Boady's arm and turned him to face her. "Is he a suspect? Do they think he killed Jennavieve?"

"They haven't named him as a suspect. He's understandably concerned. He wants me to be his lawyer, hold his hand as he goes through this." Boady could feel her studying his face, searching for signs of the struggle she must have suspected raged in his head. Boady dumped the chopped onions into the pan.

Diana slowly walked to the kitchen table and sat in a chair. She didn't speak for what seemed an eternity. Then she said, "He wants you to defend him?"

"He's not charged, so there's nothing to defend."

"He must think he's going to be charged. Otherwise he wouldn't come to you."

"Not necessarily. Back in the day, I represented quite a few clients who were under investigation who didn't get charged. Ben has an alibi. We just need to put the proof together. A simple thing even for a marginal defense attorney like myself."

"But you're not a defense attorney. He of all people knows that. He knows why you quit practicing. How can he ask you to go back to that? He can't ask you to do that."

"Honey, he trusts me. He doesn't want just another lawyer out for a cash-cow client. He needs someone who believes in him. If I were in his shoes, I'd feel the same way."

"And do you believe in him?"

"Diana... you're not saying... this is Ben Pruitt we're talking about. Ben and Jennavieve. You once said that they were as perfect a couple as we are. Remember?"

"But we haven't been a part of their lives for a long time now. We've seen them maybe four times in the last six years."

"He was my law partner. I'm Emma's godfather. I know Ben. He didn't have anything to do with Jennavieve's death."

"I'm not saying he did. I just don't know how he can ask you to go back into a courtroom. He knows how the Quinto case nearly killed you."

Boady turned the heat off and moved the pan to a backburner. He walked to the table and sat down with Diana, holding her hand in his. "I know you're worried. I went though some bad times after Quinto, and that means that you went through those bad times too. I wouldn't take this case if I had any doubt about Ben. I know you're concerned about how I might react, going back to court. I'd be lying if I said I wasn't a little nervous myself. A lot of rust can build up in six years."

Boady smiled, but she remained hard. "How would I feel about myself if I didn't help my friend? He was there when I needed him. He picked up the pieces of my crumbling practice. For almost two years, he kept things going while I wallowed in my self-pity. No one ever knew how self-destructive I'd become because he kept the practice going. He didn't turn his back on me. So how can I turn my back on him?"

Diana raised Boady's hand up to her lips and kissed him. "I know you have to help Ben. I'm sorry. You have to do this. I can't help it if I'm a little selfish when it comes to you."

"There's one more wrinkle in all this."

Diana closed her eyes. "I'm almost afraid to ask."

"Max Rupert is the lead investigator."

Diana sat back in her chair, her eyebrows raised. "Does Max know you're representing Ben?"

"Not yet. I was thinking about telling him tonight."

"Tonight?"

"It's the anniversary of Jenni Rupert's death. I was planning on going to the cemetery anyway—just to make sure he's okay. If the topic comes up, I'll mention it to him."

Diana leaned in, kissed Boady on the forehead, and nodded her understanding. "It's going to be dark soon. We'd better get you fed so you can get going."

Chapter 15

Boady pulled up to the northwest corner of Lakewood Cemetery and parked. He looked around at the quiet street, no walkers, no traffic, no one to see him heave his body over the fence—again—the second time in three years. The last time had been on the first anniversary of Jenni Rupert's death, and Boady prayed that this visit would be far less distressing.

That time, Boady had been at home, already in bed as it was nearly midnight, when his phone rang.

"Hello?"

"Boady, this is Alexander Rupert, Max's brother. I hope I didn't wake you."

Boady put the phone to his chest and cleared the slumber from his throat in a futile attempt to sound awake. "No, Alexander, I was up grading some papers. What's up?"

There was a slight pause, then: "I was hoping that Max might be there. I know it's a Tuesday and you guys usually play poker on weekends, but I was just thinking that he might have stopped by."

"I don't understand. Is Max missing or something?"

"He's not answering his phone. I've been trying to get ahold of him for a couple hours now. I just thought I'd call a few of his friends and see . . . well, it was a year ago today that Jenni died."

"Oh." Boady sat up, slipping his legs over the side of the bed.

"We had lunch today and he was acting strange."

"Strange?"

"I don't know, what's the word . . . *morose* maybe? He couldn't concentrate. Kept losing his train of thought. Hardly touched his lunch. Finally, I came out and asked him what the hell was wrong. That's when he pointed out that today was the first anniversary. I felt like an idiot for not remembering."

"When's the last time you heard from him?"

"I called him around five. He said he was going home for the night. I thought I'd drop by there to check up on him around ten, and he wasn't there. I thought maybe he might have contacted you or . . . I don't know. I mean he's a big boy. He can take care of himself, but he seemed so out of sorts at lunch."

"So, what now?"

"Well, Max isn't the kind of guy to go out to bars all by himself, but there are a few places he and I go to have a beer. I thought I'd check around and see if anyone's seen him. Maybe he can't hear his phone ringing."

"Would you do me a favor?" Boady asked.

"Sure."

"If you find him, can you call me and let me know."

"Sure, Boady."

Boady hung up and walked to the kitchen, opened the fridge, and grabbed a small handful of carrot sticks out of a bowl of cold water. As he nibbled on the carrots, he thought about his wife, Diana, asleep in the bedroom. How would he react if he ever lost her? How would he handle the anniversary of her death as the years passed?

Boady went back to the bedroom and sat on the edge of the bed next to Diana, the movement stirring her from her thin sleep. "Max is missing," he said.

"I heard," she answered. "Are you worried?"

"No. Max isn't the kind of guy that needs looking after." Boady rolled back into his nest and pulled the comforter up around his shoulders.

Diana turned onto her right side, her face nuzzled into her pillow, her eyes closed, her words still half-asleep. "If I ever lost you, I'd probably never leave the cemetery," she said.

Boady let a heavy sigh leave his chest. *Of course,* he thought.

He slipped out of bed, put on a pair of jeans, a sweatshirt, and sneakers, and headed out the door.

On the drive to the cemetery, he tried to remember where Jenni Rupert had been buried. Lakewood Cemetery was two hundred and fifty acres of rolling hills riddled with thousands of grave markers, everything from small, bronze placards to large statues of angels. He got lost trying to drive out of that cemetery after Jenni's interment, and that was in broad daylight. He held little faith that, at night, he would be able to find a single, brown-marble stone tucked away in the heart of that enormous labyrinth. But he went anyway.

He remembered that, as they gathered around the casket, there'd been a small lake to his back, a basin of still water for mourners to gaze upon as they contemplated their sorrow. Boady also seemed to remember a moose—no, it was an elk, a life-sized bronze elk about a hundred yards from the grave site. The elk had been facing in the general direction of the ceremony. And then there was the silver maple tree, one of the largest Boady had ever seen. He stood in the shade of that tree as they lowered Max's wife into the ground.

Boady tried to remember these markers as he pulled up to the cemetery gate, a closed gate with a sign that read that visiting hours ended at 8 p.m. He paused at the entrance for a moment and examined the length of wrought-iron fence that reached into the distance as far as he could see. The black pickets stood in formation, six feet tall and pointed, but not sharp—the kind of fence intended to discourage intruders but not prevent them, even late-middle-aged men with questionable knees, like Boady.

He eased back onto the road and drove slowly along the northern border of the cemetery, looking for a good place to enter, and found a spot on the northwest corner, a spot where streetlights cast very little light and a pine tree inside the fence reached its branches out over the iron spikes. Boady pulled to the side of the street and put his car in park. It was then that he saw Max's car parked a few feet away. Boady walked up to the car, just to make certain that it was Max's car and that Max wasn't in it. He was right on both assumptions.

Boady placed a call to Alexander to let him know that he'd found Max's car, then Boady went for a stroll.

He paused opposite the pine tree inside the fence and glanced around. No one around. He hoisted himself onto the top rail of the fence, the iron spikes pressing against his forearms. He swung a hand up, grasped a pine branch, and pulled his weight up enough to get a foothold atop the rail. From there, it was a simple matter of climbing down a tree, something he'd perfected as a boy growing up in in the Ozark hills of Missouri.

He believed that the lake he remembered lay somewhere near the center of the cemetery, so he set a course into the heart of the field of gravestones.

About the time that he crested his second hill, he began to doubt his memory. But on the third hill, he glimpsed the shimmer of the full moon rippling on the surface of water. He headed for the lake, stepping a bit slower now that he knew he was in the right neighborhood. The elk had to be nearby. Twice he stopped to peer through the darkness at what he believed to be horns but turned out to be branches catching the moonlight. He had to duck behind a statue of an angel as a car with a security guard in it rolled past.

He found the elk, slightly larger than life-sized, its hooves anchored to a granite mound. Boady stood beneath the elk and faced in the direction of the animal's stare. There he saw the giant silver maple tree, the one he stood beneath at the funeral. He walked to the base of the tree and looked into the shadows cast by the moonlight until he saw the form of a man sprawled out in the grass. Max lay prostrate, his mouth open, his face flattened into the ground, one hand clutching a tuft of sod, the other hand pressed up against the smooth granite of a headstone.

Boady knelt at Max's side and immediately smelled the odor of whiskey radiating up from his friend. He tried to roll Max over, but Max resisted, muttering "no" and wrapping his protest with impotent threats and slurred expletives. When Max's squawking grew too loud, Boady gave up his effort and let Max settle back into the grass.

The moon painted the surface of the lake with a wide swath of light that flickered off tiny ripples, giving the water a sequined cover. The shadows cast by the trees created patches of black on gray that swayed in the light breeze. Boady sat up against a nearby headstone to wait for Alexander to arrive. He closed his eyes and breathed in the scent of freshly cut grass. In the distance he could hear a mockingbird singing to the full moon. *This would be a nice place to spend eternity, if such things mattered to the dead*, Boady thought.

Soon, Boady heard a hollered whisper coming from the direction of the elk statue.

"Max? Boady?"

"Over here," Boady called back.

Alexander scampered through the shadows, partially crouching as he ran, as if he were advancing on an enemy pill box. He slid to a stop at Max's side.

"Holy shit, he's smashed." Alexander gave a nervous chuckle and poked his brother in the side with his thumb. "I haven't seen him this drunk since, well, never. Max, wake up."

Alexander rolled Max over and started tapping his face. Max swung blindly at imaginary flies. As he did, an empty whiskey bottle slid out of his jacket.

"Christ, what was he thinking?" Alexander whispered. "Max never did handle whiskey well."

"Leave me alone," Max stammered as he rolled back over to resume his prostrate position at the base of his dead wife's gravestone.

Alexander relaxed his grip on his brother and sat back to assess things. "If they catch us here after hours, it'll be a problem, especially with Max being smashed."

"It's just a cemetery security guy. Surely, he'll understand. He probably sees this all the time."

"Maybe. But then again, maybe not. Let's say he turns out to be a dick and calls this in. If the press catches wind of it, we might make the evening news. They're always looking for cops-gone-bad stories."

"How do we get him out of here? We can't hoist him over that spiked fence. And he's in no condition to climb over it himself."

"Due west of here, there's a gate. That's where I parked. If we can get him there, I have a bolt cutter in my trunk."

"A bolt cutter in your trunk?"

"Hey, I'm a narcotics detective. Bolt cutters come in handy. You'd be surprised how many drug dealers think a padlock will make a difference."

"I'm not complaining."

Alexander sat beside his brother and patted Max between the shoulder blades. "Max, I need you to listen."

Max grunted something loud and unintelligible, something that sounded like a word and a belch combined.

"Max, I need to get you out of here. I know you want to stay, but that's not in the cards."

"Fuck you, Festus!" Max spoke with a snarl in his throat.

"Festus?" Boady said.

Alexander waved off Boady's curiosity with a shake of his head. "Childhood nickname," he said. Then he patted his brother's back a little harder. "Max, I need you to get your shit together and stand up."

"Fuck off," came the reply.

"Fine. I'll just drag your ass to the fence." Alexander stood up and grabbed one of Max's ankles. "Come on, Boady, grab a leg."

Boady picked up Max's other ankle, and the two began dragging Max, facedown, through the grass.

"God dammit! Leave me alone," Max yelled. He began to kick and twist and claw at the grass, but Alexander and Boady kept walking.

Max continued to cuss and twist for about twenty yards before they heard him mutter, "Okay. I'll walk. Just let me go." Alexander gave Boady a smile, and they dropped Max's legs. They let him catch his breath before lifting him off the ground, each pulling one of Max's arms across their shoulders.

Max walked on billowing legs, his body lurching sideways every few steps. They had to duck behind a clump of arborvitae shrubs at one point to let the security car roll past, but the march to the gate went smoother than Boady expected.

Once there, they lay Max on the grass behind one of the larger headstones, and Boady stayed with him while Alexander went to get the bolt cutter and open the gate. While they waited, Max heaved up the contents of his stomach, the sound of his retching seeming to blast through the night like a siren. Boady walked to a clearing to watch for the security guard, but the car never appeared.

Soon, Boady heard the clinking of the chain being pulled free of the gate. He and Alexander found Max lying next to a puddle of stomach acid and whiskey, his eyes closed and a snore catching in his throat as he slept.

"I've never seen Max drunk before," Boady said. "I mean, we drink when we play poker, but he never has more than a couple beers. He's always so in control."

"He and Jenni were together since high school." Alexander squatted beside his brother and laid a hand on the back of Max's head. "I think, maybe next year, I'll keep an eye on him when this comes around."

Alexander grabbed one of Max's arms and Boady the other, and they lifted the passed-out man to their shoulders again and walked him through the gate to Alexander's car.

Boady brushed back the stubble of that memory as he once again climbed over the wrought-iron spikes protecting Lakewood Cemetery. Alexander Rupert had been true to his word in attending to his brother every year on the anniversary of Jenni's death. But it had been nine months now since Alexander died in the line of duty. Max had stopped coming to their monthly poker games. He'd only returned a couple of Boady's phone calls, and when he did, he claimed that his absence from the card games was fallout from being overworked. Boady didn't believe him, not entirely, but he heard nothing in Max's voice to warrant any further uninvited intrusion.

Boady brushed pine needles from his sleeves, glanced over his shoulder at the last traces of the sun's penumbra fading from the sky in the west. Then he began to make his way into the cemetery, his eyes once again searching for the lake and the bronze elk.

Chapter 16

Over the years, Max had found it easy to avoid detection when he would visit Jenni's grave. A security guard patrolled the cemetery at night, but a caretaker's shed blocked the view of Jenni's tombstone when it passed. Max liked leaning against her headstone because from there he could view the lake, and he liked looking at the lake when he talked to Jenni.

Max looked up at the splinters of moonlight slipping between the branches of a silver maple tree. He tried to find her face in the shadows it cast. He used to see her there, back in those early months when her vagabond memory moved through the periphery of his world, dropping him to his knees when her presence was strongest. Now he looked at the tree and all he saw were shadows.

"I miss you," he whispered. He brought his legs up and rested his forearms on his knees. "I feel like I miss you more now than I ever did. Just think, our child would have been three years old by now. Walking and talking up a storm, I bet."

But there had been no child, only a pregnancy. Max had pretty much given up on that dream, but Jenni never did. Maggie Hightower had been the one who performed the autopsy on Jenni's body. Maggie had been the one who told Max about the pregnancy, so new that Jenni herself may not have known about it. The day he buried his wife, only Max and Maggie knew that they were laying two souls to rest.

"The world seems so quiet now, so empty. That one twist of fate changed everything. I could be sitting beside you, watching our child tear through the house right now. But instead, I'm here and you're . . ." Max reached down and stroked the grass beside him.

"I get the feeling Niki's worried about me. The other day, she asked me what I had going on besides work. I made a joke about it, but it got me thinking. Maybe she's right. Maybe I need to have something else to focus on, something to distract me. So, I'm thinking I might go down to the pound and see if they have an old dog, the kind of mutt that everyone else overlooks."

Max stopped talking when he heard footsteps approaching from the hill above him. He started to pull out his badge, a move he'd contemplated doing if he were ever discovered in the cemetery after hours.

"Max?" The whispered voice sounded like Boady Sanden.

Max peeked over the top of the headstone. "Boady? What the hell are you doing here?"

"Just came by to see how you were doing."

Max leaned back against the headstone. "You're babysitting me, you mean?"

"Can't a guy break into a cemetery after dark to say hi to a buddy?"

"I know all about you and Alexander thinking I need watching on this particular night. Alexander told me."

"Well, you have to admit, it's not without reason. I mean, three years ago you were a bit of a mess. I just stopped by to see if you might need a bolt cutter."

Max smiled. "Pull up a seat." He pointed at the next headstone over, a gray, granite slab with the name "Hoover" on it, the one that Boady leaned against three years earlier as he waited for Alexander to arrive.

"I thought this might be a tough year for you, with Alexander being gone as well."

Max nodded. "I can't say the thought didn't cross my mind."

"And you haven't been to a card game since he died."

"Haven't felt like playing cards, I guess."

"With all that's happened, I thought . . ."

"I didn't bring any whiskey this time." Max patted his shirt as if to show his pockets empty.

"And here I was hoping you'd offer me a shot. Climbing that damned fence has me a little shaky."

The two men slipped into a comfortable silence, both staring at the lake for a few seconds that seemed so much longer. Finally it was Boady who spoke.

"In all seriousness, how are you holding up?"

Max gave the question some consideration before answering. "I may have backslid after Alexander died." He pressed his head to the cool granite. He could feel the engraving of her name against his scalp. He rolled his head slowly across the letter *N*. "And today—I swear, it seemed like every time I turned around, there was something to remind me of Jenni."

"If I ever lost Diana . . ." Boady paused mid-thought. "Well, I don't know where I could go that wouldn't make me think of her."

"That's not the half of it. Today we found a body in Kenwood . . . well, you probably heard about it on the news. It was Ben Pruitt's wife."

"Jennavieve Pruitt. Yeah, I heard."

"It threw me at first. With her red hair and all, she reminded me of Jenni."

"Before you say any more," Boady interrupted. "Ben came to see me today."

"That's right, you two used to be partners back in the day."

"He's asked me to be his attorney . . . if things get . . . well, you know."

Max turned to look at Boady, hoping to see some sign that he was joking. Boady kept his gaze fixed on the lake.

"I thought you quit practicing law," Max said.

"I still have my license. I can take a case if I choose to. Just because I teach, doesn't mean I forgot how to practice law."

"This isn't the case to come out of retirement for, Boady."

"I know you and Ben have issues, Max, but that's—"

"Boady, this isn't about what happened between Ben and me. I'm telling you that you don't want this case."

"We shouldn't be talking about it, Max. I just felt that you should know before you said anything to me that might be in confidence."

Max turned back to the lake, suddenly irritated that his time with his wife's memory had been interrupted. As if Boady could sense the change in Max's mood he said, "I probably shouldn't have come tonight. I just felt that I owed it to Alexander. To make sure . . ."

Max didn't say anything.

"Well, I'll leave you to your evening."

Boady stood up and brushed the grass from his jeans. Max could tell that Boady was waiting for some final word from Max, something to let them part as the friends they were before Boady mentioned Ben's name. When no words came, Boady started walking away.

Max said, "Tell Diana I said hi."

Boady stopped and turned back to Max, smiled, and nodded. "Will do," he said.

When Boady had gone, Max felt more alone than he'd felt in a long time. He reached behind his head and grazed his fingers across the letters of his wife's name. He tried to talk to her again, but it didn't feel right. So instead, he tipped his head back against the stone and looked up at the sky where a gap in the trees framed a swath of stars so deep and so beautiful that it almost brought tears to his eyes. He wanted her to be there with him. He wanted her to come down from those stars and whisper into his ear that everything was alright, that she forgave him for all of his failings. Max watched the heavens and waited in silence for an answer that would never come.

Chapter 17

On Monday, Niki and Max brought their investigation to the office of Frank Dovey, an Assistant Hennepin County Attorney in the Adult Prosecutions Division. Frank had summoned them and when they arrived, they were ushered into the conference room where fresh coffee steamed up through the mouth of a white coffee pot, surrounded by four coffee mugs on a tray. They had scarcely taken their seats before Dovey walked in. He slid the coffee tray in front of Niki and sat down.

"I thought we could have some coffee while you filled me in."

Dovey, a large man whose spikey military cut and sagging jowls reminded Max of a dollop of cookie dough, sat across from Max and drummed on the table with his thumbs. Max looked at Niki, who seemed to be lost behind the coffee tray. Max slid the tray away from in front of Niki, moving it to the opposite end of the table.

"No coffee? Sure. That's fine. I just thought, you know." Dovey spoke like a man with a thousand-dollar-a-week cocaine habit, but that was just his way. The man stayed on high speed until he walked into a courtroom. There, Dovey had a talent for reigning in his motor mouth when the situation called for it. In front of a jury he could instantly turn his tap dance into a waltz.

"The Pruitt case has been assigned to me." Dovey said. He looked at Max as if waiting for him to speak. "So, what you got?"

Max nodded to Niki, who opened her investigation file and began to summarize the case.

"The victim is Jennavieve Pruitt. Socialite. Philanthropist. Daughter of Emerson Adler."

"I met Emerson Adler once," Dovey said. "It was a fundraiser for Chief Justice Patten. It was quite the Who's Who of the mucky-mucks."

Niki shared a glance with Max, then continued. "She runs a number of foundations, but her main focus was a wetlands preservation group. She was married to Ben Pruitt, the criminal-defense attorney, and they have a child, Emma."

Max took over, opening his file and pulling out the preliminary autopsy report. "Friday morning, a jogger found Mrs. Pruitt's naked body wrapped in a blanket from the daughter's bed and lying in a parking area behind a bookstore in Kenwood. Secluded. No one saw any vehicle going in or out. ME puts her time of death within an hour of midnight the night before. She was stabbed in the throat with a knife, double-bladed. We have a knife case at the Pruitt house that is missing a knife. It fits our murder weapon."

Niki pulled out the pictures from the house and picked up the narrative. "We believe she took a shower and was getting ready for bed. When she came out of the bathroom, she was attacked. There's little sign of a struggle. It looks like the attacker caught her off guard, stabbed her, and maybe held her on the bed while she bled out."

"No defensive wounds," Max added. "Nothing under her fingernails."

Dovey examined the pictures, pausing on the pictures of Mrs. Pruitt's naked body in the parking lot. "Forced entry at the house?"

"No."

"We're looking at the husband for this, I hope." Dovey said.

"We think he's a good possibility, except he may have an alibi," Max said.

"Alibi?"

"He says he was at a legal conference. We have him on a flight to Chicago Thursday, and he flew home on Friday after I called him. He sounded surprised, but he could be a good actor."

"Phone records?"

"We show a call that he made to Mrs. Pruitt's cell phone at 5:27 p.m. Thursday evening," Niki said. "Mrs. Pruitt didn't answer. We then have a text message from Mr. Pruitt's phone to Mrs. Pruitt's phone. We've requested the cell-phone-tower data."

Dovey rubbed a hand over his bristly scalp. "So, the husband has an alibi?"

"Not necessarily." Max smiled. "We have a neighbor who swears that she saw Ben Pruitt drive up in a red car, park on the corner, and walk up to the house around midnight."

Dovey flopped back in his chair, a smile spreading across his face. "Are you shitting me? Is she solid?"

"Rock solid," Max said.

Dovey sat back up and leaned into the conversation. "So how'd he get back here?"

"We're still working on that," Max said. "He had to acquire a car in Chicago. I doubt it's a rental, because that'll leave a paper trail, but we'll check on it."

"It's possible he stole a car," Niki said. "But that seems overly risky."

"What do you think, Max?"

Max looked at Niki, then back at Dovey. "I think that Niki has some thoughts on that."

Niki waited for Dovey to acknowledge her before she continued. "It's possible he simply bought a car in Chicago, responded to an ad, gave the seller a wad of cash, and drove off. Pruitt drives here, kills his wife, and goes back to Chicago in time to be at the conference in the morning."

"Do we have any evidence to back this up?"

"Not a shred," Max said.

"So how do we get it?"

Max laced his fingers together and brought them to his lips as he thought. "We'll need to go to Chicago. I'll retrace his steps. I can get hotel surveillance footage, maybe hotel key-card information showing when he entered his room. Maybe staff might remember him. I'll drive there and back. There might be surveillance cameras on the way."

"Tollbooths," Niki blurted out. "I-90 has a bunch of tollbooths. They must have cameras."

Dovey nodded agreement. "If they have video footage, I can get that subpoenaed from their Department of Transportation. Give me a window of time for each tollbooth and I'll get the footage."

Max said. "If we can catch him driving through a tollbooth, coming back from Chicago, we have absolute proof of premeditation."

A thin smile lit Dovey's face, and he spoke as though he were thinking aloud. "And with premeditation we have first-degree murder—life in prison—so we'll need a grand jury. I can get started on that. If I can get the indictment, this'll be the biggest homicide to hit the airwaves in years: the daughter of Emerson Adler murdered by her high-powered, lawyer husband. Damn, this'll be national."

Max could almost see the drool seeping from the corner of Dovey's lips. "We still haven't received the report from the techs, and forensics from the computers is still a long way away. Should we be starting the grand jury already?"

"I'm moving on this," Dovey said. "This is a hot one, and I don't want any delay."

Max could see something in the twitch of Dovey's smile that suggested there was more to Dovey's haste than the pursuit of swift justice. These big-name cases tended to flow in a current of political maneuvering. Dovey held a bag of gold and needed to move fast in order to keep ahold of it. "You get me the evidence of how he got back here," Dovey said. "That's all I need. Well, that and a motive. Do we have one of those yet?"

Max shrugged. "We have an interview with Mrs. Pruitt's sister today. We don't know much about the state of the marriage. Hopefully she can fill in some of that."

"How many red sedans can there be on I-90 at that time of night?" Niki wondered.

Dovey again looked at Max, as though Niki weren't in the room. "I've never met a married couple yet that didn't have enough problems to explain why one might want to kill the other," he said. "And I'm betting the Pruitts had more than their share. You get me that motive and I'll have enough to take this to a grand jury."

Chapter 18

Boady stared at Ben Pruitt's two-hundred-thousand-dollar check and reminisced about a time when he had extra cash at his disposal. "Fuck-you money," he called it. Small wads of equity buried around town in bonds and certificates of deposits and a junior-league stock portfolio, the kind of money that allowed him to say "fuck you" to any client who became too much of a jerk. Many of them had been raised on mob movies where the attorney held the shovel as the client tossed the body onto the freshly dug grave. "I paid you blah-blah dollars, so you do what I tell you to do."

That's not how it worked with Boady. On that rare occasion when a client ordered him to cross a line, Boady would walk them to the door and offer to return the remaining retainer. Not once did the client take him up on that offer. "There are rules," he'd tell his clients. "We operate within those rules. Always. No exceptions." The key was to know the law better than your opponent, and work harder than they did. You could never outspend the State, but you could usually outwork them.

What most people didn't understand was that cases were won or lost well before the attorneys stood to give their opening statements. Each side of a case knew what arrows filled their opponent's quiver. Witness statements and exhibits crossed back and forth weeks, sometimes months, before the trial began. The secret, as Boady often told his protégée Ben Pruitt, was to have more than one chess board going at a time. Get used to calculating multiple moves by the prosecution and have an answer ready for each contingency.

Chess—a game. That's how he once viewed the practice of law. Abstract notions like justice and truth didn't play into his strategy. They were distractions one could learn to ignore, like people living in a path of an airport runway who no longer noticed the jets. Boady had been one of the best at playing that game. No flash, no sparkly ta-da, just a finely tuned grasp of the rules and a talent for tuning out distractions.

Miguel Quinto brought all of that crashing down around him. Boady could still see Miguel's face, the boy's eyes searching for hope in every visit that Boady made to the jail. He could still hear the words of Miguel's mother as they were leaving the funeral: "You did everything you could"—the lie that sent Boady into a dark spiral. All these memories churned in Boady's stomach as he waited for Ben Pruitt to arrive.

Ben came to Boady's house a few minutes before ten that Monday morning, parked his car in front, and walked around to open the back door on the passenger side. Emma Pruitt stepped out of the car as if she were touching her foot down on the moon, her movements hesitant and deliberate, her father holding her hand, raising her up to a standing position. Neither looked well.

Boady had called Ben to come over, and it slipped his mind that he would naturally have Emma with him. Boady went to a closet and dug around for a game or something to entertain a ten-year-old girl while the grown-ups talked. He found a lantern and binoculars, and tried to imagine how he could present these items to Emma—how could he entice her to busy herself with these random artifacts. He shook his head and put them back on the shelf.

Then he saw a sketch pad, one on which Diana would sometimes design home-makeover ideas for her clients. He pulled the sketch pad out, threw it on the couch, and grabbed a couple of pencils from his study.

Boady opened the door to a father and child who looked like they had just survived a month at a prison camp. Ben hadn't shaved since Boady last saw him. Fatigue lingered in the rings beneath his eyes. He stared at nothing in particular, as if it had worn his vision to a dull point.

Boady gave Ben a light hug, one that Ben returned. He then knelt on one knee to be at Emma's level. Her eyes betrayed a fear that tore at Boady's heart. Boady had lost his own father before he was old enough to know the man, and that loss painted every corner of Boady's world. He couldn't imagine the size of the wound that filled this little girl.

"Hello, Emma," he said.

"I'm sorry that I don't have anyone here for you to play with. I don't even have any games, but I have a sketch pad. Do you like to draw?" Boady stepped back and pointed. Emma reached for her father's arm and held him tightly.

"Emma," Ben said, in a calm, soothing voice. "Mr. Sanden and I have something we need to talk about. I need you to sit here—just for a little while. Can you do that?" Ben walked her to the couch and turned her shoulders so that she faced him. "I promise, I'll just be in the next room." He lowered her to the seat and put the sketch pad on her lap.

Boady handed her the two pencils. "Would you like a glass of water? A cookie, maybe?"

Emma looked to her father, then to Boady, and shook her head.

Boady waited for Ben to step away from his daughter before leading them to his study. He closed the French doors and took a seat behind his desk. "How are you holding up?"

Ben opened his mouth to speak, but stopped. He closed his eyes, rubbed them with the heels of his hands, and wiped tears onto his sleeve. "I haven't been able to sleep. I try. I know I have to be strong for Emma, but every time I close my eyes, I see Jennavieve's face. I see her pushing Emma on her swing. I see those two opening Christmas presents and dressing up in matching princess Halloween costumes. I see her in her wedding dress and on the beach in St. Thomas."

Ben paused as he drew in a shaky breath.

"And then I see her laid out on that table in the medical examiner's office. I haven't slept and I don't think Emma has, not more than a couple hours at a time. She wakes up out of breath and calls for her mother."

"Where have you been staying?"

"We went up to our lake cabin near Brainerd. I can't go back to the house and I wanted to take Emma to some place familiar."

"How is she doing?"

Ben shook his head. "Probably no better than I am. She's so fragile anyway. I told her that her mom is dead, but I haven't explained how.

I can't bring myself to say it out loud—not to her. I mean, how do you tell a child that her mom was murdered?"

"So what did you say?"

"I just said that the police are trying to figure that out. I left the TV off at the cabin, so she didn't see any reports. I know I have to tell her, but I keep thinking that I'll wait a little while, they'll find who did this, and I can tell her then. At least then I might be able to explain why. That's the hard part. There's no sense to it right now."

Boady leaned back in his chair and laced his fingers together. "Let's see if we can make some sense of it. Tell me about Chicago."

Ben, who had been staring at a pen lying in the middle of Boady's clean desk, looked up, a trace of confusion tucked into the folds of his brow. "You want me to go over my alibi?"

"Why not?"

A slight smile edged up from the corner of Ben's lips. "A wise teacher once told me not to ask my clients about the facts of the case, at least not until after I had all the State's evidence. I think he told me that he didn't want clients locking themselves into a story until they knew all the points to cover. Can't have them changing their story on the stand."

"I'm not sure that man was as wise as you remember."

"Don't worry, my version of events won't change," Ben said. "That's the thing about the truth; the truth doesn't change. Only a lie will change over time. I'm not lying. I was in Chicago. I had nothing to do with Jennavieve's death."

"Then what am I missing?"

"What do you mean?"

Boady debated how to step into this next part of the conversation, in the end erring on the side of complete disclosure. "You know that Max Rupert and I are friends."

"That's not a problem, is it?"

"No," Boady said. "But I went to his wife's grave on Friday. He visits her grave on the anniversary of her death every year. I went there to see if he was okay. As we were talking, I told him that you came to see me, and he said that I shouldn't take your case."

"I told you he has it in for me. I can't believe he—"

"No. That's not it. He wasn't telling me not to take the case because he hates you. He was warning me off because he knows something we don't. That's what's been bothering me. There's something out there that has him believing that you're his man." Boady stopped talking and made room for the silence that would bring a response from Ben.

Ben shook his head. "I . . . I have no earthly idea. Wait . . . it's bullshit. He can't know anything, because there isn't anything to know. I didn't kill Jennavieve. That's all there is to it."

Ben's words came out sure and strong and with enough volume to carry through the French doors. He caught himself and lowered his voice. "I didn't kill my wife. I don't care what Rupert says. I'm not concerned about what he thinks he has, because I can prove that I didn't do it. I was in Chicago for Christ's sake."

"We can prove that?"

"Absolutely. They want to waste their time on some wild goose chase, let them. I'm going to figure out who killed my wife. I'm going to find the sonofabitch that stole that little girl's mother from her." Ben had turned red as he spat out his words.

Boady slid a box of tissues toward Ben, but Ben again wiped his tears onto his sleeve.

"I could really use your help, Boady. I don't think I can do this alone."

Boady smiled. "You won't be alone. I'm your attorney and I'm your friend. I'll do everything I can to take care of you and Emma." He held out his hand, and Ben grabbed it like he was a drowning man grasping a lifeline.

"Thank you. Thank you." Ben closed his eyes and breathed a heavy sigh.

Boady slid his chair back far enough to open his drawer and pull out a legal pad and a pen. "I've always said that if you have the truth on your side, it's just a matter of finding the proof of that truth. So let's get looking."

Chapter 19

As Max waited for Anna Adler-King to come in for her interview, he read the laboratory report authored by Bug Thomas. Bug had found enough hair and fingerprints and other trace evidence to put Ben Pruitt at the scene of the crime, but the scene of the crime was his home, his bedroom. One would expect his essence to be littered throughout the place.

Bug had been thorough, and his report listed everything from the hairs they found in the shower drain, which appeared to match Jennavieve and Ben Pruitt, to partial shoe prints found on a spot of bare earth by the driveway, which belonged to Jennavieve. Max would reread that report over and over in the coming days, as he did in every case, waiting for the right clue to jump out at him, but in his initial perusal, very little seemed helpful.

Anna Adler-King arrived for her appointment wearing a tight black dress, tailored, belted at the waist, a V-neck unbuttoned just enough to give a hint of cleavage, definitely not off-the-rack. Max wondered if this was Mrs. Adler-King's idea of bereavement attire, a suit that whispered "I've lost someone" but screamed "Hey, everyone, look at me."

Max introduced himself and walked her to the interview room. "I appreciate you coming in to see me. I'll try not to take up too much of your time." Max motioned to a chair for Mrs. Adler-King as he took his seat. She remained standing, her eyes fixed on a coffee stain on the chair's seat, a brown blotch about the size and shape of a gherkin pickle. Max pointed again. "Please, have a seat."

"I don't suppose you have a chair that's clean, by any chance?"

Max leaned forward to look at the brown splotch on the orange material. "Oh, that's been there for years. It won't harm you."

"It's disgusting," she said, looking at Max as though he were trying to make her sit on a dog turd.

Max closed his eyes so that she would not see them roll. "Would you prefer my chair?" He stood up so she could inspect it.

"That would be very kind of you," she said.

Max switched his chair for the stained chair, and Anna Adler-King sat down with her back straight—careful not to lean against the back of the chair—and her hands folded together on her lap. She didn't touch the tabletop, as though contact with its surface might infect her with whatever disease pulsed through the veins of the many criminals who had been in that room before her.

"Detective Rupert," she said. "I want to do everything I can to convict the man who killed my sister."

"You know who killed her?"

"Well, isn't it obvious? Ben Pruitt. It had to be him."

"Why do you say that?"

Anna Adler-King appraised Max Rupert as if to discern whether he was playing stupid or if stupid was his natural state. Max waited.

"Who else would do something like this?"

"Mrs. Adler-King, how well do you know Ben Pruitt?"

"He's my brother-in-law, but we aren't close."

"When's the last time you spoke to him?"

She thought for a moment then answered. "It would have been at a fundraiser for the St. Paul libraries, just under a year ago."

"When was the last time you saw your sister?"

"That same evening."

"Would you say that you were particularly close to your sister?"

"We were sisters. Of course we were close."

"But you didn't talk to her for almost a year . . . and you live in the same city."

"Detective Rupert, there are bonds between sisters that make us close. We didn't need daily visits."

"I understand, Mrs. King—"

"Mrs. Adler-King," she corrected. "Unlike my sister, I chose to keep my maiden name. I am quite proud to be an Adler."

"Okay. But if you haven't talked to your sister in a year, you don't know how things stood between the Pruitts. I understand that you may not like Ben Pruitt, but that gives me nothing to add to the investigation."

"You want something to add to the investigation, I'll give you something. Jennavieve and Ben had a prenuptial agreement. Ben Pruitt had every reason in the world to kill Jennavieve."

"A prenup?" Max picked up his pen and slid a pad of paper off of a stack at the end of the table. "Tell me about it."

Anna smiled and crossed one leg over the other, her skirt sliding up just enough to expose a hint of the lace garter at the top of her expensive hosiery. "To begin with, you should know that my sister and I are rich. Not our own doing. Everything we have comes from our father and his father before him. My grandfather made a fortune in paper milling, a business he handed down. Our father diversified and built on what Grandfather did, and now Adler Enterprise is estimated to be worth nearly a billion dollars."

"Are your parents alive still?"

"Mother died five years ago. Father is fighting bone cancer right now."

"I'm sorry to hear that."

"He's a tough old bird. A lesser man would have been dead by now."

"With him being sick, who runs the ... enterprise?"

"It's a closely held corporation. He still owns the majority of the shares, but he gave his proxy to Jennavieve and me. Jennavieve has one vote more than me, so we won't tie."

"Excuse me if this seems indelicate, but what happens to those shares, now, if your father should pass on?"

Anna cast her eyes down as she prepared her response. When she raised her head and spoke, she seemed to be channeling Lauren Bacall from *The Big Sleep*, her eyelids weighted and her voice a note or two lower than before. "Detective, I know you have to ask these questions, and quite frankly I thought I had prepared myself for this before I came in here. But it's difficult for me to sit here and think that a part of you, even a very tiny part, suspects that I may have had anything to do with my sister's death."

"I didn't say that." Max said.

Anna looked at Max with a quiet intensity that cut through the pretense. "You wouldn't care about the control of my father's company if that thought hadn't crossed your mind. Or am I mistaken about that?"

Max kept his face expressionless and didn't answer.

She held her gaze on Max for a few beats, then smiled, bringing a touch of warmth to her otherwise-serious features. "It's a valid question, I suppose. As the will is written right now, I become the sole owner of Adler Enterprise after my father passes."

"'As the will is written right now'?"

"My father may be sick, Detective Rupert, but he still has his wits about him. If he thought for a second that I had anything to do with Jennavieve's death, he'd cut me out."

"Did you kill your sister? I mean, you have a pretty understandable motive, wouldn't you agree?"

"Ben Pruitt killed my sister, and the motive is in the prenuptial agreement."

"How is a prenuptial agreement a motive for murder?"

Anna leaned forward and, for the first time, deigned to put her fingertips on the edge of the table. "Jennavieve and I have trusts set up for us. My father wanted to make sure that we would never want for anything. When I heard that Jennavieve was dead, that she'd been murdered, I called our family attorney, the one who handles all of this stuff."

"You learn that your sister is dead and your first call is to an attorney?"

Anna recoiled a little at Max's accusation, and he could see anger seeping out from behind the stony façade that she struggled to maintain. "I've never been the weepy, sentimental type. That was Jennavieve.

That was her weakness, not mine. I'm more like my father. My reactions start in my head, not my heart."

"I suppose it takes a great deal of detachment to run an empire?"

"It's not detachment, Detective. I feel for the loss of my sister; I miss her dearly. But you will excuse me if I choose to grieve in my own way. I will honor my sister, not by curling up into a fetal position and bawling my way through a box full of tissues, but by getting the man who killed her. That's why I came here today—not to apologize to you for being strong, but to bring you something that could help put Ben Pruitt in prison."

This woman was a piece of work. Max couldn't tell if she was the strong, take-charge woman as she claimed, or a heartless manipulator. Either way, Anna Adler-King was a woman of considerable discipline. There would be no Perry Mason moment with this one.

"Okay," Max said. "What do you have?"

"I asked our attorney to look at Jennavieve's prenup and tell me what would happen if Jennavieve died versus what would happen if they got divorced."

"Was your sister thinking about getting divorced?"

"I'm not sure. She never said anything to me directly, but I got the feeling that she wasn't happy."

"So what did the attorney say?"

"He said that if Jennavieve and Ben were to ever get divorced, they would trace their assets to determine who paid what. In other words, if they both own a car, and they each paid half, they would split the asset. But if Jennavieve paid for it with money from her trust, and she put it in both their names, the car would go to Jennavieve. The idea being that if they ever got divorced, the stuff they bought with Jennavieve's trust money would go back to her."

"And if she dies?"

Anna looked coolly into Max's eyes. "If Jennavieve dies, all of the jointly owned assets go, by statute, to the co-owner."

Max leaned back in his chair to let those words sink in. He remembered Dovey's instruction to get him a motive so he could start the grand-jury proceeding. This had all the markings of a first-rate motive. "Do you have any notion of what they bought with trust money?"

Anna smiled. "Everything. Over the years, Jennavieve and I figured out that our father could never say no to us. We were able to raid the trust to buy just about anything we wanted. I know that Jennavieve paid for their mansion in Kenwood with trust money. And then there's the cabin up north, the condo in Aruba and another in France. I don't know the extent of it, but Jennavieve paid for pretty much everything they owned."

"And Ben Pruitt's name is on all those titles?"

"Co-owner and heir."

"But we don't know if there was any discussion about a divorce."

"I can't say. We had very different lives. We were both so busy that it became hard to get together."

"If she were going to tell someone about her plans to get a divorce, who might she tell?"

"Honestly, Jennavieve didn't have many close friends, not the kind she might confide something like that to. She lived for that foundation she ran, the one trying to protect the wetlands. Every time we got together, that was all she talked about. I think that if she had any friends close enough to answer your question, I'd look there."

"You've been a great help, Mrs. Adler-King."

"Thank you," she said with a slight nod of her head. "So, you think Ben did it, don't you?"

Max pursed his lips and gave Anna a slight shake of his head. "I can't discuss a pending investigation in that way. You understand?"

Anna's reply came back soft but firm, like a mother coaxing a child toward a predetermined conclusion. "What I understand, Detective Rupert, is that my sister is dead and my niece is with the man who killed her. I will stop at nothing to protect that little girl—the same way that I expect you to do whatever is necessary to put Ben Pruitt in prison. I hope to hear, very soon, that you've arrested Ben for my sister's murder."

Anna Adler-King rose from her chair, so Max stood as well. She stepped toward the door and he opened it for her. He understood that she was finished talking to him, so he didn't attempt to change her mind or make her stay.

"You can get me copies of that prenup?"

"I'll have it delivered," she said. Then she turned to face him one last time. "I like you, Detective Rupert, and that's not something I say to many people. I get the feeling that, like myself, you know full well my sister was killed by her husband. I have complete faith that you won't let me down."

With that, she turned and left.

Chapter 20

Ben took a moment to check on his daughter before re-creating his movements on the day that Jennavieve died. He returned to Boady's study, closing the glass French doors with a quiet click. He informed Boady that Emma seemed to be engaged in drawing something on the sketch pad, and he didn't dare interrupt her as it was her first sustained distraction from the events of the previous Friday. He sat back down, and Boady touched his pen to paper to signify the official start of their endeavor.

"Let's start with your alibi," Boady said. "We lock that in and we nip all this in the bud."

"I've been going over that in my head all weekend," Ben said. "To start with, I parked at the park-and-ride on Lexington. I don't believe they have cameras, but I gave Rupert a receipt that has the time and date. Shuttle to the airport and on my flight by 10:15 in the morning. Taxi to the hotel—the downtown Marriott—paid on my Amex card."

"So for that part of the trip, there can be no question that you flew to Chicago. What about the hotel? Did you notice any surveillance cameras?"

"I wasn't looking for them, but I'm sure they have some. It's a nice hotel."

"I'll send a letter to the Marriott's security director requesting that he preserve the footage. I doubt they'll give it to us, but if I know Max, he'll be requesting it, if he hasn't already. So you get to the Marriott, check in . . ."

"I check in, go to the room, unpack, then I go for a walk."

"A walk?"

"The opening speeches started at noon, but it was just an overview of recent court cases. They give you that material on CD, so I opted to skip it."

"Where did you go?"

"Took a stroll down Navy Pier. It was a beautiful day."

"Any paper trail?"

"Let's see . . . I bought a hot dog from a street vendor, but I paid cash. That's about all I did there. Just walked around, taking in the fresh air."

"What time did you get back to the hotel?"

"Just before one p.m. I went to a panel on white-collar sentencing trends and then one on protecting client assets, and after that . . . let's see . . . oh yeah, a panel on preserving appellate issues. That was the last one of the day."

"Anybody see you?"

"You know Michael Tanner? From Dugan & Fitch?"

"We've met."

"He sat next to me at the panel on appellate issues."

"Okay, we have only a single gap in time so far. Between check-in and when Tanner saw you on that last panel of the day. Maybe the hotel has video of the conference center."

Ben looked puzzled. "Why do we care about those couple hours? They're not going to suggest that I could have flown back here and killed Jennavieve in that time."

"No, but we're going to leave no holes. So the conference gets over at . . ."

"Five. Tanner invited me to join him and some friends in the hotel restaurant for dinner and drinks. I gave him a soft yes, but I wasn't big on the idea."

"Why?"

"Tanner's one of those guys who . . . well, he's kind of a pig. I'm not saying he actually cheats on his wife, but he sure does try. He calls every waitress 'honey' and chats up the lonely hearts in the room. I've never liked socializing with him because I never want to be put in a position of being a witness to that kind of crap."

"Okay, so you stay in."

"Right. I order room service—club sandwich and some fries—and watch TV."

"Make any phone calls?"

"Just the one to Jennavieve around five. I wanted to say hi to Emma. Got no answer, so I sent a text."

"We can get cell-phone tower data to show where that call originated. Any others?"

"No."

"Go online at the hotel?"

"No."

Boady raised a hand to his face and began stroking his light beard. "Any contact with anyone?"

"Truth is, I wasn't feeling so well. I thought maybe the hot dog from Navy Pier didn't agree with me."

"That's a pretty big hole in your alibi. How long does it take to get from Chicago to here?"

"Well, not counting flight delays, just under an hour."

"No, I mean driving."

"Um. I don't think that I've ever driven from Chicago to here." Ben pondered some more, then nodded. "No, I've never driven it."

Boady pulled his computer keyboard to the edge of his desk and typed in the query. He clicked on different options and found that the most direct path to drive from Chicago to Minneapolis took just over six hours. He frowned as he did the math in his head.

"What?" Ben asked.

"You don't have an alibi at all."

"Of course I do."

"No, Ben, you can get from Chicago to Minneapolis in just over six hours. We have the phone call and texts that put you in the room between five and five thirty. There's no evidence that you stayed in your room after that. No phone calls. No computer log-in. No contact with anyone, am I right about that?"

A shadow of panic passed over Ben's face, washing away what little color he had. His eyes darted from one imaginary point to another as though he was searching his memory for some touchstone that would confirm his presence in his hotel room. "I didn't talk to anyone."

"If it takes six hours to get from there to here, and no one saw you after six p.m. . . ."

"Oh, Christ. There's got to be . . ."

"Any contact at all? Anything that might leave a trail?"

"Can the hotel tell if I turned the TV channel?" he asked.

"Not unless you purchased a pay-per-view channel. Did you?"

"No. I watched news programs."

"Key cards will record every time you unlock your door from the hallway. Did you go out for ice?"

"I . . . I don't think so. I might have, but I'm almost positive I didn't leave the room."

"So we have a problem."

"But I didn't have a car. I flew there. I have no way to drive back here."

"That's a different issue. If we could find one little piece of evidence, something irrefutable that puts you in that hotel room after . . . say, eight o'clock, then there'd be no need to discuss how you might have gotten back here. If we cannot find that piece, then we have to prove the negative—prove that you didn't and couldn't have driven back here."

"What about the hotel surveillance? If there are any cameras, that'll show I didn't leave."

"True. I'll get that letter out today."

"If they say no, I'll also put a call into Max Rupert and ask that he secure it."

Boady turned to a new page on his legal pad and wrote the word "Motive" at the top of the page. "We've covered opportunity, now let's talk about motive. Rupert's likely going through your life with a magnifying glass right now looking for reasons why you might want to kill Jennavieve. What's he going to find?"

"I had no reason to kill Jennavieve. Things at home were pretty good."

"Pretty good?"

"I mean, every relationship has its ups and downs."

"Were you in an up or a down when you flew to Chicago? Tell me about these ups and downs."

Ben didn't look at Boady as he prepared an answer. "It's been quiet around the house lately."

"Lately?"

"Maybe a year now. I don't know exactly how to describe it. It was like she didn't want to do anything anymore, at least not alone with me. If Emma came along, we all had a great time. We went and rented one of those little sailboats on Lake Harriet last month. Had a blast. We took Emma to see *Pippin* when the touring company came through in February. Got all dressed up. Ate dinner at the Capital Grille. It was a terrific evening."

Ben began to tear up again and paused to let the emotion pass. "But if I ever suggested a date night, just Jennavieve and me, she'd always have some reason why she couldn't go. Or she'd invite another couple to join us and not tell me."

"Did you ever talk to her about it?"

"I tried a few times, but she swore it was just my imagination. She seemed to need to be away from home as much as she could, going to events at the Minneapolis Club, sitting in on extra committee meetings for the theater trust, working extra hours at the foundation. I could understand wanting a break from me, but by staying away from the house, she was also staying away from Emma. That's the part that didn't make sense. Emma was her life."

Boady stared at the legal pad as he contemplated a delicate way to approach the next topic. Finally he asked the question that he needed to ask. "Is it possible Jennavieve was . . ." He looked at Ben and waited for him to finish the question.

"Having an affair?"

Boady shrugged sympathetically and nodded.

Ben seemed to lose himself in his thoughts, undoubtedly stacking and restacking his recent memories, exposing them to this new light to see if they mutated into something ugly. After several minutes, he spoke in a whisper. "I don't think so. I mean, I suppose it's possible, but . . . no, not Jennavieve. She wasn't that kind of person. You knew her. Granted, it's been six years since we spent any real time with you and Diana, but you knew her. She'd never do something like that. I can't see it."

"I'm going to hire a researcher to do some digging. Maybe we'll come up with something. I'll also be getting the hotel surveillance footage. That might be all we need to get you off of Rupert's suspect list."

"What can I do?"

"Nothing. Any evidence you bring to the table will automatically be rejected by any jury. Let me do my work. You take care of that little girl of yours."

Ben nodded and stood to leave. Boady followed him out to the living room, where Emma had fallen asleep on the couch. Beside her lay the sketch pad. Boady picked up the pad as Ben lifted his exhausted daughter, her head coming to rest on his shoulder.

Boady opened the door and watched as Ben carried Emma to his car, carefully laying her in the back seat. Ben stretched a seatbelt across Emma and shut the door. Then he waved to Boady and drove off.

After Ben left, Boady looked at the sketch pad and at the picture Emma had drawn. It almost took away his breath. She'd drawn her mother, and not the stick-figure-type drawing where you would need context to know what she was drawing. No. This picture was the product of a talented hand. The face and hair were that of Jennavieve Pruitt. She lay on her side on the ground, stretched out beneath a tree. Emma drew Jennavieve's hands pressed together and tucked under her head in a makeshift pillow, and she wore a princess dress.

Above Jennavieve's head, Emma had drawn a dialogue bubble, the little circle that animators use to show when someone is speaking. And in the bubble she wrote: "I miss my Emma."

Chapter 21

The next day, just before three in the afternoon, Max Rupert rolled up to the Plaza Nineteen tollbooth in Rosemount, Illinois. He checked his watch and wrote down the time, this being the last of the eastbound plazas. As he neared the outer ring of Chicago, his options for alternate routes multiplied, so he would want to pay particular attention to the footage from tollbooths closer to the Wisconsin border, especially South Beloit. It would have been damn-near impossible for Pruitt to get back to Minneapolis in time to kill his wife without going through South Beloit.

Max started his trip that day from in front of the Pruitt house in Kenwood, where he leaned against his car and imagined Mrs. Pruitt's murder taking place inside, doing his best to time the action: the killer stabbing her in the throat, forcing her onto the bed, holding her down as she bled out, grabbing the blankets from Emma's bed, wrapping the body, hauling the body to the car. Then the killer returned to take the bedding from the master bed. Exactly why he took the sheets off the bed, Max hadn't yet figured out. It would come to him in time. It always did.

Then Max got into his car and drove to the bookstore parking lot. He watched in his mind as Ben Pruitt backed the red sedan up to the dumpster. He tried to keep the killer faceless. He even fought against making the killer a man. But Ben Pruitt kept showing up. He saw Ben open the trunk, then open the dumpster lid. Full. So he pulls his wife's body out of the trunk and drops it on the asphalt.

Max looked at his watch. About forty-five minutes. If the killer did any additional cleaning up, the time might round up to an hour.

Then Max got back into his car and set out for Chicago. He knew that the timing of his trip would not be scientifically accurate, given the flow of rush-hour traffic, but he wanted to travel in the path that Ben Pruitt would have taken. He wanted to put himself into the killer's mind as much as he could.

The day before, he'd spent two hours on his computer, mapping and remapping various routes between the Marriott Hotel in Chicago and the Pruitts' house in Kenwood. The timing would be tight. The computer maps showed that the fastest route, the Interstate, took just under six and a half hours. The back roads, with at least one stoplight in every little town that it passed through, would not have been fast enough to fit that window.

If Pruitt left the hotel after the text to his wife at 5:30, the drive would put him in Kenwood at midnight, just like Malena Gwin said. He kills his wife. Dumps her body. That puts him on the road by 1:00 a.m. The drive back would put him in Chicago at 7:00 a.m. Add in a little morning rush-hour traffic, and he'd be back in time to catch the first speaker of the morning.

Max had just passed Toll Plaza Nineteen when his phone rang. It was Niki.

"How's the trip going?" she asked.

"I hit some construction north of Beloit, but it didn't slow me down too much. And Pruitt would have been making the trip overnight, so he'd have had even less traffic. What's up on your end?"

"I thought you should know: Dovey got the go-ahead to convene a grand jury. He wants us to have everything ready a week from Thursday."

"Oh, for Christ's sake."

"He says he has a case and he doesn't want Pruitt jumping on a plane."

"Pruitt knows he's in the crosshairs. Hell, he's hired a lawyer already. If he was going to jump on a plane, he'd have done it by now."

"That's what I told him."

"Let me guess, he ignored you?"

"Also, I'm hearing rumblings about him. Word around the hall is that he's put in for a judgeship. The Adler family has strong ties to the Democratic Party, and to the governor. If you do an image search for old-man Adler, you'll get pictures of him fishing and hunting with the governor. They go back a long way."

Max shook his head, even though there was no one there to see it. "Well, that explains a lot. I figured there was something lighting a fire under Dovey's ass."

"Dovey wants Emerson Adler's blessing for that judgeship. Dovey gets that, and he's in like Flynn. The problem he has is that old-man Adler's dying. Dovey needs to get the case moving fast so he can get the endorsement before Adler dies. My source tells me that if Dovey can get an indictment before the old man croaks, the old man will send a letter to his buddy the governor."

"Fucking politics."

"Exactly."

"We don't have a murder weapon. The forensics aren't in for the computers or the phones. All we have is motive with the prenup, and maybe opportunity."

"We have Pruitt lying. He says he never left Chicago. Malena Gwin puts him at the scene of the murder at midnight. Those both can't be true. If the jury believes Gwin—"

"But what if Gwin's wrong?" Max said. "What if I come across some hotel staff person who can put Pruitt here later that evening? Dovey's jumping the gun. If he waits, we'll have a tighter case."

"If he can get the indictment, I suspect he'll have the Adler name backing him."

"And if it all blows up, if the case falls apart, you can bet he won't take the blame. He'll hang us out to dry. He strikes me as that kind of political asshole. Fucking politics."

"Such is the life we've chosen." Niki said. "On the plus side, Dovey did send an e-mail to say that the Marriott security is expecting you. They'll have the hotel footage ready."

"And the tollbooth cameras?"

"Subpoenaed and on the way."

Max shrugged into the phone. "At least he's an organized political asshole."

"Dangle a little opportunity in front of a guy like that and you'll be amazed at the tricks he'll do."

"Ain't that the truth."

Max needed to focus on his driving so that he could finish the trip with no wrong turns—the timing had to be the centerpiece of the case. So he said good-bye to Niki and restarted his GPS navigation.

There was no way Ben Pruitt was clever enough to pull this off without a mistake. They always made mistakes. The ones who got away with it weren't good—they were lucky.

And just like that, Max's mind was back in Minneapolis, standing in the parking ramp where some lucky sonofabitch bounced over Jenni's body and drove away—unseen, unheard, and unrepentant.

Yeah, that sonofabitch was lucky, alright. Lucky that Max had been frozen out of the investigation. But if Max ever caught up to the driver, he—or she—would be the most unlucky sonofabitch that ever walked the planet.

Chapter 22

The first time that Boady Sanden met Lila Nash, she still had bandages on her wrists and the shadow of old bruises on her face. Her ordeal had been the lead story on every media outlet in the Twin Cities, although her name never appeared in any story. The newspapers referred to her as the college student who would have been the next victim of a cold-blooded killer, had Homicide Detective Max Rupert not saved her life.

At the time of Lila's ordeal, Boady had been working with Lila's boyfriend, Joe Talbert, trying to exonerate a man who they believed had been wrongfully convicted of murder. That investigation led them to a man named Lockwood, who didn't take the intrusion into his affairs lightly. If it hadn't been for Max Rupert, both Lila and Joe would have been killed.

After the story lost its steam, Lila went back to school and Boady returned to his world of academia. That had been three years ago and Boady never expected he'd see Lila again. But just over a year ago she showed up at his office door, looking to go to law school. Boady could barely contain his fatherly pride when she chose Hamline. She possessed a brilliant mind and was a born puzzle solver.

Boady stepped out from behind his memories as the first few students of the summer-session class began to file out of the room. He waited across the hall, and when the torrent turned to a trickle, Lila emerged, books in hand. She smiled when she saw him, and he waved her over.

"Can I buy you a cup of coffee?" Boady asked. He could see a flicker of surprise cross her face. "Um . . . sure."

"Unless you have somewhere you need to be."

"No, I have time for coffee."

Boady smiled and motioned toward the stairs that led to the common area in the basement of the law school.

"Are you teaching a class this summer?" she asked.

"No, not this summer. I'm just here taking care of some scheduling details. How's con-law going?"

"Not bad. It's a little dry."

They entered the common area, a smattering of tables, a bookstore, student mailboxes, and in the corner, vending machines. Boady pulled out his wallet and slid a buck into the slot and watched the paper cup fill with coffee so weak it barely deserved the name. He slid another dollar in and let Lila select her own roast.

He'd seen Lila often over the course of her first year, navigating the corridors, while debating points of law with her peers. He would wave or nod as they passed, but they never had a chance to chat. He remembered drinking coffee with her the last time they were together. On that occasion, they talked as friends do. Now that he was her professor, their conversation seemed stiff and contrived. He tried to get past that formality. "How's Joe doing?" he asked.

She smiled. "He graduated and has a job with Associated Press."

Boady nodded thoughtfully. "I see you made law review. How'd you do in your research and writing class?"

"Second in the class. I love the research part. As for the writing . . . well, let's just say it's good to have Joe around to give me advice."

"I'm glad to hear that you like research, because I have a proposition for you. I am going on sabbatical this fall. I may be going back to court to defend a friend of mine. If it comes to that, I'll need a good researcher. Someone with the eye of a puzzle solver. It's part-time so you can do it around your school work. And it pays, oh let's say, thirty bucks an hour. Does that sound fair?"

"Thirty dollars an hour? Hell yeah, I'll do it . . . I mean if you think I'm the person for the job. What kind of things will I be doing?"

"Researching case law, drafting motions, maybe a little digging into the case. Right now, I'm just doing prep work."

"What kind of case?"

"Did you hear about that woman they found in an alley last week? Jennavieve Pruitt?"

"I saw it on the news, but I haven't been following it."

"Her husband, Ben Pruitt, used to be my law partner. He's asked me to represent him."

"They think he killed his wife?"

"That seems to be the direction they're headed. And, Lila, before you agree to do this, you should know that Max Rupert is the lead investigator."

Lila's eyes flashed with surprise and then fell to the table as her thoughts turned inward. "We're going against Max?"

Boady watched as Lila subconsciously moved her fingertips over the scar on her wrist, a scar put there by a killer's rope.

"Lila, I know you owe Max a great debt, and I'd certainly understand if you can't—"

"No, I can do this," she said. She followed Boady's gaze to where the index finger of her right hand gently stroked the scar on her left wrist and she drew her hands apart, balling them into fists and let them rest on the table. "I can do this," she repeated.

Chapter 23

The grand jury was set to convene at 10 a.m. on a rainy Thursday morning, chillier than it should have been for mid-August. Max and Niki received their subpoenas along with a note from Dovey setting up a meeting to go over their testimonies. Max still didn't understand the logic—or lack of logic—in Dovey's decision to rush this case to the grand jury. Max's investigation folder still seemed thin.

He and Niki were led to the same conference room where they met with Dovey before. The room was empty, but Max spied the Pruitt file on the table. It looked every bit as thin as Max's file. Max tapped the back of a chair, the one directly across from the file, and gave a single nod to Niki, who took that seat. Max took the seat next over.

When Dovey entered, he paused, looked at Niki, then at Max, then at the file. He strode, confidently, to the seat opposite Max, sat down, and pulled the case file in front of him.

Max and Niki shared a glance.

"I'm going to lead off with you Max," Dovey said. "You'll lay out the case from beginning to end in a logical, no-nonsense way."

"I'm not sure I can do that," Max said.

"What do you mean?"

"I mean that I have the beginning, but I don't have the end yet. We have the lab reports, but we still don't have the forensics from the computer. We don't have the forensics from her phone. There are still witnesses that we haven't contacted. Don't you think we should wait until we button up those loose ends?"

Dovey rubbed his chin as if he was considering Max's concern, but his gesture seemed hollow, as though he was only pretending to ponder. "You know, Max, I thought about it long and hard before calling the grand jury. What it came down to is this: There's a killer wandering the streets. I believe Ben Pruitt killed his wife. I believe he's a smart sonofabitch. And I don't believe the computer forensics will give us anything more than what he wants to give us. Think about it, Max. Ben Pruitt knows how this works. Hell, he knows our investigation tactic as well as we do. He's not going to plan his wife's murder with this kind of care and then be stupid enough to leave something incriminating on his computer. Besides, if we find anything on the computer, we'll just add it to the pile. We have enough now to get the indictment, and every day that Pruitt roams around free is another day that a murderer is on the loose in my city."

Nice speech, Max thought. A little too rehearsed, and Max wondered if he'd given that same speech to his boss when he proposed the convening of the grand jury.

"So I'll be putting you on the stand first, Max," Dovey said. "The way I see it, our biggest weakness is the travel issue." Dovey stopped talking and looked at Max.

Max took that as his cue to pick up the thread. "We should be getting surveillance video from the tollbooths within the next week or so. The neighbor, Malena Gwin, is certain she saw Ben Pruitt park a red sedan on the street in front of his house within an hour of Jennavieve Pruitt's death."

"What's the window of opportunity for Pruitt's alibi?"

Max looked at his notes. "His hotel key-card data shows that he entered his room at precisely 4:49 p.m. on the day of the murder. Room service delivered a sandwich to his room at 5:20. After that there's no activity until his key card registers him entering his room at 8:32 the following morning."

Dovey poked his index finger on the file. "The fact that he entered his room at 8:32 in the morning is proof that he just got back from the drive. Why else would he be going into his room at that early hour?"

"Remember," Max said, "in his statement to me, he said that he'd started down to the conference, but went back to the room to get his schedule."

"Seems damned convenient," Dovey said.

"He's a smart one," Max said. "But it still leaves us with a window of time that fits. He gets to the house in Kenwood around midnight, when Malena Gwin sees him. He had an hour to kill his wife, clean up, and dump her body. Figure it'll take a little longer to get back to the hotel because of rush-hour traffic and the 8:30 return fits perfectly."

Max pulled out some still shots of a man in a tan jacket and black baseball cap exiting through the lobby of the hotel. "We don't have anything specific. This picture shows a man, the right build and height, leaving the hotel about the right time, but we have no face shot." Max pulled out a second photo of a man with a dark jacket and a red baseball cap on his head walking through the lobby of the hotel, going the opposite direction. "This was taken at 8:28 a.m. that morning. Again same height and build, different-color clothing, but his cap is pulled down over his eyes, just like the guy leaving the night before. Could be Pruitt, or it could be a couple random guys."

Dovey studied the pictures with hawkish intensity. After a couple minutes he stood up and left the conference room, came back with a magnifying glass, and resumed his examination. Dovey was focusing on the man's shoes.

Niki glanced at Max and then said, "We blew the pictures up and looked at everything. The clothing is all different. He even had different shoes on."

With those words, Dovey put the magnifying glass down. "So what I'm hearing is that . . ." Dovey again spoke to Max as if Niki weren't in the room. "Ben Pruitt changed his clothes after he murdered his wife."

"If he's smart he would," Niki said. "That gets rid of the trace evidence."

"Did you search his suitcase when he got back?" Again, Dovey looked at Max as he spoke.

Niki answered him. "We secured the contents of his suitcase when he came back from Chicago. The clothes in that picture . . ." Niki pointed at the picture from the morning surveillance camera. "Those clothes were not in his suitcase. He must have anticipated that we'd get the footage from the lobby, and he made sure that we couldn't match anything to him."

"When we get the tollbooth footage it'll seal his fate. Is there any alternative route that he could have taken to get around the tollbooths?"

"There are, but it's going to really eat into his travel time. He'll be going through suburbs and towns with stop signs and reduced speed limits. It's possible, but he'd be taking a huge risk."

"Well, then," Dovey said. "All we need is to confirm how he got back here to Minneapolis, and Pruitt's a sitting duck."

"If that's the case," Niki said, "wouldn't it be better that we hold off on the grand jury until we have that footage?"

For the first time since they arrived, Dovey turned to Detective Niki Vang and addressed her directly. His features twisted as though a foul odor had just assaulted him. "Detective, you do your job and I'll thank you to let me do mine."

Niki's cheeks reddened as she slunk back into her chair.

Max stood and leaned onto the table. "Dovey? Listen to me very carefully," he said, narrowing his eyes on the red-faced prosecutor. "This is Detective Niki Vang, one of the best minds on the force. She's my partner, and she's my friend. Although you may have never heard of her before this case, you have heard of me. And if you've heard of me, then you know that I'm a very serious man who is not one to suffer assholes lightly. I still have enough clout around this city to muck up the plans of a political hack like you. So if you ever treat Detective Vang with that kind of disrespect again—"

"Now wait a second, Detective," Dovey sputtered. "I meant no disrespect. I was merely pointing out that we each have our jobs to do. My job is to—"

"Right now, your job is to apologize to Detective Vang."

"You know I didn't mean to—"

"Not me," Max said. "Talk to her."

A deep-red blush flashed across Dovey's fat, pale cheeks, and he began to blink in quick beats, as though Max's words had dried the man's pupils. For a few seconds, a thick, gray silence filled the room.

Then, after the blinking stopped, after Dovey regained control of his breathing, he turned to Niki and spoke in a tone so removed from his normal voice that it almost held a British accent.

"I apologize," he said.

When he turned back to Max, Dovey had once again found his smugness. "Happy, Detective?"

Max looked at Niki and jerked his head toward the door. Niki rose and followed Max out of the conference room.

Chapter 24

Boady sat down at the dinner table, about to dine on the meal of broiled walleye, potato slices, and asparagus, when the phone rang. He thought about not answering it, assuming it would be the cable company calling to get him to upgrade to a more expensive package, or maybe some bogus charity with the word *cancer* or *diabetes* or *firefighter* in the name looking for a donation. But then he remembered that he had a client again, and he answered the phone on the off chance that it might be Ben Pruitt. It was.

He asked if Boady might be around for a bit and could Ben drop by? Of course. But then Ben asked if Diana would also be at home. Boady didn't know why that would matter. He answered yes, and to his surprise, Ben sounded relieved.

By the time Ben arrived, Boady and Diana had finished supper and the dishes. Boady had moved to the front porch, where a cool summer rain gave somber weight to the evening. When Ben arrived, he stepped out of his car and opened the back door for Emma. He picked her up so that they could share his umbrella as he carried her to the porch. Emma curled her face into her father's chest, her eyes staring at nothing beyond the colors of the world that moved past her father's shoulder.

Boady stood as Ben ascended the steps. Ben put Emma down, held out a piece of paper, and said, "It's starting."

"Would you like to talk in my office?" Boady opened the door for his guests.

"I think that'd be best," Ben said. "Any chance Diana could sit with Emma for a bit?"

"I'm sure Diana would be happy for the company." Boady could hear Diana still in the kitchen and called her to come to the front room.

When she walked in, Diana leaned down and in her most com-
forting voice said, "I'm so happy to see you again. Last time I saw you,
you were just a tiny thing. My goodness, did you grow up pretty."

Ben gave a slight bow to Emma. "Mr. Sanden and I have some
things to discuss. I won't be long. I promise." The men walked to
Boady's study. Once in the study, with the door closed, Ben handed the
paper to Boady to read.

"A subpoena?" Boady read some more, then looked up.

"They served me this morning. They convened a grand jury, they
want me to testify."

"Don't worry," Boady said, "I'll have this quashed before lunch
tomorrow." Boady sat in a leather chair behind his desk and motioned
for Ben to have a seat opposite him.

"Let's not be too quick here," Ben said. "Let's consider it."

"Are you out of your mind? Ben, if you were advising any other
client, would you let them testify before a grand jury where they are
being accused of murder?"

"But I'm not just any client, Boady. I know what they're looking
for. I know the traps. If I go there, I can tell them what really happened,
at least as far as my involvement is concerned."

Boady smiled at Ben and waited.

"I know it's a bad idea, but I didn't kill Jennavieve. I was in Chicago.
They need to know that."

"Did you tell that to Max Rupert when he interviewed you?"

Ben nodded.

"Then the grand jury will hear your alibi. I'm sure that Rupert has
done the math. He'll see the same hole that we did. So tell me, how will
your testimony change anything?"

Ben nodded again and didn't respond.

"Ben, I understand that impulse that makes you want to go there
and look them in the eyes and tell them that you didn't kill your wife, but
you know better. If the prosecutor wants you indicted, you'll be indicted.
If I were the client and you the attorney here, what would you tell me?"

Ben smiled a wary smile. "I'd tell you that only a damn fool would go testify. I'd tell you to start getting ready for the shit storm that's on its way. Get your affairs in order and get ready to defend yourself in court."

"That sounds like sage advice."

Ben reached into his jacket pocket and pulled out another piece of paper. "Along those lines, then . . ." He handed the paper to Boady, who read the title on the first page *Custody Agreement* and looked up at Ben. Ben said nothing and Boady continued to read the document drafted by Ben that would transfer custody of Emma to Boady and Diana Sanden should he become incarcerated.

"I don't understand," Boady said.

"If they indict me, they'll arrest me. I have to imagine my bail's going to be in the millions of dollars. Depending on the amount, I might be held in custody until after a trial. I'm truly hoping that's not the case, but this is me getting my affairs in order."

"But what about a family member. Doesn't Jennavieve have a sister?"

"That's exactly what I'm trying to avoid. Jennavieve's sister hates me. Has for years. If she gets her hands on Emma, she'll poison my little girl against me. She'll have Emma convinced that I killed her mother, and then it won't matter what the jury says. I'll always have that cloud over my head. I can't have that."

Boady laid the paper on the desk and eased back in his chair. "Are you sure about this?"

"I've never been surer of anything. I can't imagine what the prosecutor has, or thinks he has, to convene a grand jury, but I'm preparing for the worst. If it comes to it, I can handle getting thrown in jail. I can even live with the prospect of not getting out until I'm acquitted." The corners of Ben's eyes took on a shine as the tears began to well up. "But the thought of Emma in the hands of my witch of a sister-in-law, that's something I can't abide. I need you and Diana to protect her. Please tell me you'll do it. Please."

"I have to talk it over with Diana, but, yeah, I'll agree to it."

Ben leaned forward, his elbows on his knees, his face in his hands. He kept his face hidden as he worked to settle his breath. "Thank you," he whispered in a voice so soft that it barely took flight. "Thank you."

Chapter 25

Everett Kagen lived in a modest, blue Cape Cod on a corner lot across the street from a park—the kind of quiet neighborhood that has little experience with homicide detectives or murder investigations. The house struck Max as being less than he expected. It was clean and comfortable and gingerbread in every way, but Max expected more considering this was the house of the attorney for the Adler Wetland Preservation Foundation.

Max and Niki approached, pausing at the door to hear the banter of at least two children, girls, preteen, going back and forth about the relative merits of toenail polish. Max knocked.

A woman in her late thirties, and more than a bit on the heavy side, opened the door. She had the kind of face that had probably been attractive when she was younger but had been dulled by time, and stress, and too much daytime television. She smiled a Stepford smile when she saw her visitors, a smile that disappeared when she saw the badges.

Niki took the lead. "We're here to see Everett Kagen. Is he home?"

The woman glanced over her shoulder and then nodded at the detectives. "He's downstairs. I'll get him." She turned, leaving the door open, a gesture that Max and Niki took as an invitation to enter, which they did. The two girls had stopped their jabbering and came to the dining room to observe the visitors. They pretended to be interested in the woodgrain of the table but kept glancing at the detectives in the front entry.

From somewhere in the belly of the house, Max could hear the woman's voice sputtering in short, angry bursts. A male voice, too muffled to understand, sputtered back. Soon the rumble of the couple climbing the stairs replaced the bickering. Everett, a man with rugged features, a cowboy washed clean of dust, approached them with a joyless half-smile.

"Mr. Kagen, I'm Detective Niki Vang and this is my partner, Max Rupert. Could we have a word with you? It's about the death of Jennavieve Pruitt."

"Of course." Kagen looked over his shoulder at the two girls, then said, "Maybe we could go for a walk in the park and talk?"

Niki looked at Max and then nodded to Kagen.

As they walked down the sidewalk to the street, Kagen spoke first. "I figured you'd be by sooner or later."

"When did you last see her?" Niki asked.

Kagen headed toward a bleacher at the edge of a soccer field.

"We were at the office all day, the day she died. We're starting a new case."

Kagen took a seat on the bottom bench. Max and Niki flanked him. He began to massage his thighs with his hands, as though wiping sweat from his palms. "We worked until . . . oh, it had to be maybe eleven o'clock at night before we quit."

"Were you and Mrs. Pruitt often in the habit of working late at the office?" Niki asked.

Kagen sat up and turned to her. "I don't like what you're insinuating. I'm a happily married man. Jennavieve and I were business associates. That's all."

"I'm not insinuating a thing, Mr. Kagen," Niki said. "You said that you worked late on the night Mrs. Pruitt was murdered. I merely asked if that was a regular occurrence."

Kagen went back to squeezing his thighs. "I'm sorry," he said. "This whole thing's crazy. Jennavieve was one of the nicest people I've ever met. The thought that someone might kill her . . . it makes no sense."

"So, you left the office at the same time?"

"Huh? Oh, yeah. Like I said, we worked until about eleven and called it a night. I walked her to her car—just because I'd hate for her to get mugged or something. Then I went to my car and came home. I got home sometime between 11:30 and 11:45."

"How did Mrs. Pruitt seem when you parted? Did she seem worried about anything?"

"No."

"Ever mention any concerns or fears—anyone that may have wanted to hurt her?"

"No, I mean, nothing beyond the normal."

"Normal?"

"We are a foundation set up for one purpose. We stop developers from draining wetlands for commercial purposes. We spend our time, our energy, our full resources bringing lawsuits. This, of course, makes some people angry."

"So you stopped people from building on their own land?" Max asked.

Kagen now turned to face Max, addressing him for the first time since they met. "That land is vital to the future of this state and this planet. It's the home of hundreds, maybe thousands of species of wildlife. People love living in this state because everywhere you go, you're surrounded by nature. Even in Minneapolis there's wildlife all around you if you just stop and look. That doesn't happen by accident. We need those wetlands to stay natural. Someone has to fight for that, and that's what we are doing."

"Slow down there, Mr. Kagen," Max said, holding his palms up. "I'm not attacking your cause. Just gathering information. How many people work at the Adler Wetland Preservation Foundation?"

Kagen gave a wry smile. "It sounds bigger than it really is . . . or, was. It's just the two of us. Jennavieve is the driving force and the primary financial backer. She raised awareness. She managed our web presence and social media, and she set up the fundraisers. I did the legal work. If I needed help, we brought in temps. There's been a glut of new attorneys on the market for years now. If I need a motion drafted or some research done, I can just contract it out. It keeps overhead low."

"I assume you've met Mr. Pruitt?" Niki said.

Kagen's face went slack and he leaned forward, his elbows resting on his knees, his fingers lacing together into a church steeple. "Yeah, I know Ben."

Niki waited for Kagen to elaborate, but the man went silent. Then she asked, "How did Jennavieve Pruitt feel about Ben Pruitt?"

Kagen continued to stare out into the distance, where four kids were kicking a soccer ball around. Then he said, "She was going to divorce him."

Both detectives perked up. "Are you sure?" Niki asked.

"I'm sure. You don't work with someone as closely as we did and not get to know them personally. She was unhappy in her marriage. She didn't love him anymore, but she stayed with him because of Emma. I tried to get her to . . . I could see how miserable she was. She deserved better. Then about a month ago, she asked me if I'd ever done a divorce. I told her I had, but not in years. I told her that she needed to get an attorney who does nothing but family law. She needed the best, especially given her . . . well you know, her family money."

"Did she talk to an attorney?"

"I don't know. I think she was working up the courage to do it. Emma was her life. There was no way that divorce would be a smooth one."

"So you don't have the name of any attorney she might have contacted?"

"No. Sorry."

Niki looked at Max and nodded a signal that she was out of questions for the moment. Max nodded back. Niki said, "I'm going to go have a chat with your wife—just need to confirm what time you got home that night."

Kagen's eyes darted back and forth between the detectives. "Is that necessary?"

Max cocked his head and gave Kagen a *what the hell?* look. How could a man with a law degree ask such a stupid question? "You were with Mrs. Pruitt the night she was murdered. You say you were home at 11:30. That's important. How would it look if we didn't even confirm that information with your wife?"

Kagen nodded his understanding.

All three stood and Niki headed across the street to where Mrs. Kagen watched from the front door, arms folded across her chest.

"We're not here to cause problems," Max said, "but we're looking into everything, so if you have any more information, now's the time to open up."

"I can't think of a thing. Believe me, I want to do everything I can to help. Jennavieve was . . ." Kagen looked like he might break into tears. He didn't complete his thought. "If there's anything I can do, anything at all, please don't hesitate."

"Now that you mention it," Max said. "If you don't mind, we'd like to have you come down and give fingerprints and DNA. Just a routine thing in a case like this. We may need to exclude you."

Kagen's breath caught in his throat, and he looked back and forth between Max and his wife, now talking to Detective Vang. "You'll find my fingerprints at Jennavieve's house. I've been there on a number of occasions."

There was more to this. Max could tell. Kagen was leaving something out—something that tangled the man's fingers and kept pulling his gaze to the missus.

"I take it your wife wasn't invited on those occasions?" Max asked, giving a nod toward Kagen's house.

"Okay, Detective, here's the thing. Sometimes Jennavieve and I would work at her house. She preferred it to working at the office. It was just more comfortable. But it was strictly work, and we only did it now and then."

"And your wife was okay with you working at the Pruitts' home?" Max asked.

Kagen looked at a dandelion beside his toe. "My wife was never a big fan of that idea. We had more than a few fights about it. Just between us, I didn't always tell her when we worked from Jennavieve's house. Like it or not, Jennavieve Pruitt paid our bills. She was my sole source of income. If she wanted to work at home a day or two out of the month, I wasn't going to argue. And it was just easier to leave that information out of our family dinner discussions."

"So, you'll come down and give us the fingerprints and DNA?"

Kagen looked at his house, at his wife whose life seemed to emulate the fabricated normalcy of a television commercial. Kagen smiled for her benefit and gave a little wave. "I'm sorry," he said. "But I'm going to decline that offer."

Chapter 26

Getting Ben's grand jury subpoena quashed had been a simple matter. The Court could only order Ben to testify if the State agreed to grant immunity, which Dovey wasn't about to do. The subpoena had been served as a matter of policy, but neither side believed that Ben Pruitt would actually give testimony.

With that behind him, Boady began the process of turning his home into a law office, cleaning out a bedroom on the second floor for Lila, and stocking it with the bare necessities: a desk, a couple chairs, a laptop computer, a copier/fax machine, and a drawer full of paper and pens.

Boady invited Lila over to check out the setup. "I want you to make yourself at home," he said, tossing her a key to the house. "Come and go as you like. If you need anything, just ask. You get hungry, my kitchen is your kitchen."

Lila sat at the desk and opened the laptop, examining the programs and testing the Wi-Fi connection. "This is perfect. When do you want me to get started?"

"As soon as your class schedule allows."

"All I have left is one take-home final, so . . . what do you want me to do first?"

Boady considered this and said, "I need you to find out who killed Jennavieve Pruitt."

Lila's eyes grew large and her mouth opened in anticipation of responding, but nothing came out.

Boady turned another chair around and sat backward on it, facing Lila. "Ben Pruitt is an innocent man, which means that there's a person wandering around out there who killed Jennavieve Pruitt. I suspect that the State isn't looking too hard for that person. So we will."

"If we can come up with anything important, we get it to Max and maybe have it presented to the grand jury, although that's a long shot."

"So you'll just call up Max and say, 'Hey, I got something for you'?"

Boady smiled. "We've been friends for a long time. I'm pretty sure he'll take my call."

"I thought that cops and defense attorneys hated each other."

"Sometimes things can get ugly. I once had a cop follow me home after a hearing where the cross-examination got a little heated. But that's the exception, not the rule. Max knows we all have a job to do."

"How'd you and Max become such good friends anyway?"

Boady smiled at the memory. It had been so long ago, he hardly ever thought about it anymore. He folded his arm across the back of the chair and rested his chin.

"I was a public defender back then, handling felonies in Hennepin County. I had this client, Marvin Dent, a huge man with this enormous mane of matted hair and tattoos running up his neck. Just a mean sonofabitch all around. He'd been accused of beating another man with one of those mop wringers—you know, they attach to the inside of a bucket and have a handle . . ."

"Yeah, I used one back when I worked at McDonalds."

"Right. Well I'd met with this guy once at my office, and the bottom line is that he was completely insane. I mean full-blown, untethered schizophrenic. He sat in our meeting and talked to people in the room who weren't there. I explained to him what a Rule 20 evaluation was. I told him that he was likely suffering under the throes of his schizophrenia when he clobbered his buddy."

"He hit his friend?"

"His only friend, which made it more likely that he was insane at the time. I told him my plan, and he continued to speak to the voices in his head. I should have paid more attention because he kept repeating that 'he wasn't going back' and 'I couldn't make him go back.' I thought it was just gibberish."

"Prison?"

"Security hospital. Turns out he'd spent six years there and he was trying to tell me that he wouldn't let anyone take him back there. So we get to court and I present a motion to have my client evaluated to see if he's competent to stand trial. I barely get the words out and he jumps out of his chair and tackles me to the ground. I mean he was on me in a flash. Hands around my throat. Pounding my head into the floor. I thought he was going to crush my larynx."

Lila's eyes grew big as she listened to Boady's story.

"The bailiff was a retired sheriff's deputy. No match for my client. I started to black out. But then, from out of nowhere, Max Rupert comes flying in. He was a patrol officer back then, and he'd been in court, waiting for a hearing. He ripped that three-hundred-pound behemoth off me and pinned him to the ground using pressure points. Had his arm twisted in the air. Dent was screaming and swearing, but Max had him good. I'd never seen anything like it."

"So Max kind of saved your life too?"

Boady nodded thoughtfully. "Yeah, I suppose he did. After that I demanded that he let me buy him a beer. We met to settle up and discovered that we had a lot in common, including a love of poker. We started a poker group and we've been friends ever since."

"Have you ever gone against him before? Ever cross-examine him?"

"A few times. Smaller cases, early in both of our careers. Never in a murder case."

Lila puzzled over a thought, maybe unsure how to ask the question that jabbed at her. Finally, she said, "What happens if you have to go after him, I mean really tear into him? Does that worry you?"

Boady considered the question, remembering a lecture he gave in his Legal Ethics class and said, "*Fiat justitia ruat caelum.*"

"Fiat what?"

"*Fiat justitia ruat caelum.* It means 'let justice be done, though the heavens may fall.'"

Lila looked puzzled, so Boady explained. "You ever heard the story of the Scottsboro Boys?"

"It sounds familiar, but I can't say I remember any details."

Boady turned his chair around to get more comfortable, crossing one leg over another. "In 1931, these nine black teenaged boys were pulled out of a train boxcar and arrested for raping two white women in Alabama. The charge was a complete load of crap, but the case went forward anyway, as those kinds of cases usually did back then. All nine were found guilty, but those convictions were overturned by the US Supreme Court because of the shoddy defense given the boys.

"On retrial, the case was moved to the court of a judge named James Horton. He presided over a trial where the only question in most folk's minds was whether the boys would get life in prison or the death penalty. The first defendant to have his trial before Judge Horton was a young man named Haywood Patterson. As expected, Patterson was found guilty by a jury of white men. The case was a sham and the evidence was completely unreliable, but that didn't matter.

"After Patterson was found guilty, his attorney brought a motion for an acquittal notwithstanding the verdict, basically asking the judge to overrule the jury. It's a standard motion that everyone, even the attorney, expected to be denied. But Judge Horton knew that the trial was a sham, that the evidence was cooked. And to everyone's surprise, he acquitted Patterson.

"Well, Judge Horton lost his judgeship and a great many friends because of his decision. The press had a field day with him. The decision to acquit Patterson came at a great price for Horton. Years later, when asked if he would do anything differently, he said no, and his explanation was *Fiat justitia ruat caelum*—let justice be done, though the heavens may fall. If a person is ever presented with the choice, that person must always do what is right even though it may bring on great personal loss. So in answer to your question, if justice for my client demands that I tear into Max Rupert on a cross-examination, I'll do what I have to do. I have no choice."

Chapter 27

Boady Sanden slipped a toe into the pool at the St. Paul Athletic Club a few minutes before six in the morning. He was alone. He broke the glass surface of the water and slid in, bobbing in the water a few times, listening to the soft slurp of the ripples resonating through the empty room. Then he started with a breaststroke.

As he moved through the water, he contemplated the possibility of stepping foot back into a courtroom after six years away from that life.

He thought about his last appearance before a jury, the shaking in his hands, the pressure in his chest as he rose to deliver his last opening statement. He stood in front of that jury for three agonizing minutes before he could utter his first word. More than anything else, Boady feared sending another innocent man to prison.

Boady switched from the breaststroke to freestyle. Stroke—stroke—stroke—breath. He could still see Miguel Quinto's face, the look of shock, maybe even betrayal, when the judge read the jury's verdict of guilty. He remembered his own thoughts: "win some—lose some." That's not what he told Miguel, of course. He didn't remember the exact words, but he was certain he'd done his best to exude confidence in the appeal, another lie. Boady knew he wouldn't be handling the appeal. The family had run out of money just getting through the trial. He would pass the appeal on to the State Public Defender's Office. Wash himself of this kid.

He turned to kick into another lap, and his feet didn't reach the side of the pool. He'd turned too early. Stroke—breath, stroke—breath. He was out of rhythm. *Calm your breathing*, he thought. *Get your timing back*. Stroke—stroke—stroke—breath.

Miguel's family had hired him too late—at least that's what Boady

told himself back then. Miguel had gone to the police and given a statement. That was a mistake. If only he hadn't given a statement. You can't
make a silk purse out of a sow's ear, right?

And the story he told the police ... he should have simply confessed instead of making up such a whopper. It would have saved the
family a lot of money. They wouldn't have had to sell their hardware
store to pay for Boady to defend him.

Turn. This time Boady was too close to the wall and his heels
scraped against the side of the pool. Had he not tucked enough? He
pushed off at a bad angle and had to work harder with his left-side
stroke to pull himself back to his line.

Of course, the police weren't going to believe Miguel's lame story.
He said that he went to his dealer to buy some pot, just a little to get him
through finals week. He gets to the guy's apartment and finds the door
ajar. He eases the door open and sees Kevin Deavor, his dealer, lying dead
on the floor, blood still draining from a hole in the man's head. Does
Miguel leave? Does he call the cops to report the homicide? No.

Miguel ransacks the place. He needed a little college money and,
hey, if he finds some free pot along the way, all the better. He spreads
his fingerprints and skin cells all over Deavor's apartment. He leaves his
shoeprints in blood swirling around the kitchen linoleum. And when
he finds $5,800 in cash tucked under the dead man's mattress, he keeps
it neatly stacked in the same plastic baggie where Deavor put it, ready
and waiting for when the cops would later search Miguel's apartment.

The police would match the fingerprints in Deavor's apartment to
Miguel Quinto. They would find Deavor's baggie of money in Miguel's
backpack. They would find Deavor's fingerprints on the baggie. They
would find Deavor's blood on Miguel's shoes. They would find everything except the .22 caliber gun that sent the bullet into Deavor's brain.

And then Miguel Quinto's heartbroken parents would take a loan
against their hardware business in West St. Paul to pay for the great
Boady Sanden to represent their son.

The day that Miguel's verdict came down, Boady had a dinner
to attend. He was being given an honor by the Warren E. Burger Inn

of Court for his service and skills as a trial attorney. He remembered thinking that it would be nice to get an acquittal for Miguel Quinto that day in advance of the dinner. It would have been a perfect processional for his evening. He also remembered that he was concerned that the jury might keep him in court, waiting for their verdict, and cause him to be late to his dinner.

How many laps had it been? Twelve? Fourteen? Boady struggled to pull in oxygen, feeling as though he'd swum twenty laps, but he knew he hadn't been in the water that long.

In the end, the jury came back in a timely fashion, so as not to ruin Boady's dinner. They found Miguel guilty of killing Kevin Deavor. Boady would not be going to the event as the triumphant hero he'd hoped, but this was a dog of a case. He'd kept the jury out for a day and a half. That had to be something of a victory, although Miguel Quinto might not see it. He whispered encouragement into Miguel's ear—lies about the good appeal they had—intending to buoy the young man, give him something to hope for as he grew acclimated to his new life in prison.

Boady went to his dinner. He received his honor with grace and just a touch of practiced humility. He looked out at that sea of judges and accomplished attorneys applauding him and smiled, proud of how far he'd come since his days with the public defender. He went home to Diana that night and slept soundly in his bed, not giving a second thought to Miguel Quinto.

Those second thoughts wouldn't start for another three months.

The call came from the public defender handling Miguel's appeal. When Boady heard who was waiting for him on the phone, his first thought went to the potential issues for appeal. It's common for appellate attorneys to consult with trial attorneys to get their take on where issues may be hiding. He started flipping back in his mind to any problems he remembered from Miguel's case. It had been a pretty clean case and nothing came immediately to mind. When he picked up the phone, the woman on the other end informed him that Miguel Quinto had been found dead in his cell. His throat had been cut. She thought Boady should know.

Boady's hand smashed into the pool deck, sending a shudder of pain up his right arm. Boady curled his head to the left as his shoulder slammed into the side of the pool. He'd missed his turn—completely lost track of where he was in the water.

He let his body float to the surface, pain shooting up from his wrist. He inspected his shoulder and saw a slight abrasion. The air seemed thin and he gulped in deep breaths, holding the side of the pool like a scared child. He looked around and saw that he was no longer alone. A woman with a swimming cap peeled lazily in the farthest lane away. Another woman, older, probably in her late seventies, was getting ready to enter the lane next to him. Boady rolled over onto his back. He filled his lungs with air to make his body buoyant and kicked his legs, his arms floating limp at his sides. He took short, quick breaths, keeping his chest mostly inflated.

The news of Miguel's death saddened Boady the way the death of a distant relative might. He had no real connection to the boy. He was the kid's attorney, not part of the family. Would they expect their plumber or their mailman to break down and cry at a customer's death? No, and why should Boady? He was hired to do a job, and he did it.

But now those second thoughts began to leak into his consciousness. Had he done all that he could have? He didn't focus his energies on that case—not like he did when he handled his first murder case. But he didn't need to be that focused anymore. He had experience.

Boady attended Miguel's funeral, drawn there by those second thoughts. When Miguel's mother thanked Boady for doing all he could for her son, Boady gave her his best look of empathy, but in his mind he thought, *This is what happens when you kill your drug dealer*.

Two months later, Boady got a call from Max Rupert. He thought Boady should know, before it hit the news. A recent drug raid turned up a .22 caliber revolver. Ballistics matched the gun to the bullet that killed Kevin Deavor. Phone-tower data placed a man named Robert Wallace at Deavor's apartment just minutes before Deavor was murdered. Armed with this new evidence, they brought Wallace in for questioning. After a short interrogation, Wallace confessed to killing Kevin Deavor.

Miguel's lame story about finding Deavor dead and then ransacking the apartment had been the truth. Miguel Quinto had been innocent.

Chapter 28

Max walked into his bedroom and slipped off his tie, placing it on a rack in his closet. He hated wearing ties and only did so when the occasion demanded it, like weddings, funerals, and giving testimony at grand-jury proceedings. The grand jury had very few questions for him this time—his third time up, and he had very little additional information for them, as it had only been two weeks since his first appearance before them.

By now, they knew about Kagen's belief that the Pruitts' marriage was on the rocks. They knew about the prenuptial agreement that would screw Ben Pruitt if Jennavieve were to ever divorce him. They knew that Ben had the motive to kill his wife, although technically motive isn't an element of a crime that needed to be proven at trial.

The grand jury heard Malena Gwin's testimony about Ben Pruitt showing up in a red sedan around the time of Jennavieve Pruitt's death. None of the jurors thought to ask about the tollbooth surveillance tapes, which still hadn't arrived.

After that third trip to the grand jury, Dovey told Max that he would be asking the jury to deliberate with what they had.

"We don't have the tollbooth footage yet," Max said. "We don't have computer forensics yet."

"Max, are you having doubts? Is that what I'm hearing?" Dovey's tone, both snarky and smug, reminded Max of a grade-schooler on the verge of taking his ball and leaving. "If you think someone other than Ben Pruitt did this, then by all means, enlighten me."

"Ben Pruitt killed his wife," Max said. "But if we move too fast—"

"Are you telling me how to do my job, Detective?"

"No, but this guy has to pay. It's not enough to just get the indictment; we need a conviction. Pruitt's smart. Don't underestimate him."

"I've done this long enough to know that the goal is a conviction. Trust me, Max. I'll get the indictment and then I'll get the conviction. Ben Pruitt will pay."

Max rubbed his eyes and shook his head. "It's your show, Frank."

After that, Max had gone home to switch out of his good suit and slip into a pair of jeans and a less formal jacket. It was not yet noon and he still had a lot of work on his desk back at City Hall. He threw a hot dog into a pan of water and fired up the stove. No sense going back to the office before he ate a bite for lunch.

While the water heated up, he went to his porch and grabbed his mail. Flipping through it as he returned to the kitchen, he tossed the bills into one pile on the countertop and the junk mail into another. When he'd finished, he still held a large, white envelope. His name and address had been printed on it with a laser printer. No return address. He looked at the postmark and saw that it came from a post office in Minneapolis. In the center of the envelope, a lump protruded against the paper. Max felt the lump, about the size of bullet, and next to it, something round and flat like a silver dollar, only not as heavy.

He tore open the envelope and slid the contents onto the counter. It wasn't a bullet. Rather, it was a key, short and round, the kind used on bicycle locks or a storage unit. It was attached to a key ring, and on the key ring, a rubber circle, blue, with the number 49 written on it. Max examined the key for a moment and set it aside.

Also in the envelope was a letter. He pulled the letter out and opened it. The letter held three short sentences in simple type, but the words of those three sentences burned him as though the paper itself had somehow caught fire. He dropped the letter and stepped back. His heart pounded in his chest. His hands and fingers trembled.

The letter lay open on the counter where he'd dropped it. Something inside of him refused to believe what he'd seen. He went to pick it up again but stopped. It might have DNA or fingerprints on it. He stood over the letter and read it again.

Your wife's death wasn't an accident. She was murdered. Here's the proof.

Chapter 29

Boady was staring at a blank yellow sheet of paper on his legal pad when the doorbell rang. He'd been looking at that page since just after supper, waiting for an idea to come to him, some brilliant thought that would allow him to derail the grand-jury process. He welcomed the doorbell, the distraction from his clogged brain. It didn't matter that it was almost nine o'clock, a time of night that Diana always said was too late for visitors.

Boady opened the door to find Ben and Emma Pruitt on his porch. Ben had his eyes fixed on Summit Avenue, looking one way, then the other. "Can we come in?" he said before Boady could offer.

"Of course," Boady said and stepped aside.

Ben walked into the front room and put Emma on the couch. "Can you stay here for just a bit, sweetie? I need to talk to Mr. Sanden for a minute."

Emma nodded without saying a word.

Ben nodded toward Boady's office and the two went there, and Ben closed the door.

"What's going on, Ben?"

"I'm not sure, but I think something's happened."

Boady took his seat behind the desk, and Ben opposite him. "We went to the house tonight. We hadn't been there since Jennavieve died. We've been staying up at the cabin. But Emma needed clothes and I needed some stuff. The crime-scene tape wasn't up. We could have been living there if we wanted, but, I just couldn't."

Boady saw the shake in Ben's hands and said, "Would you like something to drink?"

"No, thank you," Ben said. "I thought that since we were in the neighborhood it might be nice for Emma to spend some time with her friend, Catie Kolander. She's a neighbor. So I parked in the driveway, as usual. We loaded our things and got the car packed. Then we walked down to the Kolander house. I spent the evening with Catie's mom, Terry, and her husband, Bob, while Emma and Catie played."

Ben looked over his shoulder, through the glass of the French doors to where Emma sat on the couch. "I've been so worried about her. I thought it would be nice for her to have just one evening of normalcy. Just a few hours with a friend, like before."

"Did something happen to Emma?"

"No, I'm sorry. We had a perfectly nice evening. The Kolanders have always been very nice to me and to Emma. But when we left, we were walking back to our house. I saw a police squad car in front of the house. I crossed the street to get a better view and saw a second squad car in the driveway. Two officers were at the front door. Two others were standing back a ways, in the driveway. They had their guns drawn."

"What?"

"I'm sure of it, the two in the driveway had their guns out of the holster and the two at the door had hands on their grips. Then a third squad pulls up and parks in the street."

"What'd you do?"

"I casually took Emma around the corner and watched from a distance. Pretty soon, I heard some yelling and then they broke through the front door and went in."

"What were they yelling?"

"I couldn't hear the words, but it looked to me like they were executing an arrest warrant. They must have spotted the car and figured we were there."

Boady stood and turned to look out the window behind his desk. He saw no suspicious activity, no squad cars, no unmarked cars.

"How did you get here?"

"I took Emma down to the soccer field nearby and called a taxi."

"You never heard them actually say 'arrest warrant,' did you?"

"No."

"So as far as I'm concerned, you and Emma are my guests. You will be spending the night here."

"Let's assume that those cops were there to execute an arrest warrant—"

"Then the grand jury has come back with a true bill, and you've been indicted for murder. That's the most logical assumption."

Ben began to shake. His breath puffed in short spurts. "How . . . I don't understand. I wasn't even in Minneapolis. They know that. What's going on?"

"They must know something we don't."

"What the hell could they possibly know? I didn't kill my wife. They can't know anything because there's not anything to know. It didn't happen. It couldn't happen, I was in fucking Chicago." Ben's voice rose and Boady could see Diana on the other side of the French doors; she was sitting with Emma but looking at the office.

"Calm down, Ben. Emma needs you to keep it together. I need you to keep it together. We don't know that you've been indicted. We'll walk you down there tomorrow. If we're wrong, then all this worrying is for nothing."

"And if we're not wrong? If they indicted me for murder?"

Boady sat back down. "Well, that's what we've been preparing for." He tried to offer a reassuring smile. "You know the old saying, a grand jury will indict a ham sandwich. If that is the case and you've been indicted, we walk you down to the police station on our terms. And we're not going in until Monday. No sense spending the weekend in jail before we get to see a judge. We'll check it out first thing Monday. No photographers. No press. We walk in with our heads high. They still have to prove the case beyond a reasonable doubt. That's the battle we've been preparing for."

"They'll hold me over for a bail hearing."

"We'll get you in and out as fast as possible."

"And what if the judge denies bail?"

Boady stopped talking and just looked at Ben for a few seconds, long enough for Ben to realize that he already knew the answer. If he can't make bail, he'll sit in a jail cell and watch the clock tick away until he goes to trial.

"You know the worst-case scenario, Ben. We need to go make a bedroom for Emma. You'll stay with her through the weekend. We don't know whether there is a warrant. Until we do, you and Emma are guests here. We can spend the weekend getting her comfortable. You can explain what you need to explain to her. On Monday morning, we'll take you downtown and see where things stand."

Ben sat back in his chair and started to laugh under his breath, a laugh that grew the more he tried to control it.

"I can't believe this," he said. "It's like some farce—I mean, this is Monty Python kind of stuff. It'd be funny if it weren't for the fact that it's going to kill my daughter. She lost her mother, and she's devastated. How do I explain to her that I'm going to jail because they think I killed her mother? What do I tell her? What do I say?"

Boady pondered that question for a long time, unable to come up with a good answer. Finally, he said, "You tell her that you love her. You tell her that you'll be back with her as soon as you possibly can. You tell her to have faith." Boady looked Ben in the eye, his words offered for Emma, but meant for Ben. "You tell her that you will win this case. You will make it back to your little girl. I promise you, you'll be back here, together. Tell her to believe that."

Boady offered his hand to Ben, and as Ben shook it, the tremor in Ben's fingers seemed to fade away. Then, Ben smiled first genuine smile he'd been able to manage in some time.

Boady smiled back. "Now let's go see what we can do to turn our guest room into a room worthy of your little girl."

Chapter 30

There is a fog that can infect a person's brain, a thick, feverish sludge that engulfs sound and thought with an effect similar to being submerged in a tub of water. Max had experienced that fog after his wife died. He visited it once again the week his brother died, that time finding the fog in the bottom of a bottle of scotch. And in the hours after getting the anonymous letter, the fog returned. Max's world shrank—from murder investigations and grand juries down to a letter, and a key with the number 49 attached to it.

Max didn't return to work that day. He stared at the items on his kitchen counter for an eternity, which barely spanned the lunch hour. That's when Max the cop stepped in to relieve Max the stunned husband.

This will reopen Jenni's case, the cop said to himself. *I need to turn this in.*

But the husband piped up. *They've had this case before and it went nowhere. They don't care about Jenni. She's just another name on a page to them.*

I can't investigate Jenni's death. There's a policy. I've been ordered to leave it alone. My involvement could create problems of proof.

But it could be a prank, the husband said. *This could be nothing more than a wild goose chase.*

Maybe, the cop said. *It could be some dick I arrested in the past, come back to fuck with me. Yeah, that's possible. I should keep this private until I know it's legit, at least.*

Max shut off his phone and put the new evidence in a paper grocery bag. He could ask Bug to take a look at it. Test it for DNA and other trace evidence. Bug would do it for him, and Bug would keep it quiet.

Before he went to bed that night, Max checked his phone. He'd missed four calls from Niki. The first three were Niki asking Max where he was and why he hadn't come back to the office after testifying at the grand jury. The last message was different.

"The grand jury came back," Niki said. "They indicted Ben Pruitt. We have squads out looking for him now. Dovey's calling him a flight risk, so everything's under seal until we have him in custody. Also, the County Attorney and Dovey will be holding a press conference once we have Pruitt in custody. Dovey wants us to be there. Window dressing. Call me. Or not. Hope you're okay."

He wants us at the press conference, Max said to himself. *A show of unity. Let the public see the team that's going to put Ben Pruitt away— and put Dovey on the bench.*

Fuck 'em, the husband said.

Yeah, fuck 'em.

Max didn't sleep well that night. He tried, but terrible dreams pummeled him with every attempt. Finally he gave up, sat on his front porch, and watched the sky grow blue until the time came to drive in to the office.

"Good to see you're still alive." Niki said. "You forget how to dial a phone?"

Max plopped into his chair and took the first sip of his third cup of coffee that day. His eyes burned with fatigue, and every blink added weight to his lids. "Sorry, had a tough afternoon. Personal stuff."

"You look like hell."

Max fired up his computer, rubbing the rust from his eyes as he waited. "Didn't sleep well. I'll be okay."

"Come on, Max. What's going on?"

Max let her plea hang in the air for a few seconds before pulling out his phone. He pulled a photo of the letter, its words clear and readable. He handed the phone to Niki and typed a search for "storage units Minneapolis" into his computer. When he turned back to Niki, she was still staring at the letter on his phone.

"My God," she whispered.

"Like I said, it was a rough night." Max then showed Niki a picture of the key. "That was in the envelope with the letter."

"What's it a key to?"

"I think it's a storage unit." Max turned his monitor toward Niki. The screen showed a map of the Twin Cities and the surrounding suburbs covered with hundreds of red dots. "I think whatever evidence this letter's referring to is in one of these units. But I don't know. Hell, for all I know it could be a storage unit in New Jersey, or not even a storage unit at all. That's just my best guess."

"Where's the key now?"

"At the crime lab. Bug Thomas swabbed the key and the envelope for DNA or prints. Nothing. He wanted to keep it another day to see if he could come up with anything."

"And the letter?"

Max didn't answer.

"You didn't show him the letter, did you?"

"Not yet."

"Because if you show him the letter, he'll know what you're doing."

"I just need a little time."

"Max, what the hell?"

"This is where you say, 'I have your back, partner.'"

"Don't you—" Another detective walked past their cubicle and Niki bit her lip. When he'd gone, Niki said, "Come with me." She stood and walked past Max, who made no move to leave his seat. "Max!"

He looked at her, and she wore a serious expression that he rarely saw on her. He stood and followed. She led him out of the Homicide Unit and down the long hallway to the front door of City Hall. She pushed through the door without saying a word. Max followed her across the light rail tracks to the courtyard of the Hennepin County Government Center, a red-stone plaza with a pool and fountain centerpiece.

At the edge of the courtyard she stopped and turned to Max. "This is not your investigation, Max. I know it's your wife, but you can't be involved. You know that."

"I know it's not my investigation. It *was* Louis Parnell's investigation. He didn't find a goddamn thing. He closed the file as a hit-and-run. He's retired now, so it's nobody's investigation."

"But you can't be the one looking into your wife's death. It's not just forbidden by policy, but it's a bad idea."

"So, do what? Give this over to someone else to sit on, the way Parnell did? Do you really think any other detective will do what needs to be done? I'm reopening her case. I stayed out of it last time, and nothing got done. That won't happen again. I'll go to every single storage unit in the state if I have to. I'll find the lock that goes with that key. No other detective would do that."

"I would," Niki said.

"You're my partner. They'll no more give that file to you than they would give it to me."

"I'm your partner, yes, but I'm also a friend. I know what it means to you to find out what happened to Jenni. But that doesn't mean that I'm going to sit by and watch you mess up your career. I have your back—that'll never change. But know that I don't approve."

"I won't put you in the middle."

"I'm already there, but you're missing my point. I'm not worried about how this might rub off on me. I know that if anyone finds out what you're doing, you'll protect me. But I'm trying to protect you. You might be putting yourself out on the plank for a hoax."

"And what if it's not a hoax?"

Niki said nothing at first. Then a sad smile pulled at her lips. She reached out her hand, gently holding onto Max's arm, as though she needed the physical connection before she could speak. And when she spoke, her words came out soft and kind—the words of a friend, not a partner. "I know there are things more important than this job. In the grand scheme, I know you don't have a choice. I just needed to say what I said. And I need you to know that I will always have your back. No matter what. We good?"

Max smiled and nodded. "We're good."

Chapter 31

On Monday morning, bright and early, Boady parked in the ramp on the corner of Fourth Avenue and Fifth Street, in the very heart of the world of law enforcement. Across Fourth Avenue stood the Government Center, littered with courtrooms and prosecutors. Across Fifth Street was the jail, the building where he and Ben Pruitt were headed to see if a warrant had been issued, and if so, to surrender Ben's freedom. And kitty-corner from the ramp was City Hall and the various investigative units including Homicide. He and Ben had to walk less than a block through the densest concentration of cops in the city without being identified. The last thing Boady wanted was a show-of-force takedown just shy of the finish line.

When they stepped out of the parking ramp, they were met by the clang of a train signal stopping them from crossing Fifth Street. The Green Line light rail was approaching from the east. Boady looked over his shoulder and saw two uniformed officers coming up behind them, about a block away. They were talking to each other and paying little mind to anyone else.

The train, three cars long, had slowed for its stop in front of City Hall. The uniformed cops were within thirty feet now.

"Don't look behind you," Boady whispered.

"What?" Ben started to turn but stopped himself.

"Two uniforms headed this way. Don't let 'em see you—just in case there is a warrant out there."

Ben nodded and stiffened a bit in his stance.

The patrolmen came to the corner where Ben and Boady stood, but instead of waiting for the train to pass, they turned west and crossed the street to the Government Center. Boady let out the breath he'd been holding. After the train passed, Boady and Ben crossed the street and strolled into the lobby of the Hennepin County Sheriff's Office, Central Records. They approached a deputy standing beside a metal detector.

"My name is Boady Sanden, Attorney at Law." Boady didn't have a business card to hand to the man. "I'm here to inquire whether there is an arrest warrant out for my client, Benjamin Lee Pruitt." Boady indicated to Ben. "And if so, we're here to surrender him."

The man looked at Boady, then at Ben. "Let me check on that." He turned to a computer and typed on the keyboard. "Yep, that appears to be the case," the deputy said. He picked up a phone and made a call.

Ben closed his eyes and Boady could hear his friend's breathing go shallow.

"Are you ready for this?" Boady whispered.

Ben began to breathe faster. "I thought I was. Christ. You take care of Emma. Don't let her see me on TV."

"We'll take care of her. Remember, don't grin when they take the mug shot. Try to look calm, but not thug calm. Think of Emma. We'll get you through this. Think of that. You want to look confident that your innocence will prevail. That's the picture you want."

Ben smiled at Boady. "I'll do the best I can."

"A friend of mine works for the Associated Press. He'll tip me off on when the County Attorney's press conference will be. I'll be there. I'll try and get in a few shots on your behalf."

A second deputy with thick arms and no smile came through a door and approached Ben. "Are you Benjamin Lee Pruitt?" the man asked.

"I am," Ben said.

"I have a warrant for your arrest on the charge of murder. Please place your hands behind your back." Ben did as he was commanded. The deputy ratcheted a cuff around one wrist, then the other. The deputy pat-searched Ben for weapons. He and Boady both knew the drill and came prepared. Ben had nothing in his pockets except his driver's license and $200.00 in cash.

The three deputies led Ben through the door toward the intake room where the next step of his incarceration would take place. He would be strip-searched and given an orange jumpsuit to wear. Orange socks and plastic orange sandals, too. He would be photographed and fingerprinted and locked in a cell.

Ben did not look back as they led him away.

Chapter 32

Also bright and early Monday morning, about the time that deputies were fitting Ben Pruitt with a pair of handcuffs, a mail courier dropped off a couple packages for Max and Niki. The first was the computer forensics for the laptops and cell phones belonging to both Ben and Jennavieve Pruitt. In the second package Max found twenty-eight CD-ROMs from the Illinois Department of Transportation—the tollbooth surveillance footage. Max held both packages out to Niki. "Which one do you want?"

"Tough choice. One will bore me to tears reading computer files and web histories, the other I'll be watching cars crawl through tollbooths until I'll want to put a bullet in my brain. Which do you want?"

"I'll flip you for it." Max reached into his pocket and pulled out a nickel. He tossed it into the air and slapped it to his wrist. "If it's heads, you do the tollbooth CDs, and if it's tails you do the computer forensic file."

Niki nodded and Max lifted his hand to reveal Monticello. Tails. He handed Niki the pack of computer records.

"Excellent," Niki said. "I've been fighting a bout of insomnia lately anyway."

"Who said homicide investigations aren't exciting?" Max said, dropping his packet on the desk. "I have a little errand to take care of. I'll be back in a few."

Niki looked at him, probably trying to figure out what he was up to. Max turned and walked away before she could read anything more from his face.

Max had never looked at his wife's investigation file, yet he knew most of the case. Louis Parnell had a reputation for not being able to keep secrets, so Max would take Parnell out for a beer every now and again to get updates.

Jenni Rupert had been walking in a parking garage in the middle of a Tuesday afternoon. It was the ramp where she normally parked her car, a ramp used primarily by Hennepin County Medical Center, where Jenni worked as a social worker. There were no cameras in the ramp, at least back then. No one heard anything. No one saw anything.

Her body was found on the third level, the bones in her neck disjoined by a car tire. The casing from a headlight found near her body had Jenni's blood on it, along with a serial number that told them it was a 2008 Toyota Corolla. The hit had been hard enough that yellow paint had transferred onto Jenni's clothing. They knew the make and color of the car that killed her, but despite the nationwide search for a yellow Corolla with front-end damage, the car had never been found.

After a while, Max stopped talking to Parnell. He couldn't stand to hear that nothing new had come up. And when Louis Parnell retired, Max tucked his hopes away. He wasn't allowed to touch the file, and Parnell's replacement didn't have Jenni's case on his list. The powers that be had decided that the time had come for Jenni Rupert's file to be tucked away in the archive room.

When Max stopped walking, he looked up to find himself at the door to the archive room.

He glanced down the hall in both directions before entering. Even though he often found the need to visit the archive room as part of an investigation, this time he felt like a thief. He walked in and nodded to a man with gray hair and a thick mustache, who Max knew as Felix.

"Morning, Detective."

"Morning, Felix. I need to see a cold file."

"Sure thing. You got a number?"

Max read off the ICR number for his wife's file. He'd memorized it back when Parnell had the case.

Felix came out with the file in a red rope folder about three inches thick, thicker than he'd expected.

"You going to read it here?"

"No. I'll be taking it with me." Max smiled as he talked. He looked at Felix's eyes, searching for any recognition. He waited for Felix to stop him from taking a file that he was forbidden to have.

Felix said nothing.

Max signed for the file. Then he tucked it under his arm and said good-bye to Felix.

Chapter 33

Boady drove home from the jail using back streets that would take him past parks and cemeteries and tree-lined boulevards. He rolled his window down and breathed in the scent of recently mowed lawns and oak leaves. The smell cooled the blood that pulsed in his temples. Emma would be awake by now, rising from a bed that would be hers until her father returned. That might happen in a matter of hours, or it could be months—or, if Boady didn't have it in his bones to be the lawyer he used to be, it could be never. Boady fought to keep that thought at bay.

He stopped off at a grocery store along the way to buy food and supplies for Emma. He and Diana had never had children. It was just one of those things. Now Boady walked through the store, looking at items on the shelf and wondering what, if any of it, a ten-year-old girl might want. He spent more time in the cereal aisle than ever before, trying to remember the cereals he coveted as a child, cereals that were too expensive to make it into his mother's cupboard. He bought sweet-scented shampoo and juice boxes and prepacked meals that came in brightly colored boxes. In truth, he had no idea what he was doing.

He pulled into his driveway, parked close to his kitchen door, and grabbed a handful of grocery bags to take inside. When he went outside for his second load of groceries, he saw a man walking up his drive. He'd never seen the man before, tall, handsome, with a jersey-beauhunk slickness about him.

"Are you Boady Sanden?" the man asked.

"I am."

"I understand you represent Ben Pruitt."

Boady turned to better face the man.

"What can I do for you?" Boady asked.

"I need to speak to Ben Pruitt's attorney. It's important. It's about Emma."

"I'm Ben Pruitt's attorney."

The man reached into his jacket and pulled out a manila envelope. "Read this," he said. "It'll explain everything."

Boady opened the envelope and pulled out a stack of papers—two sets of legal documents stapled at the corners.

"You've been served," the man said.

Boady looked at the papers, at the man, and back at the papers. The first document was an injunctive order. At first, Boady didn't understand what he was reading. But as he read further, he understood.

As executor of Jennavieve's estate, her sister, Anna, had been granted an injunction, freezing all of Ben Pruitt's bank accounts. The injunction relied upon the slayer statute, a law that prevents one spouse from benefitting financially if they murder the other.

Anna had convinced a judge that Ben would be depleting the estate if he were allowed to use joint assets to pay for his defense. The order referenced a prenuptial agreement. Ben Pruitt would have no claim to any asset paid for out of Jennavieve's trust money. The judge ordered that all of their joint accounts be frozen.

When Boady looked up, he saw a well-dressed woman standing on the sidewalk at the end of his driveway. Anna Adler-King wore a suit the color of platinum, a jacket and pants cut from some soft, shiny material that rippled as she walked—an outfit that straddled a line between office-power and evening-chic. She had long, dark hair that she wore up off of her neck, and her makeup gave her face crisp lines.

"We have reason to believe that Emma Pruitt is now living here with you," the man said. "If you could go get her . . ."

"Excuse me?" Boady said.

"Read the second order," the man said. "It's all there."

Boady pulled out the second set of stapled papers. As he read, his mouth went dry. Anna Adler-King had gotten custody of Emma Pruitt, pending the outcome of Ben's trial. Something primal and raw began to crystallize along the strands of Boady's DNA as he read the custody document.

He heard the click of high heels on the concrete of his driveway. He glanced up to see Anna Adler-King making her way up to where he and the process server stood. Boady went back to reading. He looked for a date of filing. That morning. He checked the other document as well. Same thing.

"How did you know about the indictment?" Boady asked. He failed at his attempt to conceal his rage.

"Is Emma here?" Anna asked.

"Who's asking?" Boady already knew, but he wanted to be certain before he took his next step.

"I'm her aunt, Anna. We've met before. Don't you remember?"

Boady did remember. He'd seen her at Emma's baptism and at a couple of her birthday parties, early on.

"The grand jury was a secret hearing. The indictment is still under seal. How did you get these orders?"

Anna's reply was calm and well-rehearsed. "The indictment was unsealed when Ben turned himself in this morning."

"That was barely over an hour ago. You drafted both of these and got before a judge in an hour?"

"I have very good attorneys, Mr. Sanden. It's obvious that Ben killed my sister. They merely planned ahead. And when the indictment came down, Judge Hildebrandt—he's an old friend of the family—just happened to have an open slot on his calendar this morning. Now I'd like to see Emma."

The Adler name opened doors that would remain shut for most people. They likely had "friends" inside the County Attorney's Office, people who might let it slip that a grand jury focusing on Ben Pruitt had been convened. They held fundraisers for judges who wouldn't bend the law for a donor, but might hold a fast hearing for one.

Boady folded the papers into thirds and slid it into his back pocket. He was no longer angry. This was the game. They'd come out with their first-string offense, and now he needed to hit back.

"You'll need to get off of my property now."

"Excuse me?" Anna's tone rose like a cartoon sound effect.

"You heard me. Get off of my property."

"We're not leaving here without Emma," the man said. "I know she's here. I've been watching—"

For a man in his fifties, Boady Sanden was fit. He'd grown up working construction to help support his widowed mother. But more than that, Boady knew the law. He had legal custody of Emma. The custody order he had in his back pocket carried no more weight than the paper on which it was written.

Boady stepped into the face of the process server, a man in his mid-thirties, a big chest but small hands, the kind of hands that hoisted dumbbells as a means of compensating for other deficiencies. "You have exactly five seconds to get off my property."

The man squared up to Boady. "We're not leaving without—"

"One!"

The man looked at Anna then back at Boady. "You don't—"

"Two!" Boady kept his face expressionless but punched the numbers at an even pace.

"We have a court—"

"Three!" Boady knotted his fists. He had big hands that looked like hammers when they were all rolled up. He was going to take a beating if he got to five. He had little doubt about that. But this was his property. Emma was his charge. Those were things worth taking a beating for.

"Anna?" The man glanced over Boady's shoulder to where his boss stood.

"Four!"

"Come on, Roger," Anna said. "We can take care of this in court."

Anna Adler-King walked away from Boady and Roger without looking at either man. Roger paused for a second then followed her down the driveway.

Boady didn't move until they drove away. When he turned, he saw Diana standing in the doorway, her face creased with worry.

Chapter 34

That night, before driving home, Max stopped by the crime lab to talk to Bug Thomas, who told Max that he hadn't found anything more on the key. Other than residue of rubbing alcohol, evidence that the key and tag had been carefully cleaned before being placed into the envelope. The envelope had been sealed with water, not saliva, so no DNA.

At home, Max opened his briefcase, which held his wife's file, the key, the letter, and a stack of CDs from the Illinois tollbooths. He put the first CD into his laptop and waited for the self-executing file to open. As he waited, he looked at the key and tag, examining them for the hundredth time, hoping that something might jump out at him. Nothing did.

When the surveillance footage cued up, he started watching cars shuffle through the first of seven gates of Toll Plaza Nineteen, just outside of Chicago. The thought of all the footage he would need to watch already made his eyelids heavy.

Max settled in. Car after car went by, and when the occasional red sedan pulled up, Max would study it. Was there only the single driver? Yes? A man? Yes? If the car matched those criteria, Max would enlarge the screen to better see the driver and write down the license plate number. After half an hour, he'd only written down one plate number, and he was fairly certain it wasn't Ben Pruitt in the driver's seat.

This would be his homework every night until he burned through all twenty-eight discs or until he spotted Ben Pruitt and the red sedan.

He held the key and tag in his hand as he watched the surveillance footage. *There is a storage unit within five minutes of my home*, he told himself. Was it possible that his key might fit door number 49 there?

Extraordinarily unlikely. But it might. The odds were no greater or lesser that the key would fit that unit as any other in the state. Only five minutes away. He could make a quick trip there, just to satisfy his curiosity.

Max blinked and looked back at the screen. He'd been staring at cars filing through the gate, but he hadn't been looking. He stopped the footage and rolled it back to the last point he remembered paying attention. He gave his cheeks a light slap and started watching again.

They weren't paying him for this. He'd put in his eight-hour day. The bags under his eyes squeezed and pulled, begging him to get some sleep. But he knew that sleep would not come. Not unless he did something to ease his mind. One small token. A first step in an investigation he'd been wanting to do for four years.

He shut his computer down and put the key in his pocket. He would drive to the nearest storage facility and try the key there. If it didn't fit, he would come back home and hope to get some sleep. He could do at least one location every night, maybe a handful if they were clumped together. He knew this might be a wild goose chase, but if nothing else, it might clear his conscience enough each night to let him sleep.

Chapter 35

The twenty-four hours between Ben's surrender and the first court appearance moved with the speed of a crashing bicycle, a mere flash in real time, but each individual second seemed to linger forever. Boady went to the jail an hour before the bail hearing, his head full of bullet points that needed to be checked off.

Ben entered the visitor's room wearing orange scrubs, a half a smile, and hair that looked weed-whipped.

"How you holding up?" Boady asked.

"It sucks. I need a shower in the worst way. And the noise—my God. People have to yell for no damn reason. But it wasn't quite as bad as I was expecting."

"Did you see the news conference?"

"Yeah." Ben smiled. "You still got it, Boady."

Boady smiled back.

The press conference had begun with Daniel Maddox, the Hennepin County Attorney, proudly announcing the arrest of prominent criminal-attorney Ben Pruitt for the murder of his wife, Jennavieve Pruitt. After an initial statement, he'd opened the floor for questions. One reporter asked if Ben Pruitt would be representing himself, as he was a criminal-defense attorney of some renown, or if he would have his own attorney. Maddox answered that he'd been told that Pruitt had an attorney but didn't know the attorney's name.

"I'm his attorney and my name is Boady Sanden!" Boady hollered. The reporters turned to Boady, who had taken a position off to the side in the back of the room. Boady kept his eyes on Maddox.

"If you don't mind, Mr. Sanden, I'd like to finish the press conference," Maddox said, trying to get things back on track.

"*Professor* Sanden, if you don't mind," Boady said. He figured that at least some of the reporters would research his name and discover that he ran the law school's Innocence Project, an office that focused on finding those who had been wrongfully convicted and bringing their cases out of the shadows. It was the perfect background for this case—a champion of the wrongfully convicted coming out of retirement to prevent an injustice—and he hoped to tie the word *innocence* to Ben Pruitt as often as possible. "You go right ahead, Mr. Maddox. I didn't come here to interfere. Just wanted to keep the record straight is all."

Boady had a slight southern accent that he could unpack whenever it suited his purpose, a hint of country charm left over from his days growing up in Missouri. He nodded back to Maddox, who continued with his press conference. But Boady knew that when Maddox finished, the reporters would be looking to him for a quote, a snippet they could give the viewers, to suggest balance in their reporting.

And when the reporters came, Boady had a snippet ready. "The State is racing to a conclusion that simply isn't true. It's political expedience in the guise of justice, but it's not justice . . . it can never be justice when it snares an innocent man." That would be enough for the television stations—a quick sound bite to put the potential jury pool on notice that Ben Pruitt was innocent. Boady stayed at the Government Center answering more questions, but he knew which quote would be on the evening news. And he was right.

Ben sat in a plastic chair in the attorney meeting room, a visiting room where sound recordings were prohibited. Boady handed Ben the bail study, a report put together by Probation with a recommendation for Ben's bail amount. It was the first piece of bad news that Boady had to deliver that day. Ben went to the page with the recommendation, and his face froze.

"Ten million dollars?" He read it again. "Are they fucking crazy? Who do they think I am, a mob boss? Jesus Christ!"

"Calm down, Ben. You know this is only a recommendation."

"Yeah, but you know it's easier for a judge to rubber-stamp the bail study than to do any independent thinking. Who's doing first appearances?"

"Judge Moncliff. What do you know about her?"

Ben nodded thoughtfully. "Not a bad judge. Big on rules and procedure. Imagine an old-fashioned schoolmarm. She'll hold a prosecutor's feet to the fire just as often as a defense attorney."

"Any proclivities when it comes to bail?"

"She's more fair than most. If we can get bail down to between one and five million, I should be okay."

"Not necessarily," Boady said. He reached into his case and pulled out the injunctive order freezing Ben's assets and slid it in front of Ben. Boady watched the confusion in Ben's eyes meld into concern, then fear.

"They can't do this." Ben whispered as though to himself. "I have to get out of here. I have to be with Emma. Why would they do this?" Ben continued to read.

"There's a prenuptial agreement attached to the order," Boady said. "Is that legit?"

Ben turned to the eight-page attachment and flipped through it. "Yeah, but . . ."

"Are your assets all traceable back to Jennavieve's trust money?"

"Not all. I had a job too." Ben's voice rose to a level that could have been heard outside of their room. Boady held his hands up to shush Ben.

"Why didn't you tell me about the prenup?"

"I didn't think about it." Ben shrugged and rolled his eyes. "I had no idea they would try to freeze my assets. I mean what kind of a person would . . . Anna did this?" Ben shook his head in disbelief. "How can anyone be so cold-hearted? I just can't believe she'd do something like this."

"I'm not talking about freezing your assets, Ben. Don't you see? This prenup gives the State their motive."

"What?"

"This document, as I read it, says that if Jennavieve died during the marriage, you inherit everything that is jointly owned by you two. But if she divorces you, she takes everything with her that can be traced back to her trust money. I'm assuming that's a lot?"

Ben looked at Boady, his brow bent in thought, his eyes bouncing away now and then as though collecting another asset and adding it to the pile of what he would have lost in a divorce. "Good Lord," Ben whispered. "That's why I'm here? Because of that damned prenup? I have—or had—a successful law practice. I don't need her money. I don't want her money. Besides, if I kill her, I don't get a dime. The slayer statutes would stop me from inheriting a thing. Didn't they think of that?"

"They probably figured you didn't think you'd get caught."

"I can't get caught if I didn't do anything!" Ben's voice again filled the room to overflowing. His face flushed red and his eyes took on a sheen.

"I know that, Ben. I'm on your side, remember?"

Ben lowered his head into his arms on the table and took in some deep breaths. "I know that, Boady. I know you're just playing devil's advocate. It's what I'd do if I were in your chair. It's just hard to believe this is happening. This isn't supposed to be my life. I had a family and a career and everything a man could want, and now, I'm in jail getting shoulder-checked by big men with tattoos on their neck who feel a need to make some point. How'd this happen? I don't understand."

"Are you worried about your safety? We can ask for segregation."

"No. It's okay. I've got it under control. I've convinced a couple of the bigger apes that I can help them strategize their cases. They have public defenders, so now they think they have the ear of a real lawyer."

Boady smiled to himself, remembering the years he toiled as a public defender, hearing those same criticisms. "I'm going to offer to surrender your passport," Boady said.

"Absolutely. I'm not going anywhere. I just want to be out so I can take care of Emma. Not that I think you and Diana won't do a great job. But she needs her father."

"On that score . . ." Boady took a third set of papers out and slid them across the table.

Ben read the custody order and gripped the plastic table with his free hand. "No. This is crazy. We can't—"

"Calm down."

"If she thinks she's getting Emma—"

"Ben!" Boady pulled Ben's attention away from the papers. "I'm appearing on a motion to dismiss on the custody action at three o'clock. I've already filed the custody consent decree we signed. That'll be in the judge's file by the time we have the hearing. You're the sole parent here. Anna Adler-King has no dog in this fight. She can squawk all she wants to, but she has no authority. Her only possible argument is that Diana and I are not fit to take custody—and that's never going to fly. So we'll win that one."

Ben nodded. His hand grew slack and he released the table edge. "What about the order freezing assets? I need access to my accounts if I'm going to make bail."

"I'm not challenging that just yet. We'll use the Court's order freezing your assets to argue that you don't have access to funds, maybe keep bail down to a manageable amount. After the bail hearing I'll bring a motion to vacate that order as well."

"Is that one winnable?"

Boady frowned.

"We have a chance, though, don't we?"

Boady, again, thought back to his days as a public defender, sitting with clients who came to the fight with no weapons, no defense, and were facing a mountain of evidence. No matter how bleak things looked, they wanted to hear words of hope. Boady remembered how he would tell his clients that there was always hope. It wasn't a lie, even if that hope was a spider's thread holding up a guillotine blade. "Yes, we have a chance," Boady said. "I'll do everything I can."

Ben looked at Boady with a raw fear that Boady had seen in so many of his clients in the past, a fear he hadn't expected to see in Ben. Ben dropped his head into his hands and breathed the shallow breaths of a man on the brink of psychological collapse. "I'm not making bail am I? I'm not getting out?"

Boady reached out his hand and rested it on his friend's shoulder. "We need to take this one step at a time, Ben. Let's get through the first appearance before we throw in the towel on making bail. I'm going to head over to court now and organize my thoughts. They'll bring you through the back way. I want you to walk with your head held high. We're going to fight this, Ben. We're going to fight it and we're going to beat it—one way or another. You hear me?"

Ben looked up, and Boady could see the tears that Ben strained to hold back.

Boady squeezed Ben's shoulder again. "We're going to win this, Ben."

"Okay." Ben tried to sound confident, but the tremor in his voice betrayed him. "I trust you," he said.

Chapter 36

Boady had been in the courtroom many times since he ended his private practice. He ran the Innocence Project for the State of Minnesota. That role required him to appear before judges on motions to vacate convictions or grant new trials. Boady brought the miracle of DNA to old cases, prying open what had once been considered sealed, forcing the State to re-examine evidence—usually eyewitness testimony—that had falsely convicted his clients. A great many guests within the various correctional facilities in Minnesota sought to roll those dice. And on that rare occasion when the DNA could conclusively exonerate a person, Boady would get things rolling and then hand the case off to the public defender or private attorney if a retrial were ordered.

But in the years since the Miguel Quinto case came crashing in on him, he'd never stood with a client in court. His clients were all incarcerated. He hadn't sat at counsel table with a living, breathing client in years, and the last time he did, the guilt he felt over the death of Miguel Quinto nearly paralyzed him.

That malingering thought kept Boady company as he waited for Ben Pruitt to be brought up from his holding cell.

First appearances normally occurred in clusters, with deputies hauling five or six inmates at a time to court. Because of the media attention given to the Pruitt case, they set his first appearance as an individual hearing. Boady had read and reread the bail study, looking for mistakes, finding none. In the end, their recommendation for a ten-million-dollar bail came from nothing more than an educated guess. They would want a number that Ben would have a difficult time putting together, a number that would discourage him from running off.

Boady sat at the table to wait. Eight people sat in the gallery
behind him. He recognized most of the faces as being reporters from
the press conference the day before. He glanced at his watch and saw
that he had ten minutes to wait until the hearing time. As he looked
at his watch, he noticed a slight shake in his fingers. He hadn't eaten
lunch; his stomach wasn't up for it. Now he began to suspect that that
was a mistake. He drew little circles on his legal pad to give his nervous
fingers something to do.

The door opened in the back of the courtroom and a man with
flabby jowls and a black briefcase entered. With him walked Anna
Adler-King and the process-server guy whom Boady had chased off his
driveway the day before. Anna glanced at Boady but took no further
notice of him.

The man with the jowls approached the prosecutor's table, and
Boady assumed the man was Frank Dovey, the prosecutor who ran the
grand jury. He'd never met Dovey before, or if he had met him, Boady
didn't remember the experience.

"Are you Sanden?" Dovey asked.

"I am." Boady knew damned well that Dovey would have watched
the news coverage from the night before and would have seen Boady's
face. So the whole "are you Sanden" bit was nothing more than middle-
school posturing—the beginning of the dance. Boady could feel a
slight chill at the edge of his hairline where perspiration had begun to
form. "And you are?"

"Frank Dovey, Assistant Hennepin County Attorney." Dovey
opened a briefcase and pulled out a stack of papers three inches thick,
with a big manila envelope clipped to it. He handed the packet to
Boady, and Boady flipped through it to see police reports, transcripts of
witness statements, and reports from the computer forensic examination of Ben's computers. In the envelope was a large stack of CD-ROMs.
He didn't look any further. He slid the discovery into his own briefcase.

"Is this it?" Boady asked in his best ho-hum tone. He thought he
heard a slight quiver in his own voice.

"So far," Dovey said. "If more comes in, you'll get it."

Had Dovey walked in and introduced himself to Boady in a civil manner, Boady would have returned the gesture in kind. Winning had everything to do with knowing the case better than your opponent and nothing to do with feather ruffling. If Boady had his way, Dovey would form the opinion that Boady was incompetent and ill-prepared. Boady considered whether he should be working so hard to mask his nervousness. After all, a show of weakness never failed to produce over-confidence in the other side. For now, Boady decided to simply mirror Dovey's manner.

The clank of a heavy key in a steel door drew Boady's attention to his left. The door opened and Ben Pruitt entered with his jail escort. Ben wore handcuffs on his wrists with a chain that laced through a metal loop on a leather belt around his waist. He had shackles on his ankles, and he shuffled the fifteen feet to his chair.

Ben sat down and Boady leaned over to whisper in his ear. "Anna Adler-King's in the gallery. Don't look. I don't want her to think it matters, and I don't want the press to pick up on her presence. I suspect they'll have a press conference after this anyway."

Ben nodded and kept his eyes forward.

The ratcheting sound of an automatic lock from behind the judge's bench drew everyone's attention, and a woman walked in and called for all to rise. Behind her, a short, bespectacled woman with cropped black hair and a black robe entered and took a seat behind the bench. Without looking up she announced: "Please be seated." She took a moment to get situated, opened her file, and pulled out the bail study. "Call the first case," she said.

Her clerk read from a sheet of paper. "File 27-CR-16-19887, State of Minnesota versus Benjamin Lee Pruitt."

"Counsel, please state your appearances for the record," Judge Moncliff said.

"Frank Dovey for the State."

Boady stood. He cleared his throat to speak, but the words weren't there. The air in his lungs didn't move. He looked down at his legal pad, at the scribbles he'd been drawing. He thought of Diana, standing beside him, holding his hand. He cleared his throat again. "Your Honor," he said, "I'm Boady Sanden for Mr. Pruitt, and Mr. Pruitt is present in Court." With those words, his voice returned.

Judge Moncliff moved through the first appearance, reading Ben Pruitt his rights and informing him of the charges against him, an exercise required by the rules even though Ben was an experienced attorney. When the judge was satisfied that a proper record had been made, she asked Boady how he wanted to proceed.

Boady stood up. "Your Honor, we would ask that Mr. Pruitt be arraigned at this time and have his omnibus hearing set within seven days." With that, Boady laid out the first tactic of his trial strategy—speed.

"Very well. How does your client plead, Mr. Sanden?"

"Your Honor, Mr. Pruitt pleads not guilty to the indictment."

"A not guilty plea will be entered." The judge said, "Would the State wish to be heard on the issue of pretrial release?"

"The State would." Dovey stood. "Your Honor, I've received a bail study from Probation that, I believe, is woefully inadequate."

"Here it comes," Ben whispered into Boady's ear.

"Your Honor, the defendant is charged with the cold-blooded and intentional murder of his wife, a murder that was, at the very least, intricate and methodical in its planning. On top of that, Mr. Pruitt is a man of significant means. He has access to millions of dollars to pay bail. He has his primary residence here in Minnesota but also has at least three other homes that we are aware of at this time, including a residence in France and one in Aruba. There may be more that we haven't uncovered. It would be a simple matter for Mr. Pruitt to jump on a private jet and leave the country. If Mr. Pruitt is able to make it out of the country, we'll likely never see him in this courtroom again."

Dovey picked up the bail study and held it in the air. Small red blotches began to form on his neck as he amped up his tone. "Your Honor, you have to understand, if the net worth in this report is anywhere close to the truth, Mr. Pruitt will have an overwhelming incentive—once he sees the strength of the evidence against him—to just take off and live out his life somewhere where the United States cannot reach him. The State is asking that Mr. Pruitt be held without bail."

Dovey sat down, tossed the bail study into his file like he was disgusted by it, and leaned back in his chair.

Judge Moncliff's face remained expressionless. "Mr. Sanden?"

"May I approach?"

"You may."

Boady pulled out the ex parte order freezing Ben's assets, handing a copy to Dovey as he passed on his way to the bench. After giving a copy of the order to the judge, he returned to counsel table. "Mr. Dovey presented this honorable Court with speculation on Mr. Pruitt's net worth but failed to tell the Court that all of those assets have been frozen by court order. Either the State knew about this order and intentionally kept it from Your Honor, or in their zeal and rush to judgment, they made a decision before they had all the facts."

"Mr. Pruitt doesn't have the net worth set out in the bail study. If this Court set bail at one million, it would have the same effect as if bail were denied. Mr. Pruitt understands that he'll be forfeiting his passport. He has no intention of leaving the state. He wants to be with his daughter in this time of grief. He wants to prove his innocence in her eyes, in the eyes of this Court, and in the eyes of the public at large."

Boady put his hand on Ben's shoulder for the final plea. "I implore you, Your Honor; do not set bail in excess of one million dollars. He will likely not be able to make that bail with his assets frozen. But at least give him a chance. Let him return to his daughter. Let him be with her while he exonerates himself."

"Mr. Sanden, I appreciate your comments, but I feel that I would be remiss if I didn't set bail in a substantial amount, given the nature of this case."

From the corner of his eye, Boady saw Ben's head sink to the table.

"I am compelled to set bail in the amount of ten million dollars." Judge Moncliff said. "Should he make bail, he will be required to surrender his passport, remain law-abiding, not leave the state, and appear at all future hearings." The judge folded her papers together and placed them in the file.

Dovey turned, made eye contact with Anna Adler-King, and gave her a smile.

Boady sat down beside Ben, who held his face in his hand. He put his hand on Ben's back. He could feel the trot of his friend's breath shake against his chest; he could hear the sound of sobs muffling through the man's fingers. He knew, as did Ben, that there would be no release from custody until the jury rendered its verdict.

Chapter 37

A yawning half-moon slogged its way through furrows of clouds as Max pulled up to the next storage unit. The natural light, trickling over his shoulder, gave him just enough visibility to find the keyhole of door number 49—his fourth unit 49 of that night. He touched key to the lock and jimmied it, hoping once again to feel the key slide in. It did not.

He went back to his car, and in the dimness of its interior light scratched a line through yet another storage-unit address. In the two and a half weeks since receiving the mysterious note and key in the mail, he'd visited fifty-three different storage units. Working in a grid, he would eventually eliminate every unit in the state. Tonight brought him to St. Louis Park, where, according to the Internet, he had eight sites to visit. He rubbed the sleep out of his eyes and then typed the next address into his navigation.

He thought about going home and sleeping. He had a meeting with Dovey in the morning that was not going to go well. Max had reviewed every second of footage, looking for a red sedan. Max finished the last crumb of footage that night and found no Ben Pruitt. In the morning he would have to tell Dovey that he had no evidence of Ben Pruitt driving back from Chicago.

He would withhold from his report how he often found his mind wandering away from the tollbooth footage—especially in the beginning. How many times had he found his thoughts walking though the parking garage where she died, while his eyes still stared blankly at the tollbooth footage on the computer screen? He would back the footage up and try to find the last place where he'd been paying attention. He believed that he'd covered all the footage.

If he were asked under oath, he'd have to say that he wasn't entirely sure.

But he needed to prowl the storage units of Minnesota; he needed to purge his mind of that distraction—at least that's what he told himself. In truth, he knew that his hunt for unit 49 had no more tie to the Pruitt case than did the brand of bread he used to make his nightly ham sandwich. Yet, like an addict justifying his fix, Max left his home every night to once again try and find the home for that key.

As he pulled into his fifth location for the night, he glanced at the clock. 11:30. Three more units in St. Louis Park after this one, but he decided he would do only one more. After that, he would go home and sleep.

Pruitt would be appearing at the omnibus hearing in the afternoon, and Dovey was flipping out over the circumstantial nature of his case. In the two weeks since they arrested Pruitt, they'd found nothing to bolster their case. They'd hoped to find a web search showing that Pruitt mapped out a route from Chicago to Minneapolis, or maybe e-mail communications to support the theory that he bought a junker car in Chicago. But the computer forensics came back with nothing. Pruitt's phone showed no activity outside of the cell-phone towers that fed the Marriott in downtown Chicago. Their entire case rested on motive, opportunity, and Malena Gwin's testimony that she saw Pruitt outside his home on the night of the murder. Dovey expected more. Hell, Max expected more. But more never showed up.

As Max stepped out of his car at yet another storage unit, he tried to formulate a theory as to how Pruitt made it home without being seen by a tollbooth camera. As if to pile onto his sleep-deprived brain, he pondered a quote that circled in his head. Something about serving two masters. Was that from the Bible? Or did Abe Lincoln say that?

The moon had slipped behind the clouds, and he needed a small flashlight to see the keyhole for this latest unit 49.

Pruitt had to have planned an alternate route around the tolls. But that would have eaten up too much time.

He held the light in his mouth as he worked the key around, trying to make it fit.

No. It wasn't Lincoln. Lincoln's quote was about a house divided. The key clicked into the hole.

Max jumped back, startled, his flashlight falling to the ground. He stared at the key, now fitted into its home like Cinderella's foot into the slipper. His chest began to heave.

He reached down and picked up the flashlight.

He had no warrant. But someone sent him the key. That had to be consent. What was proper procedure here? Muddled thoughts of search and seizure and constitutional law began to pour into his already-saturated brain. He quieted the whole mess with a mental shout of *I don't fucking care*. He reached out and grasped the key in his fingers, turned it, and slid the locking bolt out of the door.

The latch didn't move at first, and Max stepped back and gave it a kick to loosen it up. This time, when he pulled it back, the latch popped open with a clack that seemed to echo through the darkness. He bent down, grabbed the handle, and rolled the door up.

He shined his flashlight into the black storage unit, and the beam of illumination bounced off the dusty, yellow paint of a Toyota Corolla.

Chapter 38

Boady Sanden had met with Ben Pruitt every day in the two weeks since the arrest. Some days were good and some were not.

The day that Boady told Ben about the custody hearing was a good day. Boady trounced Anna Adler-King and her two attorneys. The custody consent decree they had drafted was rock solid. Another good day came when Boady brought a full set of the discovery to Ben, all the police reports and witness transcripts. This included the grand-jury testimony of his neighbor Malena Gwin. Boady watched the confusion build in Ben's face as he read her testimony for the first time.

"What the hell is she talking about?" Ben muttered as he went back and reread the passage about the red sedan. "This is crazy."

"She gave this same statement the first time they talked to her—the day they found Jennavieve."

"It makes no sense, Boady. I swear I was in Chicago. It wasn't me she saw."

"But this explains why they locked onto you right away."

"I've never owned a red car in my life."

"We'll need harder evidence than that. We'll need to discredit Ms. Gwin."

The room went silent as both men concentrated. Then Ben perked up. "The light! There's a streetlight there on the corner, just like Malena Gwin says, but the day I left for Chicago, the bulb was burned out. Been out since . . . let's see . . . Jennavieve called the city to ask that they fix it . . . that had to be at least two months ago. They said they'd get to it when they could. I'm positive that light was still out when I left for Chicago. If it was out on the night Jennavieve was murdered, the city will have records."

"And if it was out when Jennavieve was murdered, then Malena Gwin has to be lying, or at the very least mistaken."

Ben beamed. "She claims to have been able to recognize me because I parked under that streetlight. If there's no streetlight, her whole story is blown."

"Which brings us to the next question: Why would she make up such a detailed story?"

Again Ben went silent with concentration. Then he shook his head. "I honestly have no idea. I don't really know her all that well. I mean, we say hi and wave as we pass on the street, but beyond that . . ."

"Maybe she saw someone else and thought it was you. Maybe she assumed it was you because whoever it was walked up to your house. Then she pieces the rest of the story together from a false memory, including the lit streetlight."

"And without her, they have nothing."

Boady left the jail that day in high spirits. But that would not always be the case. On the morning of Ben's omnibus hearing, Boady came to his visit with a piece of paper that had the potential to crush his friend.

When they brought Ben to the room reserved for lawyer visits, Ben entered with one of his eyes nearly swollen shut and thick bruises on his neck.

"Oh my God," Boady said. "What the hell . . . ?"

"It's not as bad as it looks," Ben said. He tried to smile, but only one side of his mouth could move.

"It looks like hell. What happened?"

"Remember when I told you I was making nice with some of the guys by giving legal advice?"

"Yeah."

"Well, the guy I was trying to help out apparently killed the brother of another swell fellow in here. That brother took umbrage."

"We need to get you segregated."

"No, I think it's over. They made their point. If they wanted to make more of a point, they would have. What I need is to get the hell out of here. Have you heard back on the injunction?"

Boady couldn't look his friend in the eye as he pulled the court order out of his briefcase and slid it across the table.

"I'm afraid you'll have to read it to me. My vision hasn't quite returned."

Boady turned red and pulled the papers back. "The Court denied our motion to quash the injunction." Boady paused to let the news find roots before he continued. "You have no access to the estate. You won't be making bail."

Boady could see the panic rising in Ben's chest, his ribs pulsing with abbreviated breaths. "I can't do this. I'm going to die in here. They have me in the middle of some fucking turf war. I have to get out."

"We can get you moved across the street to the old jail. It's not as nice as the Hilton here . . ." Boady immediately regretted the joke. Ben looked at Boady through his swollen face, a tear slipping out of his good eye. "I'm sorry, Ben. I could appeal the order, but—"

"We need to get this on the calendar for a speedy trial. The sooner, the better. Hell, if the Court has time next week, I want this on the docket."

"I'm with you on that," Boady said. "We can win this." As he spoke those words, Boady could feel his chest tighten. He had spoken those same words to Miguel Quinto in that exact same jail meeting room. He hadn't been good enough to keep an innocent man out of prison the last time he tried. Boady wondered whether Ben could hear the undertone of insecurity in his voice, the one he tried so desperately to hide.

Boady could feel his body aging, exponentially, every time he thought about the consequences of failure. He held Ben's life and Emma's happiness in his hands, and he would lose his breath on those occasions when he stopped to take in all that was at stake. Instead, Boady focused on the next task at hand. That seemed to quiet the self-doubt that threatened to drown him.

"I checked with the Court," Boady said. "If we demand a speedy trial today, we can be on the calendar by the first week in October."

At first Ben's shoulders slumped, but he took a deep breath and sat up nodding. "A month. That'll work," he said. "I can make it to

October." Ben put the back of his hand up to his good eye and wiped away the tear that had crawled down his cheek. "You know that Emma's birthday is in a few weeks. I was clinging to the hope that I might be out of here for her birthday. I've never missed one before."

"Diana and I were talking about Emma just yesterday. We think you should let us bring her here for a visit—"

"No!" Ben's answer came back fast and sharp. "Promise me you'll never let her see me like this." He pointed to his orange jump suit and at the bruise that took up half of his face. "I said my good-bye to her. That's how she'll remember me. I don't want her to see me again until I walk out of here, an innocent man. I dream about that moment. I live for that moment. It's what keeps me going. Promise me. No visits."

"I promise," Boady said.

Chapter 39

Max had spent the night carefully searching the interior of the Corolla, cataloging what little he'd found and gently putting everything back so that a crime-scene technician could repeat the process later.

Before he went to his morning meeting with Dovey, he showered, shaved, and spent an hour at a copy store making a duplicate of Jenni's investigatory file, every page—even the photos. He instructed the clerk to put the photos in a separate folder and tape it shut. He didn't want them accidentally spilling out. He had never looked at those pictures, and he would never look at them, unless he had no other option—and maybe not even then.

After his meeting with Dovey, Max would return the file to the archive room at City Hall. The time had come to turn the investigation over to someone else, someone who could coordinate DNA tests and fingerprinting, someone who was not the husband of the decedent.

As he and Niki waited in the conference room for Dovey, the exhaustion in Max's eyes pulled with both hands. He tried to shift his thoughts from his wife's murder to the Pruitt case, but his mind had become numb with fatigue.

Dovey entered with his usual confident stride. He sat down hard in the faux-leather chair and clapped his hands together in a crack that popped Max's heavy eyes open.

"Let's see what you got," he said in a booming voice. "Impress me."

Max and Niki looked at each other, and then at Dovey. Max went first.

"I've watched more than forty hours of cars going through toll plazas and . . . well, there's no red sedan carrying Ben Pruitt."

Patches of red began to work their way up Dovey's neck. He forcefully grasped his right fist in his left, cracking all of his knuckles, then did the same with his other hand. Then he took a deep breath and continued. "So we can't show that Ben Pruitt drove back from Chicago the night his wife was murdered?"

"There are other routes," Max said. "He must have skirted the cameras."

"I thought you said he'd have to take the Interstate to make it back here on time. Didn't you say that? Or have I been hearing things?"

"He would have had to break speed limits if he took the back roads. That's risky when you're on your way to murder your wife. But it's theoretically possible."

"So I'm left with 'theoretically possible' for my case? Do you have any idea how far theoretically possible is from 'proof beyond a reasonable doubt'?"

"I can't change the tapes. You asked what I found and I'm telling you. Besides, you have Malena Gwin. She saw him here, so all you need is 'theoretically possible.' Her testimony makes it a fact. He made it back here from Chicago to kill his wife. Whether he drove the Interstate or a back road doesn't matter. He was here."

Dovey brought his hand to his chin and rubbed. "What can Boady Sanden get on her? Anything I need to be worried about?"

Niki, who'd been sitting motionless next to Max, spoke up. "I've looked into her and there's not much to know. She's a widow. Doesn't work. Has some money left from her husband's insurance policy that she lives off of. I've asked around the neighborhood, and other than being a bit nosey—which works in our favor—she's absolutely normal. No criminal history. No ax to grind with Ben Pruitt. They're going to have a tough time knocking down her credibility."

"What about the computer forensics?" Dovey asked. "Find anything there?"

Niki shrugged her shoulders. "Nothing that moves the ball forward. I was hoping to find evidence that Mrs. Pruitt was talking to an attorney about divorce. I looked at her search history, and there's nothing there. No venomous e-mails to her husband, or from him. I haven't seen a thing about their relationship."

"Great. Brilliant," Dovey said. "We've had Pruitt in custody for two weeks, and we're no closer now than we were then. What happened? You're supposed to be the A-Team."

"Watch it, Dovey." Max leaned onto the table.

"You told me Pruitt did it."

"He did."

"Then, damn it, get me my proof!"

Max stood, angry enough to spit nails. A dozen insults whirled in his sleep-addled brain. But before he could open his mouth to speak, a memory blew in cold and swift like winter through an opened door.

It was his brother, Alexander, over-the-top pissed off at their wrestling coach. He'd won a wrestle-off and should have been on the A squad, but the coach put Alexander on the B squad. Said Alexander threw a punch to win his match. Max had to hold his brother back. Went so far as to carry him out of the gym.

It had always been Max's job to settle his brother down. Be the level head while Alexander got to spin like a pinwheel. "Max the Boy Scout." That's what Alexander always called him. And Jenni called him her rock. But Jenni was gone now. Alexander was gone now too. And Max could feel the ghost of that Boy Scout fading away to nothingness.

Max remained standing, let a slow breath leave his body, and walked out.

Chapter 40

When Emma Pruitt awoke on the morning of her eleventh birthday, she didn't smile. Diana made her a breakfast of pancakes and bacon, one of the few meals that Emma would actually eat. The pancakes had the words "Happy B-day" spelled out with chocolate chips. When Emma saw this, she started to cry and ran to her room.

Emma had been a guest in their house for over a month, and the number of words she spoke in that time barely surpassed the number of days she'd been there. She cried often and would sleep until noon if Diana allowed it—which she did not.

One day they brought in a psychologist under the guise of her being a family friend. The three of them attempted to engage Emma in conversation. The psychologist asked Emma about her friends and about school. Emma's responses were monosyllabic and gave no release to the pain that churned in her veins. After three attempts over the course of a week, the psychologist gave up.

"There's no sense paying me to come out here anymore. She won't talk to me. I think she suspects our ruse."

"I'm worried about her," Diana said. "She only talks when it's absolutely necessary. She's been acting up in school, refusing to obey the teachers. They tell me she doesn't talk to her friends or anyone else for that matter. I just don't know what to do."

"Going to school may not be the best thing for her right now," the psychologist offered. "The children in her neighborhood are at the heart of what she wants to avoid. Those children have parents who knew Mrs. Pruitt. They've been talking. The kids will know that Emma's father is on trial for her mother's death. Putting her into that environment may be the last thing she needs."

"So what are you suggesting?" Boady asked. "Ship her to a new school? Someplace where she has no friends? She can't even talk to us. How's she going to survive a new school?"

"I'm not suggesting that, either. I'm saying that you should look into maybe homeschooling her. Just for a semester. See how it goes. She has no one in her life she trusts—no one she feels safe enough with to open up. Until she feels safe, until she can talk to an adult, no therapist will be able to reach her. She needs time and love. You can't force her to get through what she needs to get through."

That morning, after Emma left her birthday breakfast untouched on the table, she holed up in her room with the door shut. Boady and Diana discussed whether to intrude on her privacy. In the end, they did nothing, mostly because Diana had two house showings to go to that morning, and Boady had no inclination to attempt such a maneuver on his own.

After Diana left, Boady went to his study to work on Anna Adler-King's cross-examination. Lila had been digging up old bones on the socialite, and one in particular showed promise. If Boady could coax the woman into the right trap, the jury would have to start second-guessing the State's case. But setting that trap would be difficult and time-consuming. He covered his desk with everything he knew about Anna Adler-King: her statement to the police, her testimony at the custody hearing, her affidavit supporting the injunction to freeze Ben's assets. He had newspaper articles about her and corporate filings and court records from every case that bore any imprint of her presence. Lila had been thorough in her research.

But as Boady moved the various parts around on his desk, his thoughts continued to wander up the stairs to the silence coming from Emma's bedroom. Anna Adler-King's life lay scattered across his desk like the pieces of a model airplane waiting to be assembled, yet the thought of Emma's tears stopped him from moving. He put his legal pad down and went upstairs.

As he climbed the steps, the echoes of unfulfilled hopes swirled around his mind. His childless marriage was not his choice, nor was it Diana's. From their earliest days, when they knew they would be together for life, they'd laced their conversations with plans of having a big family—filling every room of whatever house they might own with the laughter and noise of children. As the years passed, the medical truth grew roots that tangled around them, choking them in a way they would never have imagined.

Now, as Boady approached Emma's room, that memory held him back. In his dreams of being a father, he had imagined making this kind of trip. He was about to sit with a frightened, crying child and attempt to take away her pain. He'd never felt more ill prepared for any task in his life. But that was what a father would do, so it was what he would try to do for Emma.

Boady knocked on the door using a single knuckle. There was no answer. He knocked again and this time unlatched the door, letting it creak open.

"Emma?"

She didn't answer, but he saw her sitting on her bed. She had put on one of her father's T-shirts over her other clothing, and she had pulled her knees up to her chest, tucking her legs under the shirt. She rested her face on her forearms, perched atop her knees.

"Emma, can I come in?" He entered without her answering.

She made no move to acknowledge that she even heard him.

"Emma . . ." He sat at the foot of the bed. "There's no way for me to understand how you feel. Sometimes the world hits us with more than we think we can bear. And to have this all hanging over you on your birthday, I can't—"

"Did my dad kill my mom?" Emma did not look up when she asked the question.

"Emma, honey, no." Boady's words came out quick and sure. "Your father didn't kill your mother."

"The people on the news said they arrested Dad because he killed my mom. Why would they say that? If he didn't kill her, why'd they put him in jail?"

Boady moved a few inches closer to Emma as he shook off his first thoughts, explanations that delved into the history of jurisprudence and the role of probable cause and proof beyond a reasonable doubt. These were ideas that passed over the heads of many law students and were notions completely unworthy of this child's question.

"Emma, when I was a child, kids used to tell stories about the boogey man or monsters or other things that made us afraid. I grew up in the woods of Missouri, and when I was about seven or eight, a friend told me that there was this Bigfoot kind of creature that lived in the hills around my area. They called him 'Momo.' That was supposed to be short for 'Missouri Monster.' Well, after hearing about that, I was afraid to step foot in the woods."

Emma lifted her head from her arms and Boady could see the confusion on her face as she tried to fathom how this story had any connection to her father's plight.

"One night, my mother saw me staring out into the woods with this scared look on my face. When I told her that I was afraid of Momo, she sat me down and explained that there was no such beast, that my friend was just passing on a tall tale that had been whispered back and forth between kids since before Missouri was a state. I can't tell you how relieved I was when I heard that. I almost started laughing, I was so relieved.

"Well, Emma, when you grow up, it's not boogey men and monsters that make people afraid. It's things like what happened to your mother. There's no good explanation for what happened to her. It makes people afraid. And the way that people lose that fear is to lock someone up for the crime. It doesn't matter if the person that they locked up didn't actually commit the crime, as long as they believe he did. They feel safer that someone was locked up. And that's what happened here. They wanted to lock someone up as fast as possible, and your father was the only one in their sights. They moved way too quickly, and now we get to have a trial in court to show that they got it all wrong."

Emma looked at her knees as she considered Boady's story. Then she slid her knees out of her father's T-shirt and crawled to Boady. She sat beside him and leaned her head against his torso. Boady put his arm around the child's shoulders and hugged her to him.

"You'll win, right?" she asked in a voice so soft and pure that Boady felt his throat grow tight.

Again, Boady's instinct, his training to always think like a lawyer, told him to never guarantee an outcome. That notion had become so sacrosanct over the years that they made it an ethical violation to make such promises. But as Boady held fast to Emma's shoulders, he wasn't a lawyer. He was, at that moment, the closest thing she had to a friend. He considered her question and, with the steady timbre of a man telling the absolute truth, he answered: "Yes. I'll win."

Chapter 41

The first week of October rolled through Minnesota with the rumble of thunderstorms that filled the evening news with pictures of upturned tree roots and downed power lines. On a morning when the rain fell nearly sideways, Max sat at his cubicle and studied a list he'd been researching for the past week.

Whoever sent that envelope with the letter and key knew things. Deduction, induction, and a tad bit of supposition led Max to his list.

Deduction: The person who authored the letter knew that the Corolla in the storage unit ended Jenni's life. Deduction: The author of the letter knew details about what happened in that parking ramp. Induction: The words on the note were true; Max's wife was murdered. Supposition: The murderer had a motive. Supposition: The motive involved Max and his job as a cop. That conclusion seemed to Max inescapable.

So Max pulled together a list of every person he'd convicted since becoming a detective, over one hundred and fifty if he only counted cases where he was the lead. Hidden within that list had to be the driver of the yellow Toyota Corolla. Like one domino knocking down the next, it was the only logical path to explain the note.

Max expected to be shut out of the investigation once he turned everything over, but it amazed him how quickly the door closed. He'd told Lieutenant Briggs and Commander Walker about the events that led him to the storage unit and what he found there. They blinked and nodded and barely raised an eyebrow. When they took the evidence from Max, it felt as though they were peeling the flesh from his bones. Then they politely pointed him back to his cubicle. After that, nothing.

The case was assigned to Tony Voss, the newest member of the Homicide Unit, and a man Max didn't know all that well. That same day, Max invited his new colleague out for a beer. A week later, Max bought Voss another beer as they discussed the lack of trace evidence on the letter and key, a fact that Max already knew. At their next meeting, Voss confirmed that it was Jenni's blood that stained the front of the Corolla. Except for those few meetings, Max had no contact with the investigation—at least not the official investigation.

That morning he typed yet another name from his list into the computer, Artie Mesdorf, a junkie who beat his girlfriend to death when they were living in a homeless shelter. The computer answered Max with an article about Mesdorf dying of natural causes at Lino Lakes Prison a year earlier. Mesdorf was not a likely candidate, but Max decided to look at every name. They were his only leads. He thought about Mesdorf. The man was already in prison before Jenni died. He had no clout and no friends. Thus, it was unlikely that he had the ability to reach out from behind prison walls and commit any crime, much less a murder. Max crossed Artie from his list.

As he started typing another name into the computer, a knock on the side of Max's cubicle pulled him from his task. Max looked up to see Lieutenant Briggs, a squat man with jittery, gecko eyes, standing over him.

"Commander Walker wants to see you," Briggs said.

Max glanced over his shoulder at Niki, who shrugged. They both started to stand up, and Briggs said, "Just Max."

Niki eased back into her seat, and Max followed Briggs to Walker's office, where Walker sat in a chair behind a large metal desk. Max sat opposite him, and Briggs slid into a corner, off Walker's left shoulder, and remained standing.

"What've you been working on this morning?" Walker asked. The question came across the desk in a casual tone, but Walker's face and crossed arms signaled a heaviness that gave Max pause.

"Just going over some reports," Max answered. A true answer but maybe not completely honest.

"Do these reports have anything to do with the Pruitt trial that starts on Monday?"

Max saw where the conversation would be heading. "No. It's something else."

"Do these reports have anything to do with your wife's death?"

Max didn't answer.

"Dammit, Max. What the hell do you think you're doing?"

Walker paused, but again Max said nothing.

Walker continued. "I thought I made it clear that you can have no involvement with that investigation. We have rules, and those rules are there for a reason."

"Someone sent me that key," Max said. "What was I supposed to do? Ignore it?"

"You were supposed to turn it over to me and let us take care of it."

"I did turn it over to—"

"Not for three weeks." Walker let those words hang in the air for a moment. "Yes, Max, you held onto a key piece of evidence for three weeks. For God's sake, we know how to read a postmark."

"Are you telling me that if I turned that key in right away, you would have authorized a detective to drive around to every storage locker in the state and find the lock it fit? You know damn well that wouldn't have happened. It would have gone into a file and gathered dust."

"You compromised the investigation, Max." Walker leaned onto his desk and pressed his index finger into the faux wood-grain surface to make his point. The conversation had officially gone to boil. "The chain of custody for the murder weapon in your wife's case goes through you—the husband. You know damned well that the husband is the first suspect we look at in a spousal homicide."

"Are you . . . ?" Max almost stood up but held himself back. "You'd better be careful what you say next, Walker. There are things I'd gladly lose my job over, and you're stepping mighty close to that line."

"For fuck's sake, Max. I'm not accusing you of killing Jenni. But I'm not a high-priced defense attorney. It's an easy case to make that the man who would normally be the number-one suspect in his wife's murder had a hand in steering the path of the investigation."

"If I had anything to do with Jenni's death, I sure as hell wouldn't bring the murder weapon to you, would I? No defense attorney's going to care that I drove around the Twin Cities trying to match a key to a lock."

"You checked the case file out of the archives." Walker picked up a piece of paper from the corner of his desk and slid it in front of Max. Max didn't need to study it. He recognized it as the log from the archive room. He recognized his signature. Walker sat back in his seat. "You want to tell my why the hell you would take the investigation file into your custody? Don't you see how this'll look if we ever charge someone?"

"It was a cold case. Nothing was happening on it. Nothing's happened on her case since Parnell retired. Someone had to—"

"Not you." Walker smoothed his words with a touch of understanding. "We would have reopened the case. Voss is a damned good investigator. He would have found the car."

Max shook his head unconsciously as he tried to picture Voss going out every night, looking for that storage locker. He tried to picture Walker authorizing such an expense. Every man in that room knew the truth and Max didn't bother calling Walker out on the lie.

"Max, this isn't your case. It's never been your case. You've left me no choice. I'm putting an official letter of reprimand in your personnel file."

"Reprimand. Are you shitting me?"

"Detective Rupert, watch your tone." Walker's words came slowly and with a stab as chilly as the October rain that beat against his window. "I ordered you to stay away from your wife's case. Not only did you flat-out ignore me, you took it home. It's tainted with your involvement. We have policies for a good reason. And if I hear that you are working on this case—even in your off-hours, you'll be looking at another reprimand and more."

Max felt a chill wash over him as he studied Walker's face.

Now Briggs piped in for the first time since retreating to the corner. "And that includes pumping Voss for information," he said.

Walker shot Briggs a look that caused Briggs to step back into his corner. Then he looked back at Max. "Yes, we know about your meetings with Voss. And just so you don't blame him, he didn't come to us. We found out on our own."

Max looked at Briggs and remembered a day when Briggs watched him and Voss leave City Hall on their way to grab a beer.

"I got a call from Assistant County Attorney Frank Dovey this morning," Walker said. "He was on his way to a motion hearing in the Pruitt case, and let's just say he's less than happy. He thinks you've walked away from the case."

"That's bull—" Max laid up. "That's not true. The Pruitt case is as ready as it will ever be."

"That's not what Dovey says. He has real concerns. He says you haven't been able to show that Ben Pruitt made it back here from Chicago."

"We have an eyewitness saying she saw him get out of a car and walk up to the house at the very hour that the ME says Mrs. Pruitt was killed."

"Dovey said that he tasked you with finding that evidence and you dropped the ball. He says your mind's somewhere else . . . and I have to agree with him."

"Dovey's setting up his scapegoat. Nothing more."

"I've worked with Frank Dovey," Briggs said. "He's a damned good lawyer."

"Lieutenant Briggs," Walker said. "Would you mind stepping out for a minute? I want to have a private chat with Detective Rupert."

At first Briggs acted as if he hadn't heard Walker. Then the words hit him and he gave Walker an awkward nod. "Sure," he said, and he made his way out the door.

Once Briggs was gone, Commander Walker took a breath to suggest that he too disliked Briggs's presence in the office. "It's just us now, Max. Off the record. I've given you your chewing-out and believe me I don't like doing that kind of shit, but it's part of the job."

Max didn't respond.

"Truth is, I'm worried about you, Max. This thing with you delving into your wife's case, it's not only wrong, but it's unhealthy. I know you think that no one can do the case justice besides you—and who knows, maybe you're right—but look at you. You look like hell. You look like you haven't slept for a week."

"I'm fine," Max said.

"Max, I need you to be on your game here. You can't do that if you're sneaking around all night on a case you're forbidden to even look at."

"You don't understand," Max said in a way that sounded like he was talking only to himself. "It's that sneaking around that's allowed me to sleep at all. Someone sent me a key and a note saying that my wife was murdered. I can't just hand that over to someone else and go back to sleep. I found the car. I got the ball rolling again."

"That's right. You did," Walker said. "And now that it's rolling, it's time for you to put it aside. Give Voss a chance. He's bright, and he'll move heaven and earth to get to the bottom of your wife's death. In the meantime, I need you to let it go. I'm not saying forget it. I'm saying let Voss take it over, and you go back to your cases. Can you do that?"

"Can I," Max thought, *is not the same as "will I."* But such a pedantic answer wasn't worthy of his relationship with Commander Walker. Walker had been a good leader for the Homicide Unit. A man who did right by his people. Max knew that Walker had no choice in reprimanding him. Walker had Briggs to deal with, and Briggs happened to be the pet of Chief Murphy.

Max thought about his answer and said, "You picked Voss for this case, and I trust you, so I'll trust Voss . . . for now. That's the best I can do."

Chapter 42

At the motions *in limine* hearing, Boady and Dovey hashed out the details of the coming trial. They covered which crime-scene photos and autopsy photos would be admitted and which were overly prejudicial or might lead to an unfair visceral reaction from a jury. They covered procedures for jury selection, limits on *voir dire* questioning, and foundational issues for some of the State's exhibits. The last issue to be addressed was Ben Pruitt's sanction by the Minnesota Board of Professional Responsibility, a sanction that gave an official stamp to the allegation that Ben Pruitt had been dishonest with a tribunal, a sanction that Boady needed to be kept out.

"Your Honor," Dovey began, "Mr. Pruitt introduced a document at a previous trial, a letter of reprimand purportedly signed by Detective Rupert's superior, Commander Walker. This letter suggested that Detective Rupert had been reprimanded for falsifying evidence. It was later determined that the letter was a forgery. May I approach?"

"You may," said Judge Ransom.

Dovey took the sanction document to the bench, had it marked, and entered it into evidence.

"Mr. Pruitt was formally sanctioned by the Board of Professional Responsibility for permitting a fraud on the court. The State should be permitted to introduce this evidence to show the past relationship between these two men, Pruitt and Rupert, and to show the extent to which the defendant will use artifice to win his cases."

Dovey sat down.

"Your Honor." Boady stood. "The State wants to introduce Mr. Pruitt's sanction for one purpose only. He wants to denigrate the character of the defendant in the eyes of the jury. As this Honorable Court is well aware, such character evidence is inadmissible against the defendant. The sanction misrepresents the facts of that case. Mr. Pruitt was given that forged document by his investigator, a man we believe was paid off by Mr. Pruitt's client. Mr. Pruitt didn't know it was a forgery until the ethics investigation. Your Honor, the State knows full well that such evidence is prohibited as being improper character evidence."

Judge Ransom nodded slowly as he read the sanction document. "Would you agree Professor Sanden—"

"Your Honor," Dovey interrupted. "I object to the Court referring to Mr. Sanden as 'Professor Sanden.' It inappropriately elevates his status in the eyes of the jury."

"I agree with you, Mr. Dovey, but seeing as there is no jury here yet, I'll note your objection."

Judge Ransom turned back to Boady. "Professor Sanden, do you teach evidence classes?"

"Yes, Your Honor."

"And in your endeavors to teach the rules of evidence, have you explained to your students the admissibility of impeachment evidence should a defendant take the stand to testify?"

"I do, Your Honor."

"So, I would assume that you would instruct those students that evidence of a lack of veracity, especially specific incidents where that lack of veracity occurs in court, is admissible on the issue of witness credibility?"

Boady knew that this would be the outcome of the argument, but he had to pull himself over that last line. "Yes, Your Honor, but only if that witness takes the stand."

"Precisely," Judge Ransom smiled. "If Mr. Pruitt takes the stand in his own defense, I will permit Mr. Dovey to introduce the evidence of the sanction. You will, of course, be permitted to explain the specific circumstances of the sanction—if you think that will lessen its impact. But the document will come in if Mr. Pruitt testifies."

So there it was. If Ben testifies, the sanction comes in. Dovey would be able to argue that Ben Pruitt had lied to a court before. Committed fraud in order to win a case for a client. How much further would a man like that go if his own skin were at risk? Why wouldn't he do it again—and more?

But did Ben need to testify? The State would play the interview that Ben had given to Max Rupert. Ben was unwavering in his claim of innocence, he gave an impassioned plea for Max to find his wife's killer. And it laid out the details of Ben's alibi.

But then again, Boady knew that jurors wanted—needed—to hear a defendant say he didn't do it. They wanted to look him in the eye and hear those words from the man's own mouth. "Right to remain silent" be damned.

PART 3
The Trial

Chapter 43

There's a certain logic to calling the lead detective as the first witness, the same way it's logical to spread frosting on a cake before you dash it with sprinkles. The detective can tell the story from beginning to end, giving the jury an overall picture of the State's case. The rest of the witnesses then fill in their respective bits.

When Max took the stand, he saw Lila Nash sitting just behind Boady Sanden. Max tried to figure out her presence in the courtroom and remembered that she'd once told him that she wanted to go to law school. He hadn't seen her in years, and his mind flashed back to that cold winter night when he saw her tied to a barn hoist. The man who was preparing to rape Lila that night was the first man Max had ever killed, and Max never lost a wink of sleep over it.

Max gave Lila a small smile and nod, and she returned the greeting.

Dovey began his direct examination and Max recounted the events, starting with the jogger who found the body of Jennavieve Pruitt. By the time they broke for lunch, Dovey had covered the identification of Mrs. Pruitt, the search of the house, and Max's interview with Ben Pruitt. They played the video and audio of that meeting from beginning to end. Max's stomach always tightened when he testified at trials, and he didn't realize how hungry he'd grown until the judge called an adjournment for the lunch break.

The best cafeteria in the area sits in the basement of the Government Center. Max went there and ordered a cup of chili and a Reuben sandwich. He took a table as far out of the way as he could find. In his head he went over his testimony from that morning, looking for anything he may have left out or needed to clarify. He'd testified in hundreds of cases in his career, everything from speeding tickets, back when he was on patrol, to murder. He felt comfortable with his morning's work.

As he was about to finish off the first half of his sandwich, he sensed someone watching him. He looked up to see Lila Nash standing over him with a tray in her hand. Max smiled.

"Want to join me?" he said.

"I do, but I'm not sure I'm supposed to. We're kind of on opposite sides."

"I'll tell you what, we'll make it a rule that we don't talk about the case at all. Will that work?"

"Works for me," Lila said. She put her food on the table, a fruit bowl and a cup of yogurt.

"I see you're working for the defense. I had no idea."

"I'm just helping out—researching and such."

"So I take it you made it into law school?"

"Just started my second year."

"Won't your boss want you to eat with him? Where is he anyway?"

"Not during trials. He wants to be alone with his thoughts, so he brought a ham sandwich and a can of Pepsi. I saw him heading out to the courtyard, to one of the benches outside."

"Are you and Joe . . ."

"Still a couple? Yeah, we're still together."

"And what about Joe's autistic brother . . . I can't remember his name."

"Jeremy. Yes, he's with us and we have a dog named Shadow. We've become quite the little family."

"Jeremy's lucky to have you and Joe." Max dabbed a napkin to his mouth as he talked, a tick that only showed itself when he ate a meal with a female. "And what's Joe doing these days?"

"After he graduated, he took a job with the Associated Press."

"It's good to see that things are going well for you both. You deserve a happy future after . . . well . . ."

"I've been meaning to send you Christmas cards over the years, but I don't have your address, and you're unlisted."

Max pulled his wallet out and withdrew a business card. "You got a pen?"

Lila found one in her purse. Max wrote his home address and personal cell-phone number on the back and handed it to her. "Now you have no excuse," Max said.

"I figure a Christmas card is the least I can do for the man who saved my life."

Max saw Lila pull the sleeves of her blouse down to cover the scars on her wrists. "Just doing my job, ma'am." Max tipped the brim of an imaginary hat and smiled, hoping the conversation might steer away from the darkness of that night.

"Professor Sanden told me that you saved his life too."

"Well, that might be a stretch. I pulled his client off of him, but the bailiff would have taken care of it, had I not been there."

"Not the way he explains it."

Max's eyes softened into a faraway look as he remembered. "I haven't thought about that in years."

"I would think that if someone was going to cross-examine me in court and try to make me out to be wrong, I'd hold a grudge."

"Wait, Boady's going to try and make me out to be wrong?" Max exaggerated the words to show his sarcasm. Then he shrugged. "Boady has his job. I have my job. We understand that. We don't make it personal. That's just how it's been with us."

"I don't think I could ever cross-examine you—not after everything that happened. It would be like kicking my dog."

"So I'm a dog in this scenario?"

"Yeah, but I really love my dog."

Chapter 44

Dovey didn't finish his questioning of Max Rupert until just before lunch on the second day of the trial. After lunch, Dovey turned the witness over to Boady.

Before Boady could ask his first question, a strange wave of panic washed over him. He paused to let it pass. He recognized the residue from those days when the death of Miguel Quinto filled his hands with a tremble so severe that he could barely hold a pen. His insides churned and his chest worked to pull in the next breaths. But it was more than the ghost of Miguel Quinto that gripped him, and he knew it. He had prepared a blistering cross-examination for Max Rupert, one that would inflict wounds on the State's case—and on Max himself. Boady had been preparing that cross for weeks, and now the time had come.

Boady started his cross slowly, asking Max about what the State did not have in the way of evidence. The State had no evidence to explain how Ben Pruitt would have gotten back from Chicago. The State had no forensics to tie him to his wife's dead body. And other than Malena Gwin's statement, the State had no evidence that Pruitt didn't spend the night at the Marriott. That was the thing about cases built around circumstantial evidence; the defense could spend hours talking about what was *not* there—and Boady did.

Boady spent the afternoon getting Max to say "it's possible" to alternative interpretations of each key piece of evidence. He led Max through the tollbooth footage, underscoring for the jury that Max had examined each possible lane of travel, looking for that red sedan, and found nothing.

"You and your partner did a forensic search of Mr. Pruitt's computers, correct?"

"Yes."

"His computers contained no Internet searches for tollbooths or maps to Chicago."

"We didn't find any."

"And you had the hard drives examined so that any searches that may have been deleted could be found, correct?"

"Yes."

Boady nodded and flipped to the next page of notes. He took a drink of water, cleared his throat, and stood up at his table to ask the next question.

"You're familiar with Anna Adler-King?"

"Yes."

"That's the deceased's sister?"

"Yes."

"And you interviewed Mrs. Adler-King?"

"I did."

"She told you in that interview that she and her sister, Mrs. Pruitt, were the heirs to a massive family-owned business enterprise?"

"She explained that your client and his wife had a prenuptial agreement that—"

"Your Honor, I would ask that the witness be instructed to answer the question that I put to him."

"Detective?"

"Sorry, Your Honor. Yes, Mrs. Adler-King mentioned that her father was in failing health and that control of the company might soon pass to her."

"And it would have passed to the two daughters together had Jennavieve Pruitt not been murdered."

"They would have shared control of the company, yes."

"Mrs. Pruitt, being the older sister, would have held one voting share more than Mrs. Adler-King, so in fact Mrs. Pruitt would have held control of the company."

"That's my understanding."

"Don't you think that gaining control of a billion-dollar company is relevant in a murder investigation?"

"Anna Adler-King had an alibi. We cleared her."

"That's right, she was at an opening-night party at the Guthrie Theater. Is that right?"

"Yes."

Boady looked at his notes. The time had come to draw blood. "Detective, I've gone through your investigation, and I found something that I don't quite understand. You have your reports in front of you?"

"I do."

"Let me refer you to the first page of your report, written on the day you found Jennavieve Pruitt's body. Do you have that page?"

"Yes."

"How many times on that page alone did you refer to Mrs. Pruitt by name?"

Max paused to count. "Twelve."

"Now how many of those twelve times did you refer to her by the name Jennavieve?"

"Excuse me?"

"How many times did you call her Jennavieve?"

"Um . . . nine."

"And what did you call her the other three times?"

Max looked up at Boady with either concern or confusion pulling lines across his forehead.

"What name did you write in your report instead of Jennavieve, Detective?"

"I wrote Jenni."

"Your Honor, may I approach the witness?" Boady asked.

"You may."

Boady picked up a stack of transcripts and walked to the witness stand next to Max. "Detective, these are statements taken by you and your partner, Detective Vang? Would you be so kind as to go through these witness statements and find a single occurrence when a friend or relative of Jennavieve Pruitt ever referred to her as Jenni?"

Boady walked slowly back to the table, listening to Max shuffle through the pages in a halfhearted manner. Boady turned at his table and remained standing, staring at Max, who was fumbling through page after page, looking for anyone who may have called her Jenni. Boady knew that Max would find no such reference, and when Boady felt that the point had been made, he spoke. "Detective, isn't it true that no one, not one family member, not one business associate, not one neighbor, not one friend, ever referred to Jennavieve Pruitt as Jenni?"

"Possibly."

"Detective, you received a reprimand last week—"

"Objection!" Dovey was already rounding the table and on his way to the bench before Judge Ransom gave a two-fingered wave to approach.

"Your Honor," Dovey huffed. "This reprimand is completely irrelevant to the matter at issue in this case. Counsel is using it to smear the reputation of an otherwise-stellar detective, a Medal of Valor recipient. That kind of character assassination has no place in this trial."

Judge Ransom turned to Boady, who spoke next.

"First off, I'm surprised to hear that my esteemed colleague is even aware of the reprimand, because it wasn't disclosed as part of my ongoing discovery demand. We came across it by chance when we served a request directly on Detective Rupert's supervising commander earlier this week." Boady had kept an accusatory stare on Dovey as he spoke.

"Second," Boady continued. "The defense theory of the case is that this investigation was flawed from the very beginning, that Detective Rupert ignored alternative suspects. Detective Rupert was reprimanded for not following instructions, disobeying his superiors, and, most importantly, violating department policy in conducting an unauthorized investigation that distracted him from his job. It goes to the heart of my case and is absolutely admissible."

Ransom turned back to Dovey. "You knew about this letter of reprimand?"

"I learned of it last week."

"And you didn't disclose it to defense counsel?"

"It has no relevance to the case."

"Mr. Dovey," Ransom said with impatient rigidity. "You don't get to determine what evidence is relevant. That's my job. The letter comes in."

Boady returned to his standing position behind counsel table and continued. "Detective, you were given a letter of reprimand just last week, is that correct?"

"Yes." The words hissed through Max's teeth.

"That reprimand was because you disobeyed your commander's orders not to take part in a certain investigation?"

"Yes."

"And, not only did you take part, you snuck the case file out of City Hall and took it to your home?"

"I carried it to my home, yes."

"And this happened over the same period of time that you were supposed to be investigating the murder of Jennavieve Pruitt?"

"Yes."

"And what is the name of the person whose case you were investigating in violation of orders?"

"Her name . . ." Max looked at Dovey, who wore an inexplicably smug look on his face, the kind of look that said, "You made your bed, now lie in it." Boady saw a charge of tension pass between the two men. "Her name was Jenni Rupert."

Boady paused for a beat or two to let the name resonate with the jurors. Then he said, "Jenni . . . Rupert . . . your deceased wife?"

"Yes. She was my wife."

"And you decided to investigate your wife's four-year-old hit-and-run instead of conducting a proper investigation in the Pruitt case."

"I conducted a proper investigation—"

"Isn't it true that you became obsessed with your wife's case?"

"No."

"You stole her file from City Hall."

"I didn't steal it."

"So you had permission to take that file home?"

"No, but—"

"And you confused your wife's death with the murder of Jenna-vieve Pruitt."

"I didn't confuse them."

"You already admitted that you sometimes called Jennavieve Pruitt by your wife's name. You called her Jenni when no one else on Earth did."

"That was just a mistake."

"A mistake . . . in a murder investigation?"

Boady gave the jury a moment to digest that answer. He could see the well of emotion rising behind Max Rupert's eyes: anger, pain, disgust—maybe all three at once. Boady had crossed a line. He knew it.

Boady remembered what Lila had asked him. *What happens if you have to go after him, I mean really tear into him?* But then Boady thought of Emma Pruitt and the promise he'd made. He would bring her father back to her. He would exonerate Ben Pruitt. If this had been any other cop in any other case, Boady would have asked those same questions, without hesitation. It had to be done, even if it meant losing a friend. *Let justice be done, though the heavens may fall*, Boady thought to himself.

Boady took a breath to reset his mind. Then he returned to his questioning. "Detective Rupert, you zeroed in on Ben Pruitt from the very beginning of this investigation?"

"Mr. Pruitt was a person of interest."

"To the exclusion of all others."

"I would disagree with that." Max was beginning to sound tired.

"You were very thorough in investigating Mr. Pruitt."

"We sought to be thorough in all aspects of the investigation."

"Even Mrs. Adler-King?"

"Like I said before, Mrs. Adler-King has an alibi."

"So does Mr. Pruitt."

"Mr. Pruitt couldn't account for all his time in Chicago."

"Isn't it possible that Mrs. Adler-King might have slipped out of the reception at some point and returned later?"

"We found no reason to believe that she did."

"And what did you do to confirm that she was there all evening?"

"We found witnesses who saw her at the Guthrie Theater."

"But you also found witnesses who placed Mr. Pruitt in Chicago at a conference when Jennavieve Pruitt was murdered."

"Not the entire time," Max said. "There were holes."

"And so you drove all the way to Chicago, stayed overnight at the Marriott, obtained hotel surveillance footage, obtained key-card data, and viewed over . . . what would you say, forty hours of tollbooth footage?"

"Yes, something like that."

"And you gave all this effort to try to undermine Mr. Pruitt's alibi?"

"I wouldn't phrase it quite that way."

"No, I suspect you wouldn't."

"Objection."

"Sustained."

Boady continued. "All those resources, all those man hours to go after Ben Pruitt. And you barely lifted a finger to look at Mrs. Adler-King."

"We focused on Mr. Pruitt because that's where the evidence led." Max spoke sharply. Arguing instead of answering—just what Boady wanted.

"And what about other possible suspects? Did you research any of those developers who lost money in Jennavieve Pruitt's wetland lawsuits?"

"Mr. Sanden, we only have so many man hours to give; I'm not going to waste time and resources on a wild goose chase when the evidence all led back to your client."

"And yet, Detective," Boady paused to create an air of anticipation before he finished. He leaned over counsel table and lowered his voice to almost a whisper. "And yet, Detective, instead of following leads that might have exonerated Mr. Pruitt, you chose to conduct an unauthorized investigation into your wife's death. That—Detective Rupert—you had time for."

Boady shook his head and sat down before Max could come up with an answer. He pretended to go through his notes as he let the weight of Max's testimony settle onto the laps of the jurors. He allowed the silence to linger until the room bristled with Max's discomfort. Boady put his notes down. He looked at the jury and then at the judge, "I have no further questions."

Judge Ransom cleared his throat, remarked about the lateness of the hour, and called the trial to an end for the day. He told Max that he could step down from the witness stand. The courtroom remained silent.

Boady scribbled doodles in the margin of his legal pad and waited; he didn't want to look at Max's face. From the corner of his eye, Boady could see that Max hadn't moved from the chair. The judge again told Max that he could step down. This time, Boady detected movement. He stared at the doodles as Max passed by him.

Chapter 45

A trial can be like a float trip down a river. There are witnesses that bring tumult and excitement to the trial, witnesses whose words deflect and ricochet like a river shooting through rocks. There are other witnesses who are necessary but add so little to the case that one might wonder whether the river is still moving forward. After Max Rupert testified, the State put on a slew of those slower-moving witnesses, including crime-scene technicians, hotel clerks from Chicago, and, of course, the medical examiner. After all, there can't be a murder trial without someone swearing under oath that the dead body was in fact dead.

Things got a little more interesting when Everett Kagen took the stand. Kagen recounted conversations in which Jennavieve Pruitt confessed her plan to divorce her husband. During his testimony, Kagen would sometimes begin to tear up, or his breath would falter as if he were going to cry. But in those moments, Kagen would look out into the gallery, and the emotion would drain away.

The first time it happened, Boady took little notice of it. But the second time, Boady glanced to the gallery of spectators and saw Kagen's wife. He recognized Mrs. Kagen from a Facebook picture that Lila had printed off the Internet. Boady couldn't remember her first name because he and Lila had taken to calling her "the angry troll"—not because of her appearance, which somewhat resembled a female powerlifter gone to seed—but because of the way she had treated Lila when Lila went to the Kagen home. Mrs. Kagen answered the door, and once she figured out that Lila worked for the defense, Mrs. Kagen screamed at Lila and slammed the door in her face. From then on, Mrs. Kagen became known as the angry troll.

When Everett Kagen brought himself back from the brink of tears a third time by looking at his wife, something about that subtle exchange tapped at Boady's curiosity. It wasn't unusual for a family member to blur the line between moral support and control, but something about the look they passed seemed darker than it should have been, as though Everett were performing for her and not for the jury.

It may have been nothing more than a man who didn't want to cry in front of his wife, but Boady doubted it. He tucked the thought into his pocket for later.

After the State finished with the slow-moving witnesses, the trial came to its next set of rapids. Malena Gwin. Boady had spent more time preparing for her cross-examination than for any other witness's. He expected Dovey to have less than an hour's worth of direct examination. How many times could she repeat that she saw Ben Pruitt in the glow of a streetlight—a streetlight that Lila had confirmed was burned out—standing outside of his house in the hour that his wife was murdered?

Boady had enough ammunition that he expected to have her on the stand for the rest of the day, digging herself out of one hole after another. When he finished with her, Malena Gwin would be hard-pressed to swear to her own name.

Gwin took a seat on the witness chair, looking like a model from a *Town & Country* advertisement. She wore her mid-forties like a new suit tailor-made just for her. She walked with a confident stride, but short of cocky. She settled into the witness chair gracefully, as if she'd been rehearsing that part of her performance for weeks. Boady could already see that she was the kind of person that the jurors would want to believe.

Dovey plodded through the preliminary questions, setting up her credibility as a concerned neighbor and stalwart protector of the community before he launched into the heart of his examination. He took her step-by-step through her activities on the day that Jennavieve Pruitt died. He feigned concern as she told the jury about her insomnia that night and how it brought her out onto her front porch.

"Ms. Gwin, as you sat on your porch, did you see anything unusual?"

"Yes. I saw a red sedan pull up and park in the street. It parked in front of the Pruitts' house, right across the street from me."

"And what happened next?"

"A man got out—at least I think it was a man—and looked around. Then he walked up the walkway toward the Pruitts' house."

Boady sat up straight in his chair. Did he hear that right? She *thinks* it was a man?

Dovey continued, "Did you see whether that man entered the Pruitt house?"

"Yes, he did."

"And do you see that man in the courtroom today?"

Malena Gwin looked at Ben Pruitt, and her face lost its hard, matter-of-fact edge. She looked at Dovey with an almost-fearful expression. She opened her mouth to answer, but no words came out. She took a small breath, then said, "No, I don't."

"Ms. Gwin," Dovey stammered only slightly in his follow-up. "You may have misunderstood my question. I'm asking if the man you saw step out of that car that night and walk into the Pruitts' house is in this courtroom. Do you recognize him?"

Malena Gwin turned her attention back to Dovey. "I know what you're asking, Mr. Dovey, and I've given this a great deal of thought. I know how important it is that I be absolutely accurate in what I say here. I saw someone get out of a red car and walk up to the Pruitts' home. Now that I've have time to think about it, I believe that I simply assumed that it was Ben Pruitt. I didn't get a good-enough look to say with certainty that it was Ben Pruitt. In fact, now that I've had time to reflect, I'm pretty certain it wasn't him."

Boady could barely contain the urge to jump out of his seat. He fought to suppress the bolt of lightning that ripped through every nerve and corpuscle in his body. He casually wrote "we won" on his legal pad. Then, with the nonchalance of a man finishing dinner, he leaned back, crossed one leg over the other, and waited for Dovey's next move.

Dovey turned to a box he kept on the seat behind him. He rummaged through it and pulled out a binder that Boady recognized as a transcript from the grand jury. Dovey started flipping through pages.

Boady saw what was coming and prepared his objection.

"Ms. Gwin, isn't it true that you testified under oath at a grand-jury proceeding on—"

"Objection, Your Honor." Boady stood and started for the bench.

"Counsel," Judge Ransom said, raising his hand. "I'm going to excuse the jury for a few minutes. I'm also going to instruct the bailiff to have Ms. Gwin sit in a conference room outside while we address this objection."

As the jury filed out of the jury box, Ben whispered into Boady's ear. "It's a *Dexter* issue. He's going to try to get her grand-jury testimony in through impeachment."

"I know," said Boady. "And Ransom sees it too. That's why he sent the jury out. He wants this on the record."

Once the jury had departed, Boady stood. "Your Honor, Ms. Gwin testified that the man she saw entering the Pruitts' house was probably not Ben Pruitt. That's her testimony. Now Mr. Dovey's going to impeach his own witness with her grand-jury testimony. But this has nothing to do with impeaching a witness. Mr. Dovey wants the jury to ignore her testimony here today. He wants the jury to believe her testimony from the grand-jury proceeding instead. According to *State v. Dexter*, that's an improper use of impeachment."

"Your Honor," Dovey said. "I have the right to impeach Ms. Gwin. She gave a statement under oath at the grand jury which contradicts her testimony here today. I have a right to present that impeachment evidence."

Judge Ransom held up his hand to indicate that he wanted to speak. "Gentlemen, the *Dexter* case says that I have to weigh the State's right to the impeachment against the potential for unfair harm to the defendant. But the more recent case of *State v. Moua* suggests that the jury should be allowed to decide for themselves which statements are true and which aren't."

"Your Honor," Boady interjected. "The *Moua* decision is the anomaly. It is the poster child for the adage that bad facts make bad law."

"Mr. Sanden," the judge said, "I understand your concerns, and you will have every opportunity to either cross-examine Ms. Gwin or rehabilitate her testimony—depending on how she testifies—but I'm going to allow the impeachment. I'll give a curative instruction, but I'm letting it in."

Boady sat down.

"What the hell just happened?" Ben whispered.

"Don't worry." Boady fixed a mask of confidence on his face. "We have their main witness saying that it wasn't you in that red sedan. If you're not acquitted, we have a hell of a good appeal."

"I don't want an appeal." Ben gripped Boady's arm. "I need to get out of here. I need to see Emma. An appeal will take a year."

"Ben, this is a good thing. Whatever Gwin may have said before, she's on our side now. Dovey's argument that you came back here from Chicago just blew up in his face. The wind's in our favor."

To all the world, Boady exuded the look of a man who had just knocked his opponent to the mat. But inside, Boady was cursing Judge Ransom's ruling. It screwed up everything. Boady had been prepared to rip Malena Gwin to shreds. Now that she changed her testimony, he couldn't do that. She had become a defense witness, and Boady needed the jury to believe her when she said that she didn't think it was Ben Pruitt she saw that night.

But every zig has its zag. Dovey would get to show the jury that Gwin had sworn under oath that it was Ben Pruitt. Boady could do very little to attack that statement without calling into question Malena's flip.

In the end, the jury would be given two statements: one, that Gwin saw Ben Pruitt that night, and the other, that Gwin did not see him. The judge would instruct the jury that only the statement she made at the trial—that she did not see him—could be used to determine what actually happened that night. The second statement, the grand-jury testimony, could only be used to suggest the witness lacked credibility.

The jury could not use the grand-jury testimony to figure out what happened on the night Jennavieve Pruitt died. For Boady, this was the equivalent of handing two cookies to a child and telling him that only one cookie existed.

Boady looked at his friend, hoping to see some sign that Ben was buying the pep talk. What Boady saw was a man who understood the law as well as Boady, who understood that his freedom—maybe even his life—now depended upon whether the jury would believe that they really held only one cookie.

Chapter 46

Boady couldn't help but hold his breath for the rest of Malena Gwin's testimony. She had flipped once, and a flop back might come just as easily, especially with Frank Dovey hammering away at her. But she held her ground. Yes, she admitted, she had testified that she saw Ben Pruitt walking up to his house on the night Mrs. Pruitt was murdered, and, yes, a person's memory does get worse as time passes. "But, Mr. Dovey," she said, "none of that changes the fact that it wasn't Ben Pruitt I saw that night. And now that I've had more time to reflect, I'm certain of that fact."

After Dovey finished his direct examination, Boady let Malena Gwin leave the stand without a single follow-up question. He didn't want anything to dilute the power of Gwin's testimony. She was certain it was not Ben Pruitt that she saw that night. That's all the jury needed to know.

Next, Anna Adler-King took the stand. He had been looking forward to her testimony—and, more important, her cross-examination—more than any other witness of the trial. She dressed much more demurely for her turn in the witness chair than she had the day she came to Boady's house to take Emma. Gone were the power suit and runway-model makeup. Boady barely recognized her in her tweed skirt and her Sunday-school hairstyle. She'd taken significant measures to appear to the jury as one of them.

Boady watched and listened patiently as Dovey directed Anna Adler-King in her heart-wrenching performance on the witness stand. Dovey had to pause five times as Anna Adler-King broke down in tears while telling of her childhood with Jennavieve.

Anna's performance became more rigid when the testimony

turned to the prenuptial agreement. She had done her homework—
or at least her accountant had done his. Anna was able to lay out, with
unswerving accuracy, the list of assets shared by Ben and Jennavieve
Pruitt. She was spot-on with the amount of money Jennavieve drew out
of her trust to pay for those assets. The number was in the millions. The
Pruitts' house in Kenwood, their residences in Aruba and France, their
cars, investments, jewelry—all paid for with trust money. Ben had been
a successful attorney, but they treated his contribution like it was the
family change-jar. When the dust settled, Anna Adler-King had given
the jury the motive for Ben to kill his wife.

When it was Boady's turn, he spent the first half of his examination pointing out to the jury that before them sat a billionaire, a woman
who, because of Jennavieve Pruitt's death, gained control of an empire
with an estimated worth of $1.1 billion. He got her to concede that
had their father died before Jennavieve, Anna's inheritance would have
been cut in half. More than that, control of the company would have
passed to Jennavieve—and upon her eventual death, to Jennavieve's
heirs—putting control of Adler Enterprise forever out of Anna's reach.

Once Boady chiseled Anna's motive for murder into stone, he
turned to the real point of his cross-examination. Like a long-distance
runner, he had paced himself, holding back for this final burst. Now he
stood so that the attention of the jury would remain with him for the
remainder of the cross-examination.

"Let's talk about where you were on the night your sister was murdered. I've read Detective Rupert's report. You told him you were at an
event at the Guthrie Theater. Is that right?"

"Yes. There was a party for the opening of a play that night. I'm on
the board of directors of the Guthrie Theater, and as a board member, I
get invited to those events."

"And what time did the event start?"

"After the opening-night performance, so around 10:30."

"What time did you get there?"

"I probably got there around 11:00."

"What time did you leave the event?"

"I left at 1:30 in the morning."

"Are you sure about that time?"

"It could have been a little before or after that, but it was around there."

"How much before or after?"

"I don't know, ten, fifteen minutes? There were photographers; I have proof I was there. I gave those to the detectives."

Boady gave a nod to Lila Nash, who opened her laptop and began queuing up a CD-ROM disc that Lila had secured from the Guthrie Theater.

"Objection." Dovey interrupted. "Defense hasn't disclosed this footage to the State."

"It's impeachment, Your Honor," Boady said in a bored tone. "This evidence will contradict the statements Mrs. Adler-King just made under oath." Boady looked at Anna as he spoke and saw in her eyes a mingling of recognition and concern.

"You may proceed, Mr. Sanden."

The surveillance video showed people entering the lobby of the Guthrie Theater. In the top right corner of the screen was the date and time. At 10:48 p.m., a woman entered wearing a dress that shimmered in the black-and-white footage.

Boady jogged a finger at Lila, and she froze the frame. "Mrs. Adler-King, that's you entering the Guthrie Theater?"

Anna's face had taken on the expression of a woman who was watching a kitten walk in front of a moving car. She stared at the paused footage, her eyes wide, her brow furrowed, giving no indication that she had even heard Boady's question.

"Mrs. Adler-King?" Boady said. "Please tell the jury if that is you entering the theater on the night your sister was murdered."

Anna looked into the gallery at a man Boady didn't recognize, her pained expression telegraphing to the entire courtroom that something very bad was about to happen.

"Mrs. Adler-King." Judge Ransom nudged her out of her trance.

"Yes," she said. "That's me."

"And this is the opening-night reception you attended on the night your sister was killed."

"Yes." Her voice shook as she spoke.

Boady again signaled to Lila, and the footage zipped forward to the time stamp of 11:37 p.m. The footage showed Anna walking through the lobby of the Guthrie Theater, stopping at the door to glance around, then exiting. Lila stopped the footage.

"Mrs. Adler-King, you left the Guthrie at 11:37 that night, didn't you?"

"I . . . I must have stepped out for some air."

"Mrs. Adler-King, I can play the rest of this footage. Is that the answer you want to stand on?"

"Objection," Dovey interjected. Boady didn't respond. He had locked eyes with Anna Adler-King. He had expected to see the fear of a cornered animal, but instead he saw sadness. It caught him off guard.

"Sustained," the judge said.

Anna looked down at her hands folded on her lap and said nothing.

"What time did you return to the reception Mrs. Adler-King?"

"I didn't kill my sister. I loved her."

"You were gone for nearly an hour and a half, weren't you?"

"Yes, but—"

"Just a little bit ago, you swore under oath that you were at the Guthrie Theater when Jennavieve was murdered."

"Yes."

"And that was a lie."

"I . . . I can't."

"It takes about twenty minutes to drive from the Guthrie to your sister's house in Kenwood, correct?"

"Mr. Sanden." Anna sat up in her seat, her voice finding a foothold. "I did not kill my sister."

"Mrs. Adler-King." Boady shot his words back with equal defiance. "That's not the question I asked. You can drive from the Guthrie to Kenwood in about twenty minutes, yes or no?"

"I suppose . . . but—"

"If you left the Guthrie at 11:37, that would put you at your sister's house around midnight—the time that Malena Gwin says she saw a red car pull up and park in front of your sister's house."

"I didn't go to Jennavieve's house. I had nothing to do with—"

"And you own a red car, do you not? A Porsche Panamera, if I'm not mistaken."

"Yes, but what does that—"

"And you drove the red sedan that night?"

"Yes, but—"

"Mrs. Adler-King, you lied under oath to this jury."

"I . . . I—"

"You weren't at the Guthrie when your sister was murdered."

"No, but I can explain."

"Explain what? How you killed your sister—"

"I didn't—"

"To gain control of your father's company?"

"Objection." Dovey sprang to his feet. "Argumentative and—"

"Withdrawn, Your Honor."

Boady sat down and pretended to leaf through his notes. Anna Adler-King would never admit to murder, but she didn't have to. Boady had exposed that she had motive and opportunity. Boady only needed reasonable doubt. Now he let Anna's words waft through the air for a minute or two while the jury took their notes. Then he said, "I have no more questions for this witness."

Anna again had tears flowing down her cheeks, and this time, Boady thought they looked genuine. She made no effort to wipe them.

"I have a follow-up, Your Honor," Dovey said. "Mrs. Adler-King, you said you could explain where you were in that time after you left the Guthrie. Would you like to do that now?"

Anna nodded slowly. Then she raised her head and looked again at a man in the gallery. "That man there." She raised her finger to point at the man. "That's my husband, William King. He's a good man and better than I deserve."

Anna Adler-King drew in a deep, shaking breath. She slid a finger under each eye to wipe away the tears. Her mouth pulled down at the edges and she fought against the full-blown cry that wanted to get out. Then she looked at another man in the gallery, the man who came with her to Boady's house the day they tried to take Emma. Anna Adler-King raised her hand again, pointed at the man, and said, "That's Roger. He's my lover, and he's the man I left the party to be with that night."

Chapter 47

To Boady Sanden, waiting for a verdict had always been a difficult thing. His world conspired to deprive him of even the slightest measure of comfort. Chairs turned hard, clothes itched, and his bed seemed to grow lumps that hadn't been there before. It didn't help that he had to suffer this restlessness alone. He and Diana thought it best if she took Emma to Missouri to visit relatives. There would be no way to keep Emma protected from news of the trial, and nothing else Boady and Diana tried seemed to lift the girl out of her despondency. Diana and Emma would stay in Missouri until it was safe to bring her back—until the jury acquitted her father.

So Boady wandered from room to room in his house, alone, unable to escape incessant arguments that choked his brain, the second-guessing of every tactic, every decision, and every question asked in the course of the trial.

Had he done the right thing by not laying down the wood when Malena Gwin testified? He had an entire tablet of cross-examination questions that went unasked. He had proof that the streetlight had been burned out on the night that she saw the red sedan. But once she testified that she no longer thought the man in the car was Ben Pruitt, that burned-out light would have worked against his case. Boady needed Gwin to be as certain as she could be that it was not Ben Pruitt.

And what about Everett Kagen? Had he missed something there? What had been the source of that tension between Kagen and his wife? There was something he felt he missed. But in the end, Kagen's alibi rested with his wife, who was willing to swear that he was home by 11:45. If Mrs. Kagen was covering for her husband, her lie would stand.

And then there was the decision not to call Roger, the process server and Anna Adler-King's accused lover. After Anna's testimony, Lila approached him in the hallway to see what he might tell her, and he sent her away. Boady and Ben debated the merits of subpoenaing him to the stand. He was married and might deny the affair. On the other hand, if he confirmed the affair, Anna Adler-King would be off the hook as an alternative perpetrator, and the biggest part of Boady's closing argument would circle the drain.

In the end, Boady decided that he could use Roger's absence to hint that Anna Adler-King was lying about the affair, lying about her alternative explanation as to why she couldn't have killed her sister. "After all, ladies and gentlemen of the jury, if this mysterious suitor could prove that Anna Adler-King didn't drive to Kenwood that night, Mr. Dovey would have called that witness to testify. Don't you think?"

But the biggest question that haunted Boady, as he waited for a verdict, was the decision to have Ben Pruitt remain silent.

At the conclusion of each day of the trial, Boady and Ben would rehash the day's events, plan the next day's path, and discuss whether Ben should take the stand. There were hard and fast considerations that they explored and analyzed anew after every turn in the case. No matter how deep the hashing and rehashing went, it still felt like they were trying to read tea leaves.

Ben was a criminal-defense attorney and knew as well as Boady did that humans are hardwired to want to hear both sides of a story. Jurors felt that they were entitled to have a defendant look them in the eye and say that he didn't do it. It went against their nature to tell them that a guy staying silent shouldn't have his silence held against him.

But Ben had a public sanction, a punishment handed down from the Minnesota Board of Professional Responsibility. That sanction told the world that Ben Pruitt had been caught committing a fraud on the court. It didn't matter that the forged document he introduced had been given to him by his investigator. It only mattered that the sanction put a stamp of approval on the beating Dovey would have inflicted on Ben had he taken the stand.

Lila had uncovered a transcript where Dovey attacked someone with a similar black mark. He told the jury, "Credibility is like a bucket full of water. Every witness carries that bucket with them to the witness stand. If they tell the truth, they leave with their credibility intact. But if they tell a lie—if they try to defraud the judge or the jury—they punch a hole in that bucket. It doesn't matter if it's a small hole because of a small lie, or a big hole because of a big lie. It's a hole, and that bucket won't hold any water."

From the beginning, Boady leaned toward having Ben remain silent. Ben wavered. He wanted to tell the jurors, face-to-face, that he loved his wife and had no part in her death. In the end, Boady prevailed. He pointed out to Ben that everything Ben wanted to say to the jury had already been said. The interview he'd had with Max covered every point that Ben wanted to make. Boady explained to Ben that he would merely be repeating those words if he testified. The risk outweighed the benefit.

All of these competing thoughts squeezed at Boady's chest as the third day of jury deliberation began. Long deliberations tended to favor acquittals or a hung jury—at least that was the conventional wisdom. That conventional wisdom, however, didn't prevent Boady from chewing his fingernails down to the nub. At 10 a.m. on that third day, he got the call that the jury was ready to deliver a verdict. The churning in his gut and chest kicked into an even-higher gear.

Ben was already at counsel table when Boady arrived. When all the players had assembled, the judge called the jury in.

They filed in from the jury room, their eyes fixed on the floor or the back of the juror in front of them. They looked at neither counsel table. When they had all taken their seats, Judge Ransom spoke.

"I've been informed that the jury has reached a verdict. Is that true, Madam Foreperson?"

"It is, Your Honor," said juror number seven.

"Would the bailiff bring the verdict form to the bench?"

The gray-haired bailiff took the piece of paper from juror seven and handed it to the judge. Judge Ransom read the document to himself, then said, "Would the defendant rise to receive the verdict?"

Ben and Boady both stood. Boady thought he might throw up, and he couldn't imagine how Ben must have been feeling.

"In the case of the State of Minnesota versus Benjamin Lee Pruitt, to Count One of the indictment, murder in the first degree, the intentional killing of another, committed with premeditation, we the jury find the defendant—Guilty."

Chapter 48

The day had turned to night before Boady could bring himself to call Diana. He sat at his desk in his home office, surrounded by small piles of law books. He had two different legal pads, one with notes for the motion for a new trial; the other filled with precedence and case law to be used in the appeal. He would argue that a new trial was necessary because Judge Ransom allowed the jury to hear Malena Gwin's grand-jury testimony. The motion for a new trial would be heard by Ransom and the appeal would be going over Ransom's head to the Minnesota Supreme Court. He didn't expect Ransom to reverse himself, but he wanted to give it a shot.

After hearing the verdict, Boady remained at Ben's side as Judge Ransom sentenced him to life in prison—no parole. Ben could barely stand as Ransom pronounced the sentence. Boady had his hand on Ben's shoulder and could feel his friend's body convulse as he struggled to breathe.

Boady left the courthouse and drove home to begin work on the motion. He hadn't eaten lunch or supper. He looked at the clock and saw that it was almost 9 p.m. Although he didn't have the stomach for it, he knew he needed to eat. Chicken noodle soup, maybe. That usually went down easily.

When he stood to go to the kitchen, he got a look at his image in the window behind his desk. Maybe it was the imperfect reflection against the glass or the eerie glow that rose from the desk lamp behind him, but he looked half-dead, bags under his eyes, his hair cresting in an odd direction atop his head, his cheeks hanging slack from his bones. Diana would have scolded him for not taking better care of himself. If she'd spoken her mind, Boady was fairly certain that Diana would have scolded him for going back into the courtroom to begin with.

He needed to call her. He would let supper wait.

"We got the verdict today," Boady said, struggling to gather the words together. Then he added, "They found Ben guilty."

Diana inhaled sharply, but said nothing.

"I don't know what I did wrong. I thought . . ."

"You didn't do anything wrong, honey. This isn't on you."

"I'm the attorney. It's absolutely on me. I should have won this. A better attorney could have gotten an acquittal. The State had nothing. Just speculation. I don't know how I messed this up. It's Miguel Quinto all over again. I've sent another innocent man to prison."

"A better attorney? Like who, Ben Pruitt? Remember, Boady, he's an attorney too. He was there in court with you every step of the way. If he thought you were missing something, he'd have told you. This isn't Miguel Quinto. Ben was as much of a co-counsel as he was a client. You prepped the case together down to the last detail. I will not let you blame yourself for this. You did everything you could."

"No. I missed something. I had to have missed something. I don't know what, but it's got to be here, right in front of me, and I missed it."

"Boady," Diana said in a gentle voice, "honey, don't do this. Don't let this eat you up. Guilt nearly killed you before. Don't let that happen again. You'll be no good for anyone, including Ben."

Boady closed his eyes and noticed how much effort it took to open them again. "What are we going to tell Emma?"

Diana didn't answer.

"Judge Ransom already sentenced Ben. He's on his way to prison."

"Do we . . . are we Emma's parents now?"

With everything else going on, that thought never crossed Boady's mind. "This wasn't how things were supposed to go. The decree was only supposed to be for the time being, but it was binding."

"What do we tell her?" Diana asked.

"We have to tell her the truth. We tell her that her father was convicted. Tell her that sometimes people get wrongfully convicted, and we have a Supreme Court that can fix that. Tell her we're appealing her father's case, and we won't give up."

"I'll tell her. But is there a chance? Do you have a realistic shot to win at the Supreme Court?"

"I have some arguments. I'm still researching, but I think we have a chance."

"Did you eat tonight?"

She knew him so well. "Yes, I had a bite."

"A bite?"

"I'm on my way to the kitchen as we speak. I'll eat something."

"Boady, you did everything you could."

He shook his head, even though there was no one there to see it. "I wish I knew that to be true."

Chapter 49

Cases often lingered with Max Rupert, long after the jurors went back to their lives. The smell of death, the faces of the victims, the words of the guilty as they tried to talk their way out of the punishment they deserved, those fragments floated free in the waves. But the Pruitt case clung to Max heavier than most, sticking to his skin like old cigarette smoke. He would see Jennavieve's face in the sideways glance of a passerby.

In those moments when the other sounds around him fell still, he would hear Boady's words, and he would again feel the pain of that cross-examination. He had tried to exorcise that demon many times, but it continued to return. After court that day, Max drove home, where he hoped to find solace among the artifacts of a life he no longer recognized. The pictures of Jenni that adorned his walls seemed to look down upon him with reproach. He'd let her down. He'd exposed her memory to judgment. He had uttered her name amidst the push-and-shove of a murder trial, and it made him hate Boady Sanden. Boady brought Jenni's name into that trial. Boady committed the betrayal. Boady Sanden had once been the kind of guy who would sneak into a cemetery after hours to check on a friend. Max didn't have many friends like that, and now he had one fewer.

That night, Max parted the curtains of his anger and ended his friendship with Boady Sanden. He mourned that death for the few seconds that it deserved, and then he closed his eyes and fell asleep.

In the four days since Max sent Ben Pruitt to prison, a cold front had settled in over the Twin Cities, spoiling Halloween for thousands of children, forcing them to wear coats over their costumes. Max spent that morning sitting at his desk, piecing together the players in a drive-by shooting that he and Niki were now working. Two cubicles away, he heard Detective Voss tell his partner that he was heading down to the crime lab to meet with a tech.

Max stood and stretched to get Niki's attention. "I think I'm going to go for a walk. Clear my head. You want a pastry if I pass by a place?"

Niki swiveled to Max, rubbing the bridge between her eyes. "You're doing what?"

"I'm going to go for a walk. My head's too full. I need to grab some fresh air and clear things up a bit."

"It's thirty degrees out there."

"I promise I'll wear my coat, Mom."

"Fine." Niki shrugged. "Anything cream-filled."

Max nodded, grabbed his coat and left.

For a month now, Max kept away from his wife's file—at least the one Voss had on his desk. He'd not spoken to Voss, just as Briggs and Walker ordered, other than the casual hello as they passed each other in the hall. Max received no updates. He went back to being the dutiful soldier, turning his attention to putting Ben Pruitt in prison. And he'd done what he'd been asked to do.

Maybe he felt that he deserved a reward for that, nothing big, just some small update on whether Jenni's case had caught traction. But he got nothing.

As Max waited in his car outside of the crime lab, he went over the conversation he would have with Voss when they "accidentally" ran into each other in the parking lot. When Max saw Voss exit the building, Max stepped from his car and headed in the direction of the lab door. Max felt his phone buzz in his pocket. He looked and saw that it was Niki. Max shut the call down and returned the phone to his pocket.

"Hey, Voss," Max called out.

"Hi, Max. What brings you down here?"

"Checking on some prints we took in a drive-by. And you?"

"That lady in Uptown with the crease in her head. They think it may have been a wrench. I just wanted to touch base with the techs before we did a second search."

"So you're not here about my wife's case."

"Max . . ." Voss took a half-step back. "You know I can't talk to you about that case."

"Christ, Tony. I'm not asking to be part of the team. I just—"

"Briggs told me not to talk to you about it. 'Blackout.' That was the term he used. He wants a complete information blackout where you're concerned."

"Briggs is a political dick. You know that, Tony."

"That may be, but he's still my boss. Yours too."

"What if this were your wife, Tony? Would you be carrying Briggs's water if it was your wife they murdered?"

"Don't do this, Max. You don't need to know this stuff. If it was my Brenda that got killed, I can tell you right now, I wouldn't want to know this stuff."

"Yes, you would," Max said. "If that had been Brenda who got run down by a car, you'd want to know. You'd be standing in this parking lot in this cold November wind, and you'd be asking me to throw you a bone. You'd be begging me the same way I'm begging you. Let me in— just a little bit. I need to know."

"You'll get in trouble if they find out. And I'm not talking a letter of reprimand this time."

Max knew this to be true. He'd been wrestling with that thought for weeks now, ever since getting called on the carpet in Walker's office. Something about that meeting had left a bad taste in his mouth. At first he thought it was the reprimand, but as time went by, he realized that that wasn't it. He came to understand that what bothered him was how easily he put his job ahead of everything else. His job had become the most important thing in his life. His job had always come first, even when it came to Jenni. In the end he asked himself, as a man, what was more important to him? And the answer came to him.

He looked hard into Voss's eyes. He wanted the man to see that he meant what he was about to say.

"Voss, if having this job means that I turn my back on my wife, then I don't give a fuck about this job. There's right, and there's wrong. When the rules get in the way of doing what's right, do you follow the rules? Is that the kind of man you want to be? Or do you do what's right? That's a question that every man has to answer for himself. Well, I've answered that question. I have no choice. I have to see to it that my wife gets justice. And, quite frankly, fuck Briggs and fuck Walker and fuck any man who tries to stop me. I owe this to my wife. So, Voss, the question is, What kind of man are you?"

Voss shifted from foot to foot as he thought about his answer. At first, he couldn't look Max in the eye. Max could tell that the man was struggling with his decision. Eventually, Voss looked at Max and nodded. "I've been working every angle, Max. I checked out the owners of that stolen car. I mean I vetted them like they were fucking al Qaeda. But they're legit. Their car was stolen and that's all there is to that. Whoever drove the car cleaned it out good. Not even skin cells on the steering wheel."

"But they left my wife's blood on the front."

"And her hair."

The sudden image that flashed past Max's eyes must have been evident to Tony. "Sorry," he said. "I thought you knew."

"No."

"We hit a wall, Max. The name on the storage-unit lease was fake. Paid in cash through the mail. No DNA on the payment or the envelope. No cameras. No trace evidence in the car or in the storage unit—I mean, other than what belonged to your wife."

"So why keep the car in the first place? That doesn't make sense."

"It makes no sense; I agree," Tony said. "The best we can come up with is that the car was maybe leverage or held onto for blackmail purposes. Either that or the perp just didn't know a better way to make it disappear."

"But then why send me a key to the unit?"

"Like I said. It makes no sense."

Max's phone buzzed again, and Voss looked at Max's pocket and back to his face.

"You going to get that?" Voss asked.

Max ignored the phone and reached out a hand to Tony. "I appreciate the word. I promise I won't be in your hair on this."

"What hair?" Tony smiled and ran a hand across his nearly bald head. Max smiled back. "And, Max, you're right. If this were my Brenda, I'd be saying 'fuck Briggs and fuck Walker.' If anything comes up, I'll let you know."

Max gave Tony a pat on the shoulder and turned back to his car, giving up any pretense that he'd come there for any purpose other than to talk to Tony Voss. On the way to the car, his phone buzzed again, this time a single buzz indicating a text. It was from Niki. *Am at Pruitt house. You need to get here ASAP.*

Max replied: *On my way.*

Chapter 50

Max walked into the Pruitt house to find Niki standing next to two men. One wearing khakis and a jacket, the other in dirty work clothes. They stood in a semicircle around a wad of cloth. When Max looked closer, he saw sheets, cream-colored with a large patch of black—dried blood—blooming from the center.

"Jennavieve's bedding," Niki said.

"Where did you . . . ?" Max looked at Niki, who pointed to the man in the khakis.

"This is Curt Priem," Niki said. "He manages properties for Anna Adler-King. And this . . ." she pointed at the man in the dirty clothes. "This is Joe Brumble. He owns Brumble Heating and Air-Conditioning."

"I called him," Mr. Priem interrupted. "As the administrator of Mrs. Pruitt's estate, Anna is responsible to make sure that this house doesn't fall into disrepair. She asked me to take care of it. Well, I stopped by the other day and noticed that the furnace wasn't working, so I called Mr. Brumble to figure out what was wrong."

Max looked at Mr. Brumble, a man in his late sixties with thick, pickle fingers, two of which were bent unnaturally across the palm of his left hand. He wore a stained denim shirt over stained denim pants, and a hat that read "Brumble HVAC."

"You found this?"

"Yes, sir," he said. "These old houses, they have furnaces older than you. I spend a lot of my days fixing 'em, especially when fall comes around."

"Where'd you find this?" Max pointed at the sheets.

"Well, you see, a furnace draws in air from the house through this cold-air return." He nodded toward a square shaft at the bottom of the wall in the front room. A black metal grate leaned against the wall next to the hole. "The furnace pulls air in, heats it, and pushes it back out through those registers." He pointed at a vent near the front door. "If the furnace can't pull the air in, it won't work."

"Those sheets were in the heating duct?" Max said.

"Yes, sir," Brumble said. "I started the furnace to test the air flow, and damned if there was none to be found. Sometimes critters will find a way into these old ducts and build a nest. That's what I figured, rats probably. So I started digging around and . . . well, I found this. I knew about the murder that happened here. It's been in the papers, so I called Mr. Priem here."

"We didn't touch it," Mr. Priem said. "I put a call in to Mrs. Adler-King, but she's apparently out of the country, and I couldn't reach her. When I couldn't get ahold of her, I called the police."

"You did the right thing," Max said. "If you wouldn't mind, could I have both of you step into the kitchen while my partner and I have a look?"

"I think I should stay here," Mr. Priem said. "As Mrs. Adler-King's representative, I—"

"Mr. Priem, we're not going to have a debate about this." Max looked the man in the eyes and spoke in a calm tone. "It's either the kitchen or it's my squad car. It makes no difference to me."

Mr. Priem considered his choices for a couple seconds, more for show than anything else, Max suspected. Then he and Mr. Brumble left the room.

Max squatted down on one side, and Niki on the other. "We'll need Crime Scene here," Max said.

"I already called Bug. He's on his way."

"Get pictures?"

"Yep."

"Then let's take a peek." They each pulled latex gloves out of their pockets and snapped them on their hands. Then they carefully peeled back the edges of the sheet, its creases stiff with the dried blood. As they opened the center of the bundle, a glint of silver flickered and they saw the blade of a dagger.

Niki looked at Max. "Murder weapon?"

Max paused to nod. Then he carefully peeled loose another fold of the sheet; when he did, a used condom fell out. Max closed his eyes and whispered, "God dammit."

Chapter 51

As Boady Sanden waited in the reception area of the Hennepin County Attorney's Office, he again contemplated the cryptic request that brought him there, a voice message from Frank Dovey that merely stated that it was important that they meet before the motion hearing on Boady's request for a new trial. Boady had called back and left three messages for Dovey, hoping for an explanation, but he heard nothing back.

Boady, in his day, had filed hundreds of motions for a new trial. It was *pro forma*, a Latin term that meant "as a matter of form." It just as well could have meant "a waste of time." Trial attorneys were asked to give a trial court the opportunity to correct their own mistake with a post-verdict motion before appealing up the ladder. However, very few judges had the backbone to admit they had made a mistake.

Boady didn't understand why Dovey wanted to meet before the hearing, which was scheduled for that next morning.

Frank Dovey stepped into the waiting area and invited Boady back. They walked to a conference room. On the conference-room table lay a single folder. Closed. Dovey went to the chair where the folder lay and pointed Boady to a chair across from him.

When Boady had taken his seat, Dovey slid the folder to Boady. "As part of my continuing duty to provide you with discovery," Dovey said, "I thought you should see this."

Boady opened the folder. In one sleeve was a stack of photographs. In the other was a police report. Boady lifted the photos from their sleeve. He saw Detective Max Rupert standing in the front room of Ben Pruitt's house. At his feet lay a bundle of material. As he flipped through the photos, the camera moved in on the bundle as hands in blue gloves peeled away layers. At the heart of the bundle, someone had secreted away a dagger.

"Is this . . . ?" Boady tried to wrap his head around what he was seeing. "Is this the knife that killed Jennavieve Pruitt?"

"It could be. It fits the incision that caused her death."

"Is that Jennavieve's blood on the knife?"

"We've had it tested and, yes, it's her blood."

"You've had it tested? How long have you had this evidence?"

"Only a week, we—"

"A week?" It took everything he had for Boady not to launch out of his seat. Instead, he let his voice rise for the occasion. "You've had this for a week? We have a motion for a new trial scheduled for tomorrow morning—and you're just getting this to me now?"

"We wanted to test the DNA. We wanted to make sure it was Jennavieve Pruitt's blood."

"Damn it, Frank, that's not your call. You know it's not."

"It doesn't change the case."

"Again, Frank, not your fucking call." Boady's anger had moved into contempt and indignation. "You don't get to dictate what is important and what is not. You're supposed to give me everything you get, when you get it. Now I have one night to rewrite my motion. It's new evidence. It completely changes the case."

"We'll just have to agree to disagree."

"No, we won't, Frank. You're wrong. If you want me to cite case law, I can. You have the murder weapon, and I assume those are the sheets from the victim's bed?"

"Possibly."

"Cut the crap, Dovey, you know damned well they are. Where'd they find this?"

"Pruitt stuffed it into the cold-air return in his house before he left to dump his wife's body. A repairman working on the furnace found it."

"Did you test the knife for prints? DNA?"

"The only DNA on the knife was the victim's blood. No prints."

Boady shuffled through some more pictures and stopped cold.

In his hand, Boady held a picture of a condom—used. He looked at Dovey, so angry he could barely get the words out. "A condom? You found a condom and kept that from me? Are you kidding me?"

"Again, we wanted to have it tested first."

"And?"

"It was not a match for Ben Pruitt."

Boady sat back in his chair as a hundred doors in his mind flew open. "Jennavieve Pruitt was having an affair."

"That's one possibility. But even if that were true, it doesn't mean that Ben Pruitt didn't kill his wife. In fact, it bolsters the State's case."

Of all those doors that opened, not one led to the conclusion that this would be good for the State. "In what universe does this help the State?" Boady asked.

"It reinforces Pruitt's motive to kill his wife. Not only did he do it for the money, but he did it because his wife was cheating on him."

"Now I'll grant you that we can agree to disagree. What it does is introduce a lover into the picture who may have had his own reason to kill Mrs. Pruitt, or maybe it was the lover's wife who killed her." With those two words, two cogs in Boady's brain clinked together and replayed the strange glances that Kagen and his wife shared during Everett's testimony. Suddenly, it made sense. "Have you obtained a sample of Everett Kagen's DNA?"

"Kagen? No. Why would I?"

Boady eyed Dovey carefully, trying to understand if he was positioning his case in light of this new evidence, or if he actually believed that he had no reason to test Kagen's DNA. Finally, Boady said, "You're joking, right? They worked together—lots of late nights. He was the last person to see her alive. I bet he drives a red sedan too."

"As a matter of fact, he does. A red Impala. But there are a great many red sedans in this state. I drive one myself. Am I a suspect?"

"Quit being an ass, Frank. You had to see how he acted during his testimony."

"What I saw was the testimony of a close friend. I saw that Jennavieve's death hit him hard—harder than it hit your client, who never dropped a single tear throughout the trial."

"Ben did plenty of grieving in jail—and quit deflecting. Are you going to get a warrant for a sample of Kagen's DNA?"

"I will not," Dovey said with an air of finality. "I don't have probable cause. You know I don't. He testified that he hadn't been to the Pruitt house on the day of the murder."

"Of course he'd say that. His wife was in the courtroom, and she looked angry."

"Well, this angry wife backs up Kagen's alibi. He was at home with her. You're a defense attorney, Sanden. If I got a search warrant on probable cause this flimsy, you'd be the first one to demand that it be thrown out. No judge is going to sign a warrant on the basis that the man drives a red car and cried because his friend got murdered."

Boady suspected that Dovey was right, but he would rather drive a spike through his hand than admit it. "I'm going to add that to my motion. I'm going to ask Ransom to order you to obtain that DNA sample."

"Knock yourself out. You get him to order it, I'll be happy to get it for you. But it won't matter. Kagen didn't kill Jennavieve Pruitt. He was home with his wife. Ben Pruitt killed her. Even if you get that warrant and it turns out to be Kagen, all you'll have proven is that Jennavieve Pruitt had sex with Kagen. It won't change the fact that he was at home when she was murdered. Your boy is still on the hook for that part of it."

Boady stood and picked up the folder. "Are these my copies?"

"They're yours. Enjoy."

"If you'll excuse me, I have a motion to amend. I can see myself out."

Boady headed out of the conference room, pausing at the door for one last thought. "Hey, Frank." Boady leaned back into the conference room. "I hear you got named to the short list for Judge Katowski's vacancy." Boady gave Dovey a wink and a thumbs-up. "I guess having the Adler name behind you can work miracles."

With that, Boady turned and left.

Chapter 52

When Boady filed his amended motion that day, he also filed a petition for a writ of habeas corpus, an order that would require the Hennepin County Sheriff's Office to deliver Ben Pruitt from the prison in Saint Cloud, Minnesota, to the hearing. He requested the writ for two reasons: first, he wanted Ben's strong legal mind to evaluate the new evidence and hopefully provide some insight as to whom Jennavieve's lover might be. If they could find the match for that DNA, the new trial and acquittal would be almost assured.

The second reason Boady requested the writ was to gauge Judge Ransom's interest in the new evidence. If he sided with Dovey's theory, then there would be no need to transport Ben to the hearing. It would be the pro forma hearing that Boady had been expecting before the new evidence. If, however, Judge Ransom sent for Ben Pruitt, it indicated that the judge saw purchase in the discovery of the sheets.

At nine o'clock on the morning of the motion hearing, a sheriff's deputy led Ben Pruitt into the jail interview room. The skin of Ben's face clung to his cheeks like wet tissue, and seemed just as pale. Whiskers peppered his chin and neck, with splotches of gray spreading below the corners of his mouth. He had a bruise, the size of a fist, on the side of his neck, and dark smudges that angled down from the bridge of his nose—the fading remnants of two black eyes.

"Holy hell," Boady said. "What happened to you?"

Ben smiled, but his eyes remained flat. "Turns out, I have a couple enemies in prison." He sat down across from Boady and propped his elbows on the table to help hold himself upright. "I had a client a few years back who got out of a first-degree drug case by flipping on a very bad man named Rodrigo. My client had the good sense to get out of

Dodge after he testified. I think he's in South America now. On the other hand, I end up in St. Cloud, at the very prison where Rodrigo sits on a throne. He remembered me, and not too fondly."

"What'd he do to you?"

"Oh, it's not him. It'll never be him. He just gives the order. As I understand it, I have a bounty on my head. They have me in segregation, but that'll end as soon as I'm transferred to another prison. I have no doubt the bounty will follow me wherever I go."

Boady reached out and put his hand on Ben's wrist. "I'm going to get you out of there. I promise."

Ben shook his head. "No, Boady, I don't think that's in the cards. In a way, I'm okay with it. If it's a choice between watching my daughter grow up in pictures or getting a blade across my throat, I think I prefer the blade."

"Don't talk like that. I'm getting you out, and this motion for a new trial is the key."

"Boady, we both know this is a waste of time. When's the last time you had a judge grant a new trial? Ever? It's a pipe dream, although I thank you for getting me out of prison for a day."

"It's not a pipe dream." Boady slid the folder of new evidence across the table to Ben. He opened it, and Boady watched Ben's eyes as he tried to make sense of what he saw.

"Is this . . . ?" He turned the photograph of the bed sheets sideways and back. "Are these our sheets?"

"Yes," Boady said. "A repairman found them stuffed into the cold-air return of your ductwork."

"So that's Jennavieve's . . ." Ben's hand began to tremble slightly. "That's her blood?"

"That's her blood," Boady said. He pulled out a photo that showed the knife. "And that's the knife that killed her."

Tears filled Ben's eyes, and he wiped them on his sleeve. "That's the knife from our bedroom, the one Everett Kagen gave her."

"There's more."

Ben looked up from the picture, the path of his tears disappearing into the stubble on his cheeks.

Boady lifted out the picture of the used condom.

Ben looked confused. "I don't understand. Why is there . . ." Boady waited for Ben to make the connection, and when he did, his eyes bloomed with understanding. "She was having an affair?"

"I'm sorry, Ben, but that's how it looks."

"I . . . I can't believe it. Who was it?"

"They don't have a match, but they know it wasn't your DNA. If I had to bet, I'd put my money on Kagen."

Ben shook his head slowly as he contemplated this possibility. The furrow in his brow slowly melted away, and he gave a slight nod. "I liked Everett. We had him and his wife over for a barbeque a number of times. I never saw it. Did Dovey do a search warrant for Kagen's DNA?"

"No, he hasn't."

Now Ben sat up, and Boady saw a fire in his eyes, one that had been out since Judge Ransom read the guilty verdict. "Why the hell not? If it is Kagen, then he lied his ass off. He was the last person to see her alive. How can Dovey not apply for a warrant?"

"I'm on your side here, but I think Dovey's right. Where's the nexus? I don't think Dovey has enough to get a search warrant. He was with her that evening, but the only evidence that puts him at the scene of the crime is Malena Gwin saying that she saw a red sedan pull up and a man—who she originally said was you—walk toward the house. Think about it. If you were Kagen's attorney, you'd get that thrown out."

Ben sank back into his chair. "Yeah. I suppose you're right." He turned his attention back to the photos.

"That doesn't mean we won't get his DNA," Boady said. "I'm going to hire an investigator, a guy I worked with in the old days, to follow Kagen around. If he spits out a wad of gum or throws a used coffee cup away, we'll get Kagen's DNA. In the meantime, I promise you, our motion for a new trial is a lock."

"You really think so?"

Boady had never been more certain of any promise he'd ever made, short of his own wedding vows. And when he and Dovey appeared before Judge Ransom later that day, Boady's confidence was born out. Dovey's objections landed harmless, like the kicks of a petulant child.

"Your Honor," Dovey argued. "The defendant is grasping at straws. There is no basis here to overturn the verdict of those jurors."

"No basis?" Boady countered. "They found the murder weapon wrapped in the bloody sheets where Jennavieve fell after being fatally stabbed. Also in those sheets they found a used condom and the DNA of an unknown man the State knows to be someone other than Ben Pruitt. We can establish that whoever left that DNA was at the Pruitt house after Ben Pruitt left for Chicago. That puts an unknown man in Jennavieve Pruitt's bed within hours of her death. The jury never heard this evidence. The State can make no credible argument that this new evidence is nothing short of a game changer."

"Your Honor," Dovey said. "If there was another man in Mrs. Pruitt's bed, that only strengthens Mr. Pruitt's motive to murder his wife. It changes nothing—"

"Mr. Dovey, let me stop you right there." Judge Ransom held up his hand in a stopping gesture. "If I were a juror, I believe this new information would be important to a proper verdict. I don't see any viable argument to the contrary. I'm granting the defendant's motion for a new trial."

With that small victory in his pocket, Boady pivoted to his next argument. It had been Ben's idea.

"If Ransom grants the new trial," Ben said, "we should waive the jury."

Boady hadn't been completely on board at first, but Ben convinced him.

"It's the right move," Ben said. "If he grants the new trial, he's indicating that he sees enough weight in the new evidence that a jury might have reasonable doubts. I've had court trials with Ransom before. He's not a rubber stamp. If he sees reasonable doubt, he'll acquit."

"But what's the advantage of giving up our twelve-person jury?" Boady asked. "With a jury, we only need one holdout. There has to be a good reason to give that up."

"There is," Ben said. "Speed. With a court trial we won't have to go

through the entire trial all over again. Ransom's already heard the evidence. I'm betting we could get Dovey to stipulate a lot of the prior testimony. If we're not starting from scratch, we can push Ransom to set a trial date before the end of the year. I could be out by Christmas."

Boady laced his fingers together and thought this over. "You've got a point, There's really no reason to call all those witnesses again if they're just going to say the same thing."

"Exactly."

"But Dovey's going to think we're pulling a stunt. He objects to everything we ask for. It's his default setting."

"Then we need to make it seem like his idea." For the first time since he came to Boady's front porch back in that last week of July, Ben Pruitt sounded like the fearless attorney Boady had known for all those years. "He has to get all his witnesses subpoenaed and back to court to testify. And with the holidays coming up, that's going to be a nightmare. If we show him the way, he'll run down that path. I'm sure of it."

After waiving the jury, Boady began to drop bread crumbs for Dovey to follow.

"I'd like to remind the Court," Boady said, "that Mr. Pruitt's demand for a speedy trial still stands. We're asking that the Court put it on the trial calendar immediately."

Ransom nodded and said, "As a matter of fact, I just had a speedy trial settle for next week. We can put your trial into that slot and get this matter heard and concluded before the end of the month."

Dovey's eyes went wide. "Your Honor, I can't possibly have my witnesses lined up that quickly. And I'll need time to prepare my case. You have to give me at least sixty days to prepare."

Boady interjected a suggestion. "There shouldn't be all that much prep work. We've already gone through this whole trial once before. Most of the testimony is going to simply repeat what this Court has already heard. If nothing else, Mr. Dovey could pull his notes from the previous trial and ask the exact same questions. Heck, I might do that myself."

"Your Honor, the problem isn't formulating the questions," Dovey said. "I agree with Mr. Sanden that most of the retrial will be repetitive of the last trial. The problem is lining everyone up—especially with the holidays coming up. People take vacations around Thanksgiving. It's going to be difficult, if not impossible, getting everyone here on such short notice."

Judge Ransom said, "Mr. Dovey, you have subpoena power. I expect you to use it. I'm not going to delay this trial. You'll just have to make it work."

"Your Honor," Boady addressed the court as though he were thinking aloud. "I have witnesses who . . . well, I know that nothing in their testimony will change from the last time they testified. If it's okay with the Court and with Mr. Dovey, I might ask that we stipulate to their testimony—unless the State has a problem with that."

Dovey started to object. "Your Honor, I . . . um . . ."

"Yes, Mr. Dovey?" said Ransom.

Boady could see the wheels spinning in Dovey's head, just like Ben predicted. "Your Honor, if I could have a moment." Dovey rubbed his chin as he thought through Boady's idea. "If you think about it, Your Honor, now that this is a trial to the Court and not a jury trial, there may be a number of witnesses who could be stipulated to. I mean, Your Honor has already heard their testimony. You're already in a position to make a credibility determination. We could probably stipulate to a great deal of the prior testimony."

Ransom turned to Boady. "Mr. Sanden, your thoughts?"

"Let me confer with my client." Boady leaned in to Ben and whispered, "You think we set the hook deep enough?"

Ben nodded so that Ransom could see it and whispered back. "Reel away, Counselor."

Boady turned to address the judge again. "I believe that Mr. Dovey's suggestion makes some sense, especially given our demand for a speedy trial and the problems of scheduling witnesses on such short notice. I suspect we could stipulate to much of the previous testimony. If the witnesses have nothing new to add, there's really no reason not to use their prior testimony. The witnesses we call at the new trial can be those who can add something new to the record."

Again, Judge Ransom nodded. "I have no problem with such a stipulation. We'll put it on the record at the start of the new trial. Just so we're clear, neither side is required to stipulate to a witness's prior testimony. And each side has the right to call any witness they want to call to make their record. Is that understood?"

Dovey and Boady both agreed.

The judge adjourned the hearing and everyone left the courtroom except Ben and Boady and the bailiff, who stood in the back waiting to take Ben back to his cell. Ben turned to Boady with the look of a man who'd just been handed a reprieve. He put a hand on Boady's shoulder and, in a voice choked with emotion, said, "You know what this means?"

"What?"

"It means that I'll get to testify," he said. "Ransom already knows about my sanction. It won't matter if Dovey tries to impeach me with it. I can't tell you how hard it was to not take the stand last time. I know it was the right decision, but it hurts. I've regretted that decision every second since then. Even if it falls on deaf ears, I want to take the stand and tell the world that I had nothing to do with Jennavieve's death."

Chapter 53

Back in the day, when Boady rode the highest of waves through the courtrooms of Hennepin County, the county had a prosecutor named Elizabeth Moore whom many lesser attorneys feared and mocked behind her back. She had a reputation as being ruthless, but in truth, she was just damned good at her job. She came to the table prepared. She made a single, reasonable plea offer, and if you didn't take it, she prosecuted the case as promised. She was never one to fold on the morning of trial. For that straightforward resolve, a trait some attorneys, like Boady, saw as a mark of integrity, she earned the moniker "Dragon Lady."

In the summer of 2002 and again later that fall, Boady had trials against Elizabeth Moore. One case was a burglary, the other criminal vehicular homicide. Both were close calls, cases that could have swung guilty as easily as not. Boady won both. No one had ever beaten the Dragon Lady back to back. And so, fittingly, other defense attorneys began to call Boady "St. George," referencing the Catholic saint who, as legend has it, slew a dragon in order to bring Christianity to a town in Libya.

Boady feigned humility at the name and accepted it with pride. He began to privately read up on the tales of his namesake. In his arrogance, Boady would sometimes imagine himself holding Ascalon, the sword that St. George used to slay the dragon, as he marched into the courtroom to defend his clients.

That was before Miguel Quinto.

As Ben Pruitt's second trial commenced, Boady began to experience an old sensation, one that had gone dormant years ago. With each new witness, he could see the wound in the State's case grow wider and deeper. It was as though he wielded Ascalon once again.

The influx and efflux of morning witnesses included Mr. Brumble, Detective Niki Vang, the crime-scene technician Douglas Thomas, and a scientist from the Bureau of Criminal Apprehension named Donna Price, who confirmed that the DNA in the sperm sample did not belong to Ben Pruitt. Dovey kept his questioning short, focusing on his trial theme of "so what—it doesn't change the fact that Ben Pruitt killed his wife." So Jennavieve Pruitt might have been having an affair. So another man's semen was found at the scene of the crime, literally next to the murder weapon. So what? It only shows how clever Ben Pruitt was in pulling it off.

But Boady turned each witness into a weapon for the defense. Another man in the house on the night Jennavieve Pruitt was murdered went against everything they had testified to in the first go-around. They convicted Ben Pruitt on the argument that he was the only man with motive and opportunity. Now that theory didn't fit, and with each new slash of his sword, Boady exposed the depth of the State's hypocrisy.

By noon, Boady had damaged the State's case but had not yet destroyed it. It still breathed. It was still a dangerous beast that could rear up and kill. As Boady walked with Lila down to the cafeteria, he fought against the overconfidence that welled up in his chest. He tried to flush the image of Ben's reunion with Emma from his head.

This isn't over, he told himself. *Don't let your guard down.*

Boady had lost sleep after seeing how Ben had been beaten by the other inmates. His friend had barely been able to survive a couple months in a cell. He would not live long in the system. Boady had to remind himself to breathe whenever he thought about the possibility of losing the case a second time. How could he ever face Emma?

The one loose end that continued to eat at Boady was Everett Kagen.

Boady had hired a retired cop named Bill Kotem to follow Kagen around. All he needed was a single sample of the man's DNA.

Kotem had followed Kagen for twelve days and could report that Kagen only left his house one time in those twelve days. With Jennavieve Pruitt dead, he had no job. He didn't go to church or to the store. He never even crossed the road to spend time in the park. The one time he left his house, Kotem saw Kagen loading garbage bags into the trunk of his car. He then drove to a shredding facility, a warehouse in Northeast Minneapolis, where Kagen loaded the garbage bags onto a conveyor belt. The bags traveled up the belt and fell into a hopper the size of a dump truck, where Kagen's trash was shredded into a pasty mulch and mixed with a ton of the other shredded material. There would be no retrieving a DNA sample from that mess.

Kotem then followed Kagen to a breakfast restaurant where he watched Kagen eat a meal of pancakes and eggs. Kagen used a plastic fork that he brought with him and drank milk through a straw. When the meal was over, he put his fork, straw, and a napkin that he used to wipe his mouth into his jacket pocket and left.

Why would a man carry around a dirty fork and straw except to keep his DNA from being collected? And why would Kagen be so protective of his DNA if he had nothing to hide? But, odd as it may have been, Kagen's behavior proved nothing, and by the day of the retrial, Boady had no DNA sample from Kagen.

The first major snowfall of the season followed Boady to the courthouse that morning, and by noon, the city wore a fresh six inches of the stuff. Boady decided to eat with Lila in the cafeteria that day instead of eating his sandwich outside like he preferred. They went through the line and claimed a table in the back of the room.

As Boady finished the first half of his sandwich, he stopped midbite and nodded toward the center of the cafeteria. Everett Kagen had taken a seat at a small table, where he reached into his pocket, retrieved a plastic fork, and began eating his salad. He sipped water through a straw and had a paper napkin on his lap.

"Do you think he killed her?" he asked Lila.

Lila looked over her shoulder to see whom Boady was eyeing. "Kagen?" she paused to give the question more consideration than Boady thought it needed. "I think he was having an affair with Jennavieve. And if that's the case, he certainly perjured himself at the first trial."

"But do you think he killed her?"

"I still have my money on Anna Adler-King. There's something cold about that woman."

"No," Boady said with a quiet conviction. "I thought it was Anna too, but not anymore. I don't know exactly why he did it. Maybe Jennavieve threatened to end the relationship, or tell his wife. I've seen people do unbelievable things in the heat of passion. I think Jennavieve sent Emma to spend the night with her friend so that she and Kagen could have the house to themselves. I think they had sex, and after they were done, they got into an argument. Jennavieve went to shower off, and Kagen got the knife and met her as she came out of the bathroom."

"So how do we prove it?" Lila asked.

Boady shrugged. "We don't. I brought a motion to Judge Ransom, hoping to get a search warrant for Kagen's DNA. He denied it. I didn't think it would fly, but I at least had to ask."

"Why won't he sign a warrant? Kagen's DNA might match the semen in the condom. That would be the whole case right there. It proves he was there that night. It would prove he was having an affair with Jennavieve. If nothing else, it's a lock for reasonable doubt."

"'Might,'" Boady repeated Lila's word back to her. "'It *might* match the semen. That's the problem. Judge Ransom won't sign a search warrant on what *might* be found. It has to be probable. We need proof that Kagen's DNA is likely to be found in that condom. But we have no proof of the affair. Kagen denied it, and his wife puts him at home before Malena Gwin saw the red sedan pull up to Jennavieve's house. I don't know how he did it, but I believe in my gut that Kagen killed Jennavieve Pruitt. Unfortunately, gut instinct is a long way from probable cause. And without that—no search warrant."

Kagen had his back to them, but Boady could tell that Kagen took care that he ingested every morsel of food that touched his lips. He would be leaving no spit on his plate. Then, mid-bite, Kagen paused, grabbed the napkin from his thigh and sneezed into it. He paused and sneezed again. He wadded the napkin into a ball and placed it on the edge of his small table.

Lila looked at Boady. "Wait here," she said.

She stood, removed her suit jacket, laid it across her chair, and headed toward Kagen's table. She passed his table, turned, and walked up to him so that she was squarely in front of him. She leaned onto his table, one hand on either side, her blouse falling open just enough to expose the edge of her bra.

Boady watched as she spoke to Kagen, but he could not make out what she said. She then pointed at Boady. Kagen turned in his seat to look and then turned back to Lila. Lila frowned, shrugged, and then walked back to Boady's table.

"What was that?" Boady asked.

"I just told him that I worked for you, and I wanted to ask him a single question before we called him to the stand to testify."

"Question? What question?"

"I never got to ask. He told me to 'fuck off.' He really is a bit of an ass."

"So why—"

Lila held up her fist and let her fingers open up to show the snot-filled napkin that she had palmed.

"Good Lord. Let's go."

Lila went to the restroom to wash her hands while Boady scooted through the crowded cafeteria to the front counter. There he asked for and received a plastic bag from the kitchen. He thought about asking for a paper bag, the preferred method of preserving DNA evidence, but that wouldn't work for what Boady had in mind. When the time came, Boady would need Kagen to see what the bag held. He would need Kagen to know that the game had changed.

Lila caught up to Boady as he was leaving the cafeteria. When they got to the hall, they paused to look back. Kagen was just putting his fork and straw back into his jacket pocket. He then reached for his thigh—paused, stood up—then bent over to search under the table.

A look of confusion capped his face and he stopped moving. Boady could see him mentally walking through his meal, trying to find the lost napkin. When Kagen finally turned to look at the empty table where he and Lila had been sitting, Boady smiled.

Chapter 54

After lunch, Boady had to suppress a grin as he said, "Your Honor, the defense calls Everett Kagen to the stand."

A bailiff stepped out of the back door and reentered with Everett Kagen behind him. Kagen looked at Boady with questioning eyes, probably still not sure what to think about the missing napkin. He walked on shaky legs up to the witness stand and raised his hand as he swore to tell the truth. After Judge Ransom had him recite his name for the record, Kagen turned his attention to Boady.

Boady slid his hand into his jacket pocket and slowly pulled out the plastic bag with the cafeteria napkin in it. He straightened out the folded plastic, taking his time to let Kagen see what he held. Boady looked at the bag and then at Kagen—and winked. He laid the bag on his table.

Kagen never took his eyes off of the napkin.

"Mr. Kagen, were you having a sexual affair with Jennavieve Pruitt?"

Judge Ransom and Dovey both shot a look at Boady. But Kagen continued to stare at the napkin.

Boady waited, one tick . . . two ticks . . . three ticks. "Mr. Kagen? Were you having an affair with Jennavieve Pruitt?" Boady repeated with an edge of insistence.

Four ticks . . . Five ticks . . . six.

"Mr. Kagen?" Judge Ransom asked.

"I . . ." Kagen parted his lips to speak, but nothing came out. He passed a dry tongue across them and tried again. "I . . . I wish to invoke my right to remain silent."

On the inside, Boady was leaping and punching the ceiling. On the outside he looked bored, no more excited than a man reading a car manual. Out of the corner of his eye, he could see that Dovey was stunned by Kagen's response. Boady took advantage of Dovey's confusion.

"Not only were you having an affair with her, but you were at her house the day she died."

"I decline to answer that question—"

Finally, Dovey woke up and jumped to his feet. "Objection!"

"Mr. Sanden," Ransom interjected. "No more questions."

"Your Honor," Dovey said, "I strenuously object. It is completely improper to call a witness just to get him to plead the Fifth."

"Now wait a second," Boady responded with a rising voice. "I had no idea—"

"Gentlemen!" Judge Ransom sent his voice booming through the courtroom. "You will both sit down." He turned to Kagen. "Mr. Kagen, you are an attorney, so I assume you know what you are doing. You are not required to testify if there is a legitimate concern that your testimony could incriminate you."

"Thank you, Your Honor," Kagen whispered.

"Your Honor," Boady said. His next words would be a gamble, but if it paid off, it would be huge. "The State has the ability to grant Mr. Kagen immunity. That would permit him to testify."

Judge Ransom rubbed his chin as he considered Boady's gambit. Ransom was a smart man. He had to see it. It would be professional suicide to grant immunity to a murderer. If Dovey refused to grant immunity, it showed that even Dovey believed that Kagen may have killed Jennavieve Pruitt. If Dovey had faith in his case, he would grant immunity with the belief that Kagen's crime was merely perjury.

Ransom turned to Dovey. "Mr. Dovey?"

Dovey stared at Kagen, probably trying to glean some assurance from the man's expression. But Kagen didn't twitch. He stared at the floor in front of the witness stand, looking stunned.

"Your Honor," Dovey said. "The State will not be granting Mr. Kagen immunity for his testimony."

And there you have it, Boady thought to himself, *proof that even the prosecutor has reasonable doubt.*

"You are excused as a witness," the judge said.

Kagen nodded. He held the rail for support as he stood.

Ben leaned in, hugged Boady, and whispered, "I think you just saved my life."

Chapter 55

Ben Pruitt took the stand wearing the same gray suit he wore on the first day of his jury trial, although it hung more loosely on his thin frame now than it did then.

Boady jumped right into the heart of the matter. "You were Jennavieve Pruitt's husband?"

"Yes."

"Where were you on the night she was murdered?"

"I was sleeping in a bed in room 414 at the downtown Marriott in Chicago, Illinois."

"Did you drive back to Minneapolis that night?"

"No. I did not."

"Did you kill your wife?"

"I loved my wife. No. I did not kill her."

"Did you have anything to do with her death?"

"I wasn't there to protect her. If I had been there . . . if I hadn't gone to Chicago, I believe she would still be alive. But I had nothing to do with her death."

"No further questions."

"Mr. Dovey," Judge Ransom said. "Your witness."

Dovey cleared his throat. "Mr. Pruitt, do you believe that your wife was having an affair?"

"I wouldn't have believed it before this trial. Even now, I have trouble believing it. I thought we were happy . . . well, 'happy' might be a strong word. I thought we were fine. We had our daughter, Emma, and our careers, and everything was fine. At least that's what I thought. I loved Jennavieve. She was the most amazing woman I'd ever met."

"So you had no idea that she was sleeping with another man? I find that hard to believe."

"Objection," Boady said. "Argumentative."

"Sustained."

"Mr. Pruitt," Dovey continued. "You stand to inherit a small fortune with the death of your wife."

"I've lost so much more," Ben said. "If you count your wealth in dollars, you are a sorry person indeed, Mr. Dovey. I lost my best friend. I lost the mother of my child. Even if Jennavieve was seeing another man, we were a family. Things would have worked out."

"She was planning to divorce you, Mr. Pruitt. How were things going to—"

"Objection." Boady stood up. "Your Honor, the only testimony that Mrs. Pruitt had any idea of getting divorced came from the testimony of Everett Kagen. He has now pled the Fifth. Because of that I move that his entire testimony, at this trial and at the last, be stricken."

Ransom rubbed a thumb across his chin. "Mr. Dovey, he's got a point. Mr. Kagen can't pick and choose what testimony remains in the record. If he invokes his right to remain silent, his entire testimony needs to be stricken."

"But, Your Honor, we have a stipulation. The parties agreed—"

"Mr. Dovey," Ransom interrupted. "This is not open for argument. Mr. Kagen's testimony will not be considered by this Court. Move on."

"Yes, Your Honor," Dovey said.

"Mr. Pruitt, you received a sanction from the Board of Professional Responsibility for committing fraud on a court of law. Do you agree that's true?"

"I agree that the sanction exists. I do not agree that I committed fraud on the court. I had an investigator assisting me on a case. That man presented me with a document that appeared to be a reprimand handed down to the detective in that case—Detective Max Rupert. I admit that I should have looked at it more closely, but at the time, I believed the document to be authentic."

"But that wasn't the finding of the board."

"No, that wasn't. I've accepted their decision, even though I know it to be wrong. I've moved forward with my practice and my life. I refuse to let that single incident define me. Other than that one blemish, I have lived a spotless life, and no one can change that—not even you, Mr. Dovey. Because the truth is—I didn't kill my wife. The truth, Mr. Dovey, will ultimately prevail."

Boady tried not to smile as Ben hit it out of the park.

Dovey flipped through a legal pad looking for a place to pick up his questioning. He paged forward and back, pausing occasionally to consider. Boady thought he knew the source of Dovey's hesitation. Ben Pruitt was no ordinary witness. He'd spent years in trial. He'd learned cross-examination techniques from the same experts as Dovey. Ben knew how to spot traps—the same traps that he'd built during his career. Ben's answers had all cleared the fence. Dovey would only do more damage to his case by continuing. Finally Dovey tossed his legal pad onto the table in front of him and shook his head. "No further questions."

Chapter 56

The Court took a break to let the attorneys prepare their summations. Boady retreated with Ben and Lila to the holding cell, a secured room just outside of the courtroom. As Boady organized his thoughts, he listened to Ben and Lila—small talk at first, but then Lila brought up the events from the cafeteria that led to Kagen pleading the Fifth.

"I can't believe I misjudged him so completely," Ben said. "I trusted him. I had him in my home as a guest. He ate meals with us—with my daughter. I . . . I just can't believe it. But why kill her?"

"Maybe Jennavieve was going to break it off," Lila said. "Maybe that sent Everett over the edge."

"I'll get him," Ben whispered. "I don't care about the affair. He had no right to take her away from Emma."

"Now, hold on Ben," Boady said. "Nobody's getting anyone here. We're going to let the law handle this."

The muscles in Ben's jaw flexed as he seemed to work through what he now knew about his wife and Everett Kagen.

"Besides, we don't know that Kagen is the guilty one," Boady said.

"What do you mean 'we don't know'?" Ben gave Boady a beseeching gesture with his hands. "Who else would have killed Jennavieve? It had to be him."

"I haven't ruled out your sister-in-law. She had the most to gain out of all this. Or it could have been someone your wife sued and pissed off. Hell, it could have been the angry troll for all we know. Maybe . . ."

Boady stopped talking as a curious notion stepped out of the shadows. The idea of Mrs. Kagen being the killer had never occurred to him. It brought him back to that day in the first trial when Everett dried his emotions every time he looked at his wife. Boady gave a thin voice to those thoughts as they formed in his head. "Maybe she found out about the affair." The room went quiet as that new possibility hung in the air.

Lila was the one to break that silence. "But Malena Gwin said she saw a man get out of the red sedan."

"No," Boady said. He picked up a legal pad full of notes and began throwing the pages back until he found what he was searching for. "Here it is. Her actual testimony was that she saw a man get out of the car. Then she said 'at least I think it was a man.'"

"That's right," said Ben. "I forgot all about that."

"Is it possible?" Lila asked.

Before they could discuss it further, the bailiff tapped at the door and stuck his head in. "The judge wants everyone back in court in ten minutes," he said.

Boady tossed his notepad on the table. "I need to clear my head," he said. "I'm going to find a quiet corner and focus on my summation. I'll see you all in the courtroom in ten."

The bailiff let Boady out of the holding cell. Boady then walked through the courtroom and out into the hall to find a quiet space where he could concentrate. Even though it was late in the day, other cases were still being heard on that floor and all of the conference rooms were filled. So Boady made his way to a stairwell and ducked inside. He had to walk up a flight to find a clean step to sit on, but he found one and took a seat.

There he began to catalogue the facts he would hammer home to the judge in his closing argument. He preferred not to use notes, relying instead on mnemonic devices to retain the evidence in the correct order for his presentation. He'd barely gotten through half of the first trial when he heard voices approaching in the stairwell below him. He muttered a curse that his seclusion would be interrupted. The voices grew closer and he thought he recognized Dovey's.

The door opened and he heard Dovey say, "Step in here for a second."

"Are you telling me that you lost this case?" It was Anna Adler-King. "You said you had this. It was a lock. Those were your words. And now you're telling me Ben Pruitt is going to walk?"

"I can't help it," Dovey said in a hushed tone. "It's not my fault that Kagen took the Fifth. He made himself look guilty by doing that. Some things are beyond my control."

"I'm starting to wonder if you are the kind of person I want to see as a judge," Anna said coldly. "I went to bat for you, Frank, and this is what I get?"

"Judge Ransom hasn't ruled yet. He might—"

"Don't bullshit me, Frank." Anna had stopped whispering and began to scold Frank Dovey like he was a child. "We both know where this case is going. You need to find a way to turn this case around. You hear me? If you want my support, you need to show me that you can keep your word."

"How do you expect me to do that? We're doing closing arguments in five minutes."

"That's up to you," Anna hissed. "The way things stand right now, the report I'm going to give the governor won't look good for you."

The sound of Anna Adler-King's shoes scraping on the grit in the stairwell echoed off the walls as she turned to leave. Boady heard Dovey follow her through the door as well. Boady peeked over the edge of the steps to make certain he was again alone before he stood up and brushed off the seat of his pants.

Dovey was in a hot seat. But with closing arguments about to start, he had no options, at least none that Boady could see. As Boady walked back to the courtroom, he contemplated what he might do if he were in Dovey's shoes. Every option came back to the same problem—the trial was over. Dovey had no rebuttal witnesses. He had no further investigation. Kagen had pled the Fifth and was off-limits. Even if Dovey could figure out a way to get to Kagen, he had no time.

Boady smiled at the thought that Dovey's judgeship hinged on the outcome of a case that everyone knew the man had lost. Boady normally didn't take enjoyment in the downfall of others, but Dovey was a political animal, and political animals deserved no sympathy in Boady's view. And now Dovey was cornered, with his world collapsing around him. Boady reminded himself, as he walked into the courtroom, that cornered animals are the most dangerous animals of all.

Chapter 57

Boady didn't have time to share with Ben what he'd overheard in the stairwell. He'd barely made it to his table when Judge Ransom entered and called the trial back to order.

"Is the State ready to proceed with closing argument?" the judge asked.

"Your Honor, I'd like to be heard on that before we continue."

Here we go, Boady thought.

"Your Honor," Dovey began, "as you may know, this case has received a great deal of attention in the community, especially given the nature of who the deceased is. She and her family have been the cornerstone of some of this state's most important charities."

Ben leaned over and whispered into Boady's ear, "What's he doing?"

Boady whispered back, "He's panicking. Anna has his nuts in a vice and she's squeezing. He can't afford to lose this case."

Dovey continued. "I would also point out that the procedural posture of this case has been . . . well, a little unusual, to say the least. Because we had two separate trials, some of the testimony necessary for this Court to render a just verdict came several weeks ago. Also, with this Court's ruling that none of Mr. Kagen's previous testimony is admissible, well, that makes matters even more complicated. I believe it would be appropriate to permit the parties to submit their summation in writing, give us time to marshal our facts and put them in a more-coherent form before you rule. Maybe have them submitted by the end of the week?"

"What?" Ben Pruitt's voice carried well beyond the defense table. "What's he doing?"

Boady put a hand up to shush his client. He leaned into Ben's ear. "It's a stall tactic."

"No kidding," Ben whispered back. "But I can't go back to jail again. We've won this thing. It's not fair."

Ransom looked perplexed. "Mr. Sanden, would you like to be heard on Mr. Dovey's request?"

"One second, Your Honor," Boady turned back to Ben. "He knows he's lost the case. I heard him. He and Anna were arguing about it during the break. She's pissed and she's ending her support for his judgeship if he doesn't pull a rabbit out of his hat. He needs time to find that rabbit, so he's asking for written submission to get time to figure something out. That's all this is about."

"Mr. Sanden?" the judge repeated.

Boady stood up. "Your Honor, there is no legal precedent supporting the State's request for written summations. Mr. Dovey is doing a rain dance in the hopes of creating his own rain delay. It's improper, and I would ask that we proceed with closing arguments here and now."

Judge Ransom's face took on a look of genuine curiosity. "Mr. Sanden," the judge said, "are you saying that I'm prohibited from letting the State do a written submission? Because I agree, I know of no case that says I have to allow it. But at the same time, I'm not aware of a case that says I can't. If you are aware of such a case, I'd be interested to hear about it."

"No, Your Honor, I am not aware of a case saying that it can't be done. But I don't believe that this is about wanting to do a written submission. I believe that this is about stalling the outcome of this case. I think—"

Dovey jumped to his feet. "Your Honor, that's an outrageous accusation. I demand an apology. As an officer of the court, I—"

"Mr. Dovey!" Judge Ransom shouted back. "Take your seat until the Court addresses you."

Dovey stood, glaring at Boady for a few seconds before taking his seat. Boady stared back and thought he saw a flicker of panic in Dovey's eyes, a brief spark of recognition that Dovey knew that Boady saw through him.

"If I may, Your Honor," Boady continued. "I am not saying that the Court cannot grant Mr. Dovey's request. I am arguing that the Court should not grant it. Not only is it disingenuous, but there's a man's freedom at stake here. I submit that Mr. Dovey can see the writing on the wall and wants one last chance to find a savior for his case before the record closes. Not only that, but my client, a man wrongfully convicted of a crime he didn't commit, will be forced to wait for his freedom to be restored to him, while Mr. Dovey engages in this fantasy. That, Your Honor, would be a travesty. Mr. Pruitt should not have to spend one more night locked up."

Judge Ransom sat back in his chair. Dovey started to stand, but the judge put up a hand to stop him. He stroked his chin as he contemplated a decision. Then he leaned back up to his bench. "Mr. Sanden, I'm inclined to grant the State's request. Mr. Dovey has a right to present his case to its fullest extent."

Boady could see Dovey, in his periphery, breathe a sigh of relief.

"But," the judge continued, "the State's written submission will be due tomorrow, not the end of the week. Mr. Dovey, you can e-mail your written submission to me by noon. Mr. Sanden can reply by 2:00 p.m. Any rebuttal from the State will be here by 3:00. I'll have my decision filed by the end of the day tomorrow."

Boady looked at the clock on the wall. It was after 4 p.m. Just twenty-four hours until Ben would be free. He knew the verdict that Judge Ransom would deliver. Hell, everyone in the courtroom knew that Ben would be acquitted, but because of Frank Dovey's political ambitions, they would have to wait.

Then a thought struck him, and he rose. "Your Honor, I move that the Court grant Mr. Pruitt a furlough pending the verdict."

Dovey hit his fist on the table as he rose. "Absolutely not, Your Honor." Dovey yelled his objection. "This man is a convicted murderer. You cannot release him from custody—"

"Mr. Dovey!" Ransom's voice boomed. "You will maintain decorum in my courtroom. I will not tell you again."

"But, Your Honor," Dovey said in a pleading tone. "I cannot allow this man to be put back on the streets."

"Mr. Dovey, this is not your decision to make," Judge Ransom said. "I can grant a furlough if I see fit. You're the one who wants to delay this trial for written submissions. I've granted that request, but I feel that justice demands that I follow my conscience and my judgment on Mr. Sanden's request as well. I'm going to grant the defendant's motion for a furlough."

Dovey looked over his shoulder to where Anna Adler-King sat in the gallery. It seemed to Boady that he was seeking some reassurance he would not be held accountable for Judge Ransom's decision to release Ben. If that was what he was looking for, he didn't get it. Anna Adler-King stood and walked out of the courtroom.

Ransom adjourned the trial for the day, and Boady, Ben, and Lila sat motionless as the courtroom cleared. Once they were alone, Ben leapt at Boady and hugged him so fiercely that Boady thought he might lose consciousness.

"What just happened?" Lila asked.

"We won," Boady said.

"But he didn't issue his verdict," Lila said.

Ben spoke. "He furloughed me. If he was going to find me guilty, he wouldn't furlough me."

"Congratulations, Lila," Boady said. "You just won your first murder case."

Ben's knees seemed to give out and he fell back into his chair. "I can't believe it," he said. "I mean . . . I hoped and I prayed for this, but in the back of my mind . . ." Ben's eyes filled with tears. "I can't wait to see Emma again."

"And I can tell you that Diana can't wait to bring her back here from Missouri. They've been down there longer than we had planned. By the way, we didn't tell Emma anything about what was happening in court. We wanted to wait until . . . well, until today—until we got you freed. Now, let's get you processed out of jail." Boady reached for his coat and began emptying the pockets. "It's a bit colder today than when they arrested you. You'll need a coat." Boady handed his coat to Ben.

"No, I can't," Ben said. "You need it."

"I can go buy a new one. I have that two hundred grand in my bank account, just waiting to be spent. I can take the skyway to Macy's—won't even have to step outside."

"Well, if you insist," Ben said.

"I do. Need a ride?"

"No." Ben nodded toward the deputy still standing quietly in the back of the courtroom. "I'll catch a cab home. After being surrounded by men twenty-four hours a day, I'd like to be alone for one night. Get cleaned up and get my head together before I see Emma."

Ben held out his arms one last time and embraced both Boady and Lila. "I couldn't have done this without you."

Chapter 58

By the time Boady left the Government Center, the snow had stopped falling and the final tally came to eight inches. He had cursed the snow that morning on his drive in, but now the city was absolutely stunning. The world was right. He meandered as he made his way toward Macy's to buy a new coat. He felt like whistling a Christmas carol, but he and Diana had a rule: no carols until after Thanksgiving. So he whistled "Singin' in the Rain" instead.

The downtown Macy's was a mere four blocks from the Government Center, and after he bought the coat, he decided to take in the beauty of Minneapolis in winter and walk outside as he made his way back to his car.

Still a block away from the parking ramp, he spied a man standing on the corner of Seventh Street and Third Avenue. He wore a coat that looked an awful lot like the one Boady just gave Ben. The man was looking away from Boady and in the direction of the oncoming traffic. The coat collar was up, but even so, the man looked like Ben Pruitt. Boady picked up his pace slightly, and as he drew closer he could see that it was Ben watching for a taxi to come up the street. Boady was about to call out to his friend when a white SUV pulled up and stopped in front of Ben.

Ben jumped into the SUV and immediately leaned over to the driver and began kissing her. Boady stopped walking, trying to make sense of what he was seeing. He could not see the woman's face as she wrapped her hands around Ben's shoulder and neck and held him in their embrace. Boady couldn't move as he watched the kiss grow in intensity.

When they ended the kiss, Ben settled into the passenger seat of the Cadillac Escalade, and Boady could see the face of the driver. It was Malena Gwin.

The SUV pulled back out into traffic and headed toward Boady. As it passed, Ben and Boady locked eyes. The corners of Ben's mouth turned upward into a malevolent grin, as if to say *now you know my secret*. But behind Ben's eyes, Boady saw fear.

Chapter 59

Lila parked on Summit Avenue because Boady's driveway hadn't been cleared of snow yet. She stomped slush off of her boots as she crossed the porch, knocked on the front door as she always did, and then let herself in. Lights were on in the entryway and Professor Sanden's office, but the rest of the house remained dark. She began loosening the laces on her boots.

"Professor Sanden?" she called out. "I just came to clear out my room."

Still no reply.

She slipped her wet boots off and walked in her stocking feet to Boady's office. Through the glass of the French doors she could see him sitting at his chair, staring at his computer monitor.

"Professor? You okay?"

Professor Sanden looked up at her with an expression so sad, so defeated, that it confused Lila. He waved her in. "Sit down," he said pointing to a chair. When she had taken a seat, he turned the monitor so that she could see it. The screen showed a paused image from the tollbooth footage—a white SUV with a man in the driver's seat. "Recognize him?" he asked.

Lila looked closely at the image, the recognition seeping into her consciousness one sliver at a time. "That looks like . . . Mr. Pruitt."

"It is Mr. Pruitt," Professor Sanden said. "The car belongs to Malena Gwin."

"I don't understand."

"After court today, I saw Ben get into this car and kiss Malena Gwin. We were looking for a red sedan, not Malena Gwin's SUV. I mean, who would have thought of that?"

"Professor Sanden, I still don't understand."

Sanden paused as if to force out words that refused to cross his tongue. "Ben Pruitt killed his wife, and he had Malena Gwin as an accomplice."

"That doesn't make sense," Lila said. "Malena Gwin was the one who caused this whole trial. She's the one who said she saw Mr. Pruitt that night. If it wasn't for her, Mr. Pruitt would never have been charged."

"And when he gets acquitted, he'll have double jeopardy. He can never again be prosecuted for her murder. He wanted to get charged. He needed to go to trial. That was his plan all along."

"But he was convicted."

"True. I don't think that was part of the plan. I'm sure he believed that once Malena Gwin changed her testimony, he'd walk. Regardless, he had a trump card. He knew about the bedding. He knew the furnace wouldn't work as long as that duct was clogged. He stuffed that bedding down there to make sure it would eventually be found."

Lila played the case in her head, seeing it differently this time around. "That's why he moved the body."

Boady smiled at Lila's insight. "Exactly. It never made complete sense why the killer went through the trouble of moving the body to that parking lot. We all assumed the killer was trying to hide his crime and failed when he found no room in the dumpster. But it was the exact opposite. Ben dumped Jennavieve's body in that parking lot to ensure it would be found while he had an alibi in Chicago. We couldn't prove the alibi because Max Rupert was right. He did drive back here. Malena Gwin said it was a red sedan because it would get Max looking for the wrong car."

"We need to tell Judge Ransom," Lila said. "He didn't acquit Mr. Pruitt today. We need to tell him before he issues that order tomorrow."

"We can't do that."

"Professor Sanden. Ben Pruitt is a murderer. We know he's a murderer. We know he's about to go free. We can't just sit here and do nothing."

"We are bound by the rules, Lila. We have an ethical obligation to act diligently for our client's best interest. If we take any action that is contrary to our client's best interest, not only do we violate that obligation, but the evidence would be inadmissible. Ransom all but said that he intends to acquit Ben. If we went to him and told him what we know, he would have to ignore it. He has no choice either. What we know about Ben now will not become evidence. Ben will not be convicted if we go running to Ransom—at least not under that theory."

"Is there nothing we can do?"

"I've been racking my brain over that question, Lila. I have an idea, but . . . I don't know. There's no precedent for it, at least none that I know of."

"Can I help?"

"Yes. There's a book in the law library, a treatise on ethics that I use in my class. It can't be checked out, but I'll call ahead and tell them it's for my research and they'll let you leave with it." Boady wrote the title of the book on a piece of paper and handed it to Lila. "Can you drive over and get that for me?"

"Sure thing, Professor. I'll have it here in a flash." Lila ran to the door, slipped on her boots, and raced to her car, nearly falling on the slippery, snow-covered sidewalk.

The interior of her car was still warm and the windshield clean. When she got behind the wheel, she pulled her keys from her purse so hurriedly that they sailed from her trembling fingers, bounced off of the steering column, and fell to the floor. Lila reached down and patted the wet floor mat, looking for her keys, all the while cursing herself for losing her head. She was about to open her door and get out to look for the keys when her fingers felt them under her seat.

When she sat back up, she saw the headlights of a car, a black BMW, pulling up to the curb across the street to park. Lila was about to start her car when the door of the BMW opened enough to flood its interior with light. And there, behind the wheel, sat Ben Pruitt.

Lila slid down in her seat just enough to keep a thin view of Ben Pruitt stepping out of his car. He straightened up, looked around, and then bent back down, reaching into the center of his car. When he stood back up, he had a small black pistol in his hand.

Lila scrunched down even more and held her breath.

Ben Pruitt tucked the gun into the back of his waistband and started toward Professor Sanden's house.

Chapter 60

Max Rupert had gotten two calls from Frank Dovey that evening, which he let go to voice mail. When he listened to them later, he could hear the desperation in the man's voice. The first call came just after Max got home from work. The message came across as a command, telling Max that he needed to get to the prosecutor's office right away—something about only having twenty-four hours to find a smoking gun. Max deleted the message without returning the call.

The second message, left half an hour after the first, was more pleading in tone. Dovey apologized for calling Max at home, explaining that he'd gotten Max's number from Lieutenant Briggs and that he really needed Max's help. In the second message, Dovey explained that Kagen had pled the Fifth and that the case had fallen apart. He said that he'd managed to get a delay of one day to fix the holes in the case, and that he needed Max's help to do that. Dovey ended that call with a plea that rang pathetic in Max's ear. Max deleted that message as well.

Later that evening, after Max shoveled the snow from his driveway, his phone chimed again. He didn't recognize the caller and considered letting it go to voice mail, believing it to be Dovey again, using a different phone. Instead, he decided to confront Dovey and let loose the raw opinions that had been swirling through Max's head as he shoveled snow.

"Max Rupert here."

"Max, this is Lila Nash." Her voice, a whisper, came through the phone in quick spurts.

"Lila, how are—"

"Max, I can't explain, but I need you to come to Professor Sanden's house. It's urgent."

"Look, Lila, if this is some sort of trick to get me to talk to Boady, I'm disappointed."

"Damn it, Max. This is Lila. You know me. I need you to get over here."

Something in her voice convinced him that this was no stunt. "What's wrong? What's happening?"

"I don't know. I'm not even sure if I am supposed to be calling you. I don't know what to do. Can you just get here as fast as you can?"

"With lights and sirens, I can be there in ten, maybe twelve minutes."

"No sirens, at least not when you get close. Something's going down, and I don't want to make it any worse."

"Are you safe, Lila?"

"Yes, but I'm not so sure about Professor Sanden. Please hurry. I'll explain when you get here."

"I'm on my way." Max put his phone into his pocket, grabbed his gun, badge, and a coat, and ran out the door.

Chapter 61

Boady stared at the computer screen, the words of the case he'd been reading no longer in focus. Instead, he saw a vision of Emma's face. She had her mother's eyes, sad eyes that held more pain in them than a ten-year-old should have to bear. And what was about to happen, what Boady had in mind, would break that little girl's heart even more, break it in a way that could never be mended.

How could she ever forgive him for what he was about to do? But it had to be done. Boady could see no other way.

He thought back to the years he spent with Ben Pruitt and searched his memory for signs of the monster he now could see. There were ten years between their ages, but Boady felt a brotherly fondness for his protégé that still tugged at his heart, even now that he knew the truth. Had that monster been lurking inside Ben the whole time? Had the closeness he felt toward Ben blinded him? Boady thought back to all the meetings they had at the jail, the pure emotion on Ben's face, the tears and other small touches that put his performance over the top. He'd been so convincing.

As Boady tore down and restacked his memories of Ben, he came to realize that Ben's performance wasn't simply the creation of a brilliant actor. Acting was part of it, yes, but this was more than just an act. This was the work of a sociopath.

He heard the front door open and assumed that it was Lila returning because she had forgotten something. The sound didn't pull him from his thoughts. After a few minutes, he sensed a presence in his periphery. He looked up to see Ben Pruitt standing in the doorway to his office. Boady jumped on the inside but suppressed his reaction on the outside.

"Good evening, Ben," he said.

"Mind if I come in?" Ben asked.

"Be my guest." Boady gestured to a chair.

"Isn't this where you say you're surprised to see me?"

"No. There's no point in such pretense." Boady clicked his mouse to bring up the freeze-frame from the tollbooth. He turned the screen to Ben. "I don't think that's my best side, do you?"

"You killed Jennavieve?" No matter how he tried, Boady couldn't mask the hurt in his voice.

"Are you asking me as a friend, or as my attorney?"

"I think it's safe to say that we are no longer friends, Ben. Not after this."

"That's too bad, because I still like you, Boady. You did a hell of a job for me. Honestly, I've been dying to spill the beans for a while now, especially after they found the sheets and the knife. I wanted so bad to let you in on my little secret. And because we have attorney-client privilege, I could have. But then I remembered ol' Miguel Quinto. I didn't want you slacking on the job the way you did with him. Things were getting critical, and I needed your head in the game."

"Why are you here, Ben?"

"Well, Boady, when I saw you downtown, I got a little nervous. I mean, you should have seen the look on your face—like you just watched me stab a puppy or something. That got me to thinking, and, well, I just thought I'd drop by to make sure you aren't thinking of doing anything foolish."

"What could I do?" Boady asked. "My hands are tied."

"That's what I always liked about you, Boady. Everything by the book."

"You killed Emma's mother."

"I killed a shrew," Ben shot back coldly. Boady could see in his eyes that Ben had spoken a truth he hadn't meant to utter out loud. Ben took a small breath to recompose himself and then continued. "Great job, by the way, getting that napkin with Kagen's DNA on it. I was getting a little concerned that you weren't going to pull it off. But then you did your magic."

"As best I can figure out, Malena Gwin must have delivered her car to Chicago and then what . . . took a train back?"

"You're not recording this, are you?"

"It's attorney-client privilege, remember? It wouldn't matter."

Ben stood up and leaned over the desk to make sure that no recording devices had been hidden just out of sight. Then he sat back down. "Just making sure. A guy can't be too careful these days."

Boady continued to lay out the plan he'd constructed so far. "You get Malena's car keys, fly down to the conference, say hi to a few chums, and then drive back, getting here in time to see Kagen leave."

Ben didn't respond.

"You knew about Jennavieve's affair. Malena would have been watching the house for you. The odds would have been pretty good that he'd have left some DNA on the sheets."

"Do you really think it's healthy to delve into those details, ol' buddy? You know how sensitive you can be. Besides, like you said, there's nothing you can do about it."

"Well, that's not entirely true," Boady said.

Ben studied Boady carefully before speaking. "We still have attorney-client privilege. What you know can never leave this room. If you tell anyone, you'll lose your license and the evidence will be inadmissible. Trust me, Boady, I've thought this through."

Boady picked up his desk phone and turned it to Ben. "I have the number here for Judge Ransom's chambers. He's probably not there, but you can leave a message."

"And just why in the hell would I call Judge Ransom?"

"You committed a fraud upon the Court."

Ben let out a booming laugh. "Have you completely lost your mind?"

"You told the Court that you didn't kill your wife. That was a lie." Boady watched Ben carefully, looking for any sign that he might see where Boady was going.

"Oh, good Lord, you're serious." Ben's laugh faded, but his grin remained.

"Under Rule 3.3, 'Candor Toward the Tribunal,'" Boady paraphrased the rule for Ben, "if an attorney has reason to know that his client has engaged in fraudulent conduct related to the proceeding, he must take remedial measures including disclosure to the tribunal."

"That's a rule for civil court, Boady. This isn't civil court, it's criminal. Our clients lie all the time. Hell, judges and juries expect it."

"It's a rule of ethics, Ben. There's no exception for criminal cases."

Ben's face turned dark and serious. He pursed his lips and sighed. "I was afraid you might start thinking crazy. So, you see why I felt it necessary to drop by."

"The rule requires that I first give you the opportunity to correct your fraud." Boady pointed to the phone.

"And if I refuse?"

"Then the rule requires that I call Judge Ransom."

"No court in the world will back up what you're thinking. You go through with this, and you'll accomplish nothing, other than to lose your license."

Now it was Boady who chuckled.

"What's so funny?"

"*Fiat justitia ruat caelum.*"

"Excuse me?"

"I haven't used that phrase in a decade, and now it comes up twice in one case. You know what it means?"

"I'm afraid it doesn't ring a bell."

"Let justice be done, though the heavens may fall." Boady leaned forward and looked hard at Ben, the last shade of their long friendship having disappeared into the dark anger behind Boady's eyes. "Let me be clear—ol' buddy. I don't give a flying fuck if I lose my license. I'm willing to take my chances. I'm making that call. Ransom may change his decision. He may not. That's on him. But I'm calling him."

"Wait, Boady. You don't know what you're doing." Ben's tone now turned to pleading. "You didn't know the real Jennavieve. She could put up a front better than anyone."

"Better than you?" Boady asked.

"She cut my balls off, Boady. She used her money like a whip. She controlled everything in that house, and I could see her start to do that to Emma. I couldn't let that happen."

"You could have divorced her. People do it all the time."

"You don't know about money, Boady—not real money. They have the lawyers and the connections. Hell, you saw how quickly they swooped in after I got arrested. That family is vicious. I would have lost Emma forever."

"Can't you see what you've done to Emma? Doesn't that register in that self-absorbed brain of yours?"

"I'm protecting Emma, dammit! That's why I had to do what I did."

"No, Ben. *I'm* protecting Emma."

Boady turned the telephone back around and picked up the receiver. As he started dialing the number for Judge Ransom, Ben leaned forward and reached behind his back. When his hand came out, it held a gun.

Chapter 62

Max pulled up to Boady's house and parked on the street. Lila leapt from the driver's side of her car.

"Ben Pruitt just went in there. He had a gun in his belt."

"Slow down, Lila. What's going on?"

"We found something, about the case, but I don't think I can tell you."

"I don't understand, Lila."

"I think Ben came here to do something bad to Professor Sanden."

"You have to tell me, Lila."

"I can't. It's against the rules." Lila ran a hand up her forehead as she thought. "Max, do you trust me?"

The question took Max by surprise. "Of course I do."

"Then here's what we're going to do. You are coming in there with me. We go in quietly. If there's nothing to see, you can leave. But just go with me, please."

Max led the way to the porch. Lila opened the door slowly to avoid making noise. Then she and Max entered. Max had been to Boady's house many times for poker games and knew the layout. He could see light in the study and hear the muffled sound of voices. He motioned for Lila to remain at the front door as he tiptoed in.

When he was within a few feet of the office, he could see Boady through the glass of the French doors. Max took a couple more steps and saw Ben Pruitt in a chair opposite Boady. He still couldn't hear the conversation, but he had a clear view of both men. Their demeanor, the way each stared at the other, the short blasts of words that volleyed back and forth across the desk, suggested an argument.

Max felt like a burglar as he stood outside of the office. He was almost close enough to overhear what had to be a privileged conversation, and it made him feel uncomfortable. He was about to turn around and leave when he saw Ben Pruitt lean forward, reach behind his back, and pull a gun out of his belt.

Max pulled his gun and quietly chambered a round. He moved closer to the door so he could hear the conversation. Ben Pruitt sat at an angle with his back to Max, but Max could see the gun. Ben hadn't pointed it at Boady, but instead held it on his lap, stroking the barrel with his thumb.

"Christ, Ben!" Boady gasped. "What are you doing?"

"I want you to put the phone down and listen to me," Pruitt said.

Boady slowly put the receiver back in its cradle. Then he held his hands out over the desk, palms down as if to say *don't do anything rash*.

"I need you to keep your head for a few more hours. That's all I need."

"You want me to keep *my* head? You're the one with the gun. Just put that thing away before this goes too far."

"Judge Ransom needs to file that acquittal. After that, we can part ways for good."

"Except for the fact that you're threatening me with a gun."

"I'm not threatening you, Boady. I just want you to see it. Handsome, isn't it? I got it from a client some years back."

"Ben, I don't—"

"Shut up, Boady." Ben spat the words across the desk. "I'm not going back to prison. You have to know that by now. They almost killed me. They'll finish the job if I go back."

Max peeked through the glass and caught Boady's attention, the flick of Boady's eyes landing on Max and moving back to Ben as if he'd seen nothing.

"What am I supposed to do, Ben?" Boady said. "You killed Jenna-vieve. Am I supposed to pretend that didn't happen?"

"You don't do anything," Ben said. "You and I will just sit here in this comfy office and do nothing. Hell, I'll even type up your summation so you have it ready to e-mail to the judge tomorrow. After that, we wait until Judge Ransom files that acquittal. That's all you have to do. I'm asking you to do nothing. Just sit on your thumbs for one day; that's not too much to ask."

"And if I don't agree?"

"Don't go there, Boady. Please."

"I want to know, Ben—old friend—if I don't agree, what will you do? Will you kill me too? Dump me in some empty lot like you did Jennavieve?"

"Boady," Ben's words came out like they'd been dragged through broken glass. "Don't fuck with me. If you try to send me back to prison, I will stop you—by any means necessary."

Chapter 63

The blood in Boady's veins seemed to gel when Ben Pruitt threatened to kill him. At that same moment, the French doors slammed open, glass shards filling the air as Max burst through.

"Put the gun down!" Max shouted at the top of his lungs. "Put it down—now!"

Ben half jumped and half fell out of his chair.

"I said drop the gun! Do it now!"

Ben's legs pumped until his back hit the wall. Stabilized enough to gain his balance, he started to stand up straight, the gun aimed at the floor. "Don't shoot!"

"Drop the gun!"

"Wait! Don't shoot me. I need to talk to you." Ben slowly raised the gun, being careful to aim it away from both Boady and Max.

"Put that gun down, or I swear to God I'll blow you away! Do it now!"

Ben continued to ignore Max's command, and the gun continued its path until Ben turned it into his own head, the muzzle resting against his temple. "If you kill me, Detective, you'll never know who killed your wife."

All the yelling and chaos that had filled the room fell mute, leaving an unnatural silence. Max had seemingly lost his ability to speak, so Boady said, "Ben, please put the gun down."

"What about it, Detective? 'Your wife's death wasn't an accident. She was murdered. Here's the proof.' Does that sound familiar?"

"What the hell's he talking about," Boady asked.

"You wrote the note," Max said. "You . . ." Max had his gun trained on Ben's head, the end of the barrel a mere eight feet from Ben's nose.

Boady sensed a slight break in the tension, so he stood up behind his desk in the hope of turning the confrontation into a conversation. "Would someone please tell me what's going on?"

"Allow me," Ben said. Ben's voice carried a slight tremor as he spoke, although Boady could tell that Ben was doing his best to appear calm. "I had certain . . . insider information about the death of one Jennifer Rupert. Honestly, I never thought it would have any value to me."

"Where'd you get that information, Pruitt?" Max barked. "Tell me or—"

"Or what, Detective?" Ben jiggled his gun against his own temple. "Want to see who can shoot me first? Because I'm not going back to prison."

"What are you talking about, Ben?" Boady asked.

"Honestly, I didn't think that information would ever do me any good, but I put it away as a plan B, just in case. I half suspected that the city would put its best homicide investigator on my case. I mean, why not? Turns out, it was your case from the start."

As Ben talked, Boady could see him grow more determined. He stopped using the wall to keep himself upright, and he'd lost the tremor in his voice.

"Then I hear that they subpoenaed the footage from the tollbooths," Ben continued. "Now I did a pretty good job of hiding my return, but the possibility existed that our boy Max might pick me out of the crowd. So I sent him on a little treasure hunt, to distract him." Ben gave a forced chuckle. "I almost lost it when I heard that you got reprimanded over it. Icing on the cake, I guess."

"You know who killed my wife?" Max asked. Boady had never heard Max sound so vulnerable. Even that night they had to carry him out of the cemetery, Max never lost his bark. But now, he sounded almost meek.

"Yes, Max. And if I go to prison, that secret goes with me. I promise, you'll never know the truth. It's a simple bargain, Detective. You let me go and I give you your wife's killer. That sounds like a fair trade to me."

The gun in Max's hand began a barely perceptible shake. The equation had changed. It was no longer a matter whether Ben would get convicted. It had become a more rational transaction. One killer caught in exchange for one going free.

"Max," Boady said softly. "This is your call."

Sweat now glistened on the lines of Max's forehead. His eyes narrowed to a squint and his chest stopped rising with breath. Max's gun slowly sank, sagging under its weight until it pointed at Ben Pruitt's heart. Boady could only imagine the fight going on inside of Max's soul.

Then Max said, "No."

"'No'?" Ben repeated. "What do you mean, 'no'? Are you willing to live the rest of your life never knowing who killed your wife?"

"Are you willing to live the rest of your life in prison? I'm betting we can make a deal once you realize just how bad you have it. Maybe a trade in exchange for a nicer set of bars to look through."

"There will be no deal, Rupert. It's now or never."

"We'll see. I'll come and visit you every year or so. See how you're doing. See if you changed your mind. If not—so be it. But you're not walking on this. You're going to prison. Now drop . . . the fucking . . . gun."

Ben's eyes took on a quiet sadness and he slowly shook his head from side to side. "You won't be seeing me in a year, Detective, because I'm not going back."

Ben thrust the gun at Max, the muzzle flashing with exploding gunpowder. And even though he stood only eight feet away, his bullet sailed well wide of its mark. Almost as if he intended to miss his target.

Max put a bullet into Ben's chest before he had a chance to think.

Ben fell back into the wall and slid to the floor.

"No!" Max yelled, dropping to his knees beside Ben. "Why'd you do that?"

Ben gulped at air, his eyes large and full of fear.

"Who killed my wife?" Max grabbed Ben's shirt and shook him. "Who killed my wife?"

Ben's eyes fluttered. Then he smiled a limp smile.

"Give me a name!"

Ben's eyes rolled up into his forehead and his body went limp.

Boady felt his legs deflate as he eased back into his chair. He could barely breathe as he looked around the room: Ben Pruitt dead on the floor, Max kneeling over the dead man with a look of utter despair on his face, Lila holding onto the frame of the French doors, her pale eyes searching the room for some kind of answer. Boady tried to speak, but when he opened his mouth, nothing but empty breath came out.

Chapter 64

By New Year's Eve, the city had turned cold. Meteorologists were bragging that Minnesota had hit a new record low, and they saw no relief on the way. Boady parked his car on the street in front of Max Rupert's house and slipped on a pair of leather gloves.

He'd spent Thanksgiving in Missouri, trying to explain to Emma why they would be returning to a funeral in Minnesota. He'd concocted a story about a prison riot to explain her father's death, but Diana quashed that idea. "She'll read the story on the Internet someday," Diana said. "It's going to hurt, but we're going to tell her the truth. If she has any hope of getting through this, she needs to know the truth. She needs to know where to aim her anger."

Diana was right, of course.

He hadn't spoken with Max since the shooting. He'd called a few times. Left messages, but never heard back. As he stepped from his car into the icebox that was his chosen home state, he paused one last time to collect his thoughts—and maybe to collect a bit of courage. With a briefcase in his one hand, he knocked on Max's door and waited. He could hear the footsteps approach. They paused as a shadow filled a small window in the door. Then he heard the deadbolt click open.

Max opened the door but didn't greet Boady. He just stood there.

"Can I come in?"

"What do you want, Boady?"

"What I want is five minutes of your time. That's all. After that, I'll leave and never bother you again. Just five minutes."

Max considered it for a moment, then stepped back to let Boady enter.

Boady followed Max to the living room, where Max took a seat on a recliner. Boady sat on the couch. Boady had been to Max's house a number of times, both before and after Jenni's death. Nothing seemed to have been touched since the day of her death.

"Five minutes," Max said.

Boady opened the briefcase, pulled out a file about two inches thick.

"What's that?"

"I've been appointed to be the executor of Ben Pruitt's law practice." Max looked at Boady with no expression.

"When a practicing attorney dies, the Bar appoints another attorney to wrap up the practice: close files, return retainer money, oversee file retention, that kind of thing. Ben's practice used to be mine. I'm the one who set up the billing procedures and file-retention system. Hell, he still had my old legal assistant on staff. Well, it just made sense to have me go in and shutter the practice."

He paused to see if Max saw where he was headed. It didn't appear so.

"I've been going through Ben's client list for the past month. Everything seemed in order, but then I came across this file." He handed it to Max. "The man's name is Ray Kroll. This file was in a drawer all by itself. There is no record of Kroll ever paying a retainer, which probably means he paid cash."

Boady watched as Max thumbed through the pages in the file. "Got arrested for a bar fight?" Max asked.

"Charged with first-degree assault. Nearly beat a man to death with a brick. Bailed out and promptly got shot."

"The guy he beat up had friends. So what?"

"Maybe. But look." Boady lifted the pages of reports to expose the face of the file folder underneath. There, someone had scratched a note in blue ink. *Jennifer Rupert—yellow Corolla—#49—St. Louis Park.*

Max froze.

Then Boady lifted papers on the opposite side of the file to show Max a CD-ROM taped to the back of the file. "I listened to this CD, Max. It's two men having a conversation over the phone. Max, they're talking about Jenni. This is where Ben got his information about Jenni's death. I thought you should have it."

Max stared at the file in his hands, and Boady could tell that a thousand wheels were turning in the man's head. Then Max looked up and said, "I'm not supposed to have this, am I?"

Boady thought about the deep river of trouble that would come rushing in on him if anyone ever found out. He'd lose his license, his job—who knows how far the Board of Professional Responsibility would go. On the other side of the ledger, however, Boady knew that giving the file to Max would allow Boady to sleep at night and look himself in the mirror. In the end, it was an easy decision.

"I'm supposed to destroy it," Boady said. "But the way I see it, Ray Kroll's dead. Ben's dead. And somewhere out there is a murderer who got away with it. I can't destroy this file. But, if you tell anyone where this came from, I'll deny it."

"No one will ever know," Max said. "I promise."

Boady stood up. "I think my five minutes are about up." He walked toward the door.

Max remained in his chair, looking at the file.

"I hope you find what you're looking for, Max. And if you ever want to have a beer or . . . well, you know where I live."

Max folded the file closed but didn't look up. "Thanks," he said softly.

Boady nodded in silence and let himself out.

Acknowledgments

I would like to offer my immense thanks to Dan Mayer, Jill Maxick, Cheryl Quimba, Jon Kurtz, Jade Zora Scibilia, and everyone at Seventh Street Books and Penguin Random House for all of the support they have shown me over the years.

I want to thank my first editor and best friend, Joely (my wife), for being my rock.

And thank you to my superstar agent, Amy Cloughley.

I would like to thank Donna Oliva, Nancy Rosin, Robert Docherty, Leonardo Castro, Allison Krehbiel, Scott Cutcher, Professor Len Biernat, Detective Robert Dale, Margaret Koberoski, Tami Peterson, James M. Crist, and Lily Shaw for answering questions and being excellent beta readers.

About the Author

Allen Eskens is the award-winning and *USA Today*–bestselling author of *The Life We Bury* and *The Guise of Another*. A criminal-defense attorney for twenty-five years, he lives with his wife in Minnesota, where he is a member of the Twin Cities Sisters in Crime.